Silent Winter

MAGGIE JAMES

First published in paperback 2019 by Orelia
Publishing

For all the friends who have supported me throughout my writing journey. Thanks to each and every one of you. Your help is much appreciated.

Part One

Hell

CHAPTER 1

Concealed by a thick hedge, the Watchman ignored the chill that struck up from the ground into his feet. His target was late in leaving work, but so what? Rick and he had waited twenty-three years to exact retribution, so an extra half hour made no difference. After tonight, time wouldn't matter for their intended victim; a minute would seem a decade and then an eternity. Or so the Watchman hoped.

His grip tightened around the crowbar clenched in his palm, his gaze fixed on the third-floor window, which hosted the only illumination visible. After a few minutes, the window went dark, and the Watchman exhaled a noisy sigh of satisfaction. Before long his plan would become a reality.

'Bring it on,' he muttered.

Seconds later, a man left the building, his breath white plumes in the night air. He headed towards his car, never noticing the dark-coloured van parked next to the hedge. The Watchman crept forward, knowing the security cameras covering the car park were defunct. His rubber soles made no sound as he advanced, cat-like, on his prey. Anticipation pounded through his veins. The moment Rick and he had waited for so long had arrived.

He raised his right arm.

Then crashed the crowbar into the man's skull.

CHAPTER 2

Holly Blackmore paced the kitchen, anger drumming a staccato beat in her brain. The spaghetti Bolognese she'd eaten weighed heavily in her stomach; Drew's portion was congealing in the microwave. The red digits on the oven clock mocked her; five past eight, and still no sign of him. Her husband had never been this late before, although seven thirty wasn't uncommon. She'd heard all the excuses about how his deadline to deliver the firm's latest app was looming, etc. Holly no longer believed his reasons for coming home late, not given everything else that was wrong between them.

Why the hell hadn't he called? Or at the very least, texted?

Not for the first time a thought gripped her. Was he having an affair?

Holly's heart squeezed in pain. Three years into their marriage, and her love for Drew still flared hot and strong, the way it had on their wedding day. She wasn't so sure it was mutual anymore.

She chewed the skin around her nails, her feet marking a steady pace across the floor, eyes glued to the oven clock. Eight ten, and still no sign of her husband.

Had she scared him off by what she'd said that morning? But damn it, she was twenty-six, the same age as Drew, both of them young and healthy. The time was right for them to have a baby.

Eight fifteen. Her hands shaking, she grabbed her mobile, found Drew's number and placed the call. Within two rings it went to voicemail.

'Where *are* you? Why didn't you call to say you'd be late?' Angry barbs laced Holly's tone, but she was past caring.

'Selfish, irresponsible git,' she muttered. The fury that had percolated inside her all day, ever since Drew slammed his way out of the house that morning, was now brewed to perfection, and he'd be getting it full force the minute he stepped through the door.

Five minutes later, still with no sign of her husband, Holly called her brother-in-law's mobile.

Todd answered straightaway. 'Hey, Hols. How're you doing?'

'Is Drew with you?' *Say yes*, she prayed silently. Maybe the two men had gone for a run together.

'Not tonight.' Her hopes shattered like glass around her feet. 'He's not back from work, I take it?'

Tears pooled in Holly's eyes. She drove her fingernails into her palms, desperate to dispel her fear that Drew was with another woman. To her relief, her voice came out normal. 'Not yet. And he hasn't called. Or texted.'

'He'll be immersed in that project he's heading up. Lost track of time.'

Damn you, Todd, Holly thought. *Always Mr Logical.* When she didn't reply, he continued, 'You know what a pig his boss is. Rides him pretty hard.'

'Yeah,' said Holly. 'That's what it'll be.' She ended the call, then burst into angry tears. Her fingers tugged at the microwave door, then pulled out Drew's meal. With one swift motion, she flipped open the rubbish bin, sliding the food off the plate into its depths. Twin odours of meat and pasta lingered in its wake.

When her husband came home, she'd give him hell.

******

Pain gripped the back of Drew's head, jolts of fire that stabbed, hot and fierce, through his skull. For a while, he didn't open his eyes, aware something was wrong, but he had no idea what. Waves of agony crashed over him, then receded, but he found that by lying still he could lessen their blows. He floated in a sea of blackness, reluctant to think about where he was, or why his head felt like a cricket bat had clouted it. He focussed on his breathing, the regular *one-two* in and out of his belly, allowing the world to recede into another, less painful, dimension.

A memory edged into his brain. The night's chill as he walked to his car. His urge for a beer—or several—at the Red Lion. After that, nothing. He couldn't recall strolling into the pub, ordering a pint or chatting to any of the regulars. He must have done; why else would his head feel like someone had buried a meat cleaver in it? Somehow he'd made it home afterwards and into bed. *Stupid, stupid*, he chided himself. It had been years since he'd drunk himself into oblivion, and Holly would rip several strips off him. In a while, he'd use the bathroom, down a couple of paracetamols along with a load of water, and return to bed.

Without thinking, Drew lifted his head and at once regretted his folly. Agony drilled a channel into his brain, and a howl of pain escaped his lips. He lay back, concentrating on his breathing until the pain faded. Then, with care, he opened his eyes.

And saw nothing.

Blackness surrounded him. Drew strained his vision, sure that his pupils would adjust to the darkness of his bedroom—because where else could he be?—and his wardrobe, his treadmill, the window, would appear. They didn't. All that lay before him was an impenetrable nothingness, thick and never ending. His head hurt too much for him to question why, or to wonder where Holly was.

Entombed in the blackness, Drew's eyes grew heavy. Sleep—that was what he needed. Screw the painkillers and water; the en-suite bathroom seemed a million miles away, not a few feet. He'd call in sick later and take whatever crap his boss dished out. He pulled the duvet closer around him, glad of its warmth. The darkness cradled him in a welcome cocoon, and he drifted back into oblivion.

CHAPTER 3

Ten thirty p.m. Exhaustion soaked every cell in the Watchman's body, yet his mind operated in overdrive. Mission accomplished: Drew Blackmore lay shackled and helpless, at his mercy.

The Watchman's legs were stiff after long hours seated on the stone floor outside his victim's prison. Throughout that time he'd waited for signs of life behind the closed door. The makeshift sound-proofing he'd installed was only partly effective; in hindsight that wasn't a bad thing. Now, as he listened, he heard noises: a soft groan, a muttered curse. Silence for a while. Then a howl of pain.

The Watchman's face split into a wide grin. *Curse and moan all you want, Drew Blackmore*, he thought. *Won't get you nowhere. This ain't the Ritz, and room service won't arrive anytime soon.*

He shifted position with a wince, his ears still on alert. Minutes later a loud snore, then another, rumbled into the darkness. Soon they subsided into heavy breathing that rasped against the night air. Still the Watchman lingered, reluctant to leave. He derived pleasure from listening to his victim sleep, oblivious of the true nature of his plight.

Delay made revenge taste sweeter, the Watchman decided. Not revenge, he reminded himself. *Justice*. And Drew had plenty more of *that* coming his way.

With an effort, he wrenched himself back to practicalities. Time to go; Drew would most likely be asleep for hours. The Watchman eased himself upright and onto his feet, grimacing at the protests from his calf muscles. He padded up the stairs and towards the exit.

Cold air blasted against his body as he opened the door. A hard frost had set in; thank God the weather had rendered the ground impervious to tyre tracks or footprints. The faint ones he'd already left on the icy whiteness would dissipate within hours of tomorrow's dawn. Not willing to risk Drew escaping—although fuck only knew how his victim would manage *that*—he padlocked the door behind him. He climbed into the Transit van he'd stolen the day before and started the engine. Time to head to one of the rougher areas of Bristol and abandon it.

The Watchman smiled as he drove, thinking of the fun he'd have with Drew. Such gratification there'd be in listening to his victim's screams, his pleas for release. He'd leave Drew to stew in his misery—no food or water for a couple of days—before making his next move. When the horror of his situation sank in, the Watchman wanted Drew to feel alone, helpless, abandoned. The way he and Rick had done, years before. After that—oh, how he'd enjoy playing with his new toy.

Ah, Rick. Too soft-hearted by far, that one. He'd have to be careful the little bastard didn't go easy on Drew.

CHAPTER 4

Holly stared at the digital clock. Eleven p.m. and still no Drew. Anger, mixed with fear, churned in her gut.

She picked up her phone for the umpteenth time that night and called his number. Straight to voicemail. This time Holly didn't leave a message. What was the point?

She briefly considered calling Todd a second time, but rejected the idea. At this time of night he'd be in bed with Nessa, who, as the mother of two toddlers, wouldn't appreciate being disturbed for anything less than an emergency. Holly wasn't sure her situation qualified. Not yet.

******

When Drew awoke, the pain in his head had eased a little. The intense darkness continued to puzzle him, though. Had Holly bought blackout curtains and not mentioned them?

Drew's eyes strained into the void, but failed to discern any shapes. He couldn't hear anything either. Normally he'd be aware of Holly beside him: the rhythm of her breathing, the occasional soft snore, the rustle of their duvet when she turned over.

He put out a hand, questing for the curve of his wife's hip. Instead of flesh, it met with nothing.

Perhaps, in her anger, Holly had slept in the spare room. Or perhaps she'd banished *him* there instead.

Wait. He'd heard something. A clank: metal upon metal, close to his ear, but he hadn't a clue what had made the sound. What the fuck was going on?

Breathe, Drew, he told himself, as panic squeezed his chest. Perhaps he'd drunk too much in the Red Lion and banged his head on the way home, hence the ache that pounded through his brain. Why the blackness, though? The silence, broken only by that strange noise? Was this some weird nightmare?

Drew raised a hand to massage his skull, then stopped. Whatever had produced that clank of metal on metal was wrapped around his wrist. Realisation—cold and awful—slammed into him, followed by denial. Once the shock wore off, scream after scream ripped from Drew's throat.

******

One thirty a.m. saw Holly on the brink of calling the police. Or the local hospitals. Whatever his faults, not coming home at all wasn't Drew's style. She'd watched the red numbers on the oven clock tick up towards midnight, her anger boiling all the while, but once one o'clock came around, panic took over. All this time she'd been imagining her husband screwing another woman. Now her conscience was prodding her to examine alternatives.

Images flashed into Holly's head. A car accident, Drew bloodied and broken in a hospital bed, surrounded by beeping monitors. Or worse, his corpse on a mortuary slab. The thought choked her. She sank to her knees, huge sobs wracking her body.

What if Drew was dead and they had screamed their last words to each other in anger?

The fear inside her swelled until Holly stood up, shoving it firmly back down. She needed to pull herself together, and fast. At times like this she wished she had siblings. That her parents hadn't taken early retirement and moved to Spain. Holly refused to disturb them when she might be fretting over nothing. So whom could she turn to for help? Amber or Elaine from work? She hardly knew them; they'd shared a few coffees, the occasional lunch, nothing more. Long hours spent as a divorce lawyer afforded her little time for her former mates from school and university, and gradually she'd lost contact with them. Besides, after their wedding, Drew had filled her world. The result? In the chill of this dark November morning, she was alone with her fear.

This wasn't the time for self-pity, though. 'Get your act together, for God's sake,' she muttered, while searching for her phone.

She'd start with the hospitals. Her fingers shaking, she found the admissions number for Southmead, and placed the call.

Nobody who might be Drew had been brought in that night. The same story at the Bristol Royal Infirmary. Wherever Drew was, he wasn't in hospital, at least not in Bristol.

Holly grabbed her car keys. Jonas Software Solutions was a five-minute drive away. It made sense to check there before getting the police involved. Besides, wasn't she supposed to wait twenty-four hours before reporting someone missing? Or was that an American thing?

The night air slapped icicles against her face as she stepped through the door. Not a soul was around, apart from a stray cat sniffing a rubbish bin. Her fingers shook, hampering her efforts to press the 'unlock' function on her car key. *Be alive*, she begged Drew in her mind, *because I need you. Maybe I should have told you more often.*

Minutes later Holly swung her Golf into the driveway of Jonas Software, parking beside her husband's car. Thank God; he must have fallen asleep at his desk. She surveyed the grim 1960s structure; no lights shone in any of the windows, including Drew's office. She tried the main door, but it was locked. The reception area was equally dark. Holly's breath, steamy in the night's chill, fogged the window as she peered inside. The building seemed deserted.

Holly fumbled in her bag, pulled out her phone. She called Drew's number again in the hope his ring tone might awaken him at last.

No response. Wherever he was, Drew wasn't asleep in his office. Then why was his Audi still parked up?

Fear gnawing at her brain, Holly returned to her car and drove home. Todd; that was the answer. He'd know what to do. His frequent insomnia meant he was probably still awake. The second she stepped through the doorway she tapped out a text.

'Call me as soon as you get this message. Drew still isn't home.'

******

Drew's throat felt raw, yet he continued to scream. By now consciousness had fully claimed him; he couldn't delude himself some nightmare gripped him. No, his plight was terrifyingly real, and the thought petrified him. What the *fuck*?

Drew's screams ground to a halt amid a riot of pain from his injured head. His breath rattled harsh from his mouth while he struggled for oxygen. An iron hand squeezed the life from his lungs, against which his heart hammered like a pneumatic drill. He gulped in air, but it wouldn't penetrate the blockage in his chest. His throat was closing over. Had he been buried alive? Would he suffocate, alone and abandoned, in this hell-hole? *No, no, no, he couldn't die this way, dear God, just one breath, please…*

With difficulty, Drew sucked in a scrap of air. Then another. His ribs ached, and his blood boomed in his ears, but he could breathe. Barely, but enough.

He assessed his situation. Thick chains encircled his wrists, linked to a metal ring bolted to the floor close to his head. He knew that for a fact, because he'd tugged, pulled and nearly wrenched his arms from their sockets, but he couldn't free them. Enough leeway existed to cross one over the other, and to extend them fully on each side. His ankles were secured in a similar fashion.

He was lying on a bare mattress, only a few inches thick, the sort used for fold-up beds. No pillow, but a duvet covered his body. Underneath it Drew was naked; his questing hands had revealed his clothes had been removed. Something else was missing as well: his fingers were bare. His platinum wedding band from Holly, and his father's gold signet ring, both so precious, were gone.

Drew threw back the duvet and explored his surroundings as best he could. His chains allowed him enough latitude to get on all fours, and to turn his body over, but not to stand, or move more than a few inches in any direction. His hands groped through the darkness, and met plastic. A bucket. The floor on which it stood was concrete. Close to his feet he found a pile of blankets. The material was coarse, but thick, and there were plenty of them. What the *hell*…?

Whoever had chained him here had stripped him of his humanity, damn it, yet provided a mattress and blankets. None of it made any sense. A howl of anguish, raw and primitive, tore from Drew's mouth. The fear in his belly was almost physical. With that, a warm sensation spread over his groin, accompanied by the reek of urine. Strangled whimpers issued from Drew's mouth on the realisation that he'd wet himself. He shifted position, away from the soaked part of the mattress.

He sucked in more air, willing himself to ignore his humiliation. Reality check: some bastard had tethered him to the floor, damn it, in this black-as-hell place, where he couldn't see a thing or hear a sound apart from his own panic. He'd perish here, trapped in an unending nightmare, without a clue why. Fettered and helpless, left to die in the dark without oxygen.

Maybe not. A sliver of hope pierced Drew's despair. The atmosphere wasn't stale; it lacked the cloying thickness that would accompany a slow depletion of air. Instead it was cold, chilling the tip of his nose on every breath. Drew lay still, wondering if he'd imagined the subtle sensation— but no, there it was again, the faintest stir of air brushing over his skin, coming from above his head. Wherever he was, his prison wasn't sealed. He had an air supply. Terror had caused the tightness in his chest, not suffocation.

Don't panic, he told himself. Hard not to, in the circumstances. Who had done this to him? And why had he, of all people, been singled out?

A case of mistaken identity, perhaps. Some guy had angered a local gangster, with Drew unlucky enough to resemble the culprit. Or else a random psychopath had snatched him. Neither possibility offered a shred of comfort.

He ignored the voice in his head whispering a name. Someone who had ample reason to hate Drew. Who, a long time, ago, had threatened him with retribution.

Wherever you are, I will find you, and you will suffer, said the voice.

******

Todd was silent on the other end of the phone once Holly finished speaking. 'He's not been having an affair, I can tell you that much,' he said eventually. 'Think about it, Hols. He's always at work, home with you, or else out running with me and the rest of the lads.'

'How do you know he's at work when he claims he is?'

'Because I pick him up from Jonas Software on the nights we go for a run. Always at seven o'clock, and he looks exhausted every time. If he says he's at work, I believe him. He wouldn't lie to me.'

No, thought Holly. *But he might to his wife.* 'Should I phone the police?'

'You're certain he's not been admitted to hospital?'

'Yes.' Irritation edged into Holly's voice. She'd told Todd about the abortive calls to Southmead and the BRI; hadn't he been listening?

He's only trying to help, she reminded herself. Without her brother-in-law, she'd be alone with her worry, at two thirty on this icy November morning.

'I'm not sure there's much the police will do if you report him missing,' Todd said. 'Not at the moment, anyway. He's probably gone on a bender and is sleeping off the booze somewhere, which explains him leaving his car at work. Probably a last-minute office celebration that got him so drunk he couldn't call you.'

'Drew didn't mention anything about a work-related party. Surely he'd have told me?'

She heard Todd drag in a long breath. 'Jeez, Hols, then I've no idea. Look, try not to worry.

He'll most likely call you in the morning, all contrite, and tell you how sorry he is. Okay, so he's never stayed out all night before, and yes, Nessa would rip my guts out if I pulled a stunt like that, but Drew's under a lot of pressure at work. Not surprising he might get drunk to take the edge off.'

'I suppose so.' Holly was wound too tight to say much else. If Todd was right, Drew would crawl in sometime that morning, and when he did, she'd kick his arse into the middle of next century.

'Text me when he gets home,' Todd said.

'Will do.' Holly sat nursing her thoughts for a while after the call ended. She eyed the red digits of the oven clock. Three a.m. With a sigh, she headed into the hallway and plodded up the stairs. The curtains in the bedroom she shared with Drew hung open; a slice of moonlight fell on the empty bed. An icy chill embraced her, the central heating having clicked off hours before. She stripped off her clothes, tugging on a pair of fleecy pyjamas and sliding into bed. The vacant space where Drew should be mocked her, and Holly curled in on herself, hugging her knees to her chest to get warm.

'Drew,' she said into the darkness. 'Where the hell are you?'

CHAPTER 5 - Before

Twenty-three years ago, in a shabby rented flat in Bristol's Barton Hill area, a woman shouted at her seven-year-old son.

'Get yourself off to bed. And don't come out, not for any reason, or you'll get a slap. I've got a friend coming round.'

Rick didn't dare mention his empty belly. He'd not eaten since the stale cornflakes he'd scoffed at breakfast time. So tonight was going to be one of *those* nights, he thought. At first his child's brain had taken his mother's words literally; the men were simply her friends. Ones for whom she wore fancy clothes, all black and red, and more make-up than usual. After a while he realised that the sounds coming from his mother's bedroom didn't seem friendly, nor did the men. More than once she appeared the following day with a split lip or black eye, and the boy learned not to ask how she got her injuries. Every time he endured the noises echoing throughout the cramped flat, a little more of him died.

As a seven-year-old, all he wanted was a proper family. Other kids had a daddy, and mums who didn't entertain a different man most nights. Rick hadn't a clue who his father was and his mother always told him to shut the fuck up if he asked. Starved of love, he made do with one of her T-shirts that he'd stolen. By day he hid his prize under his bed. At night he slept with his head pillowed against the fabric, the scent of sweat and cheap perfume filling his nostrils.

Years later, things made more sense. He understood how his mother had supported a two packs per day smoking habit on her shop assistant's salary. Although his brain realised the truth, his heart rejected the idea. Denial won. She wasn't a whore. No way.

Once he'd heard her talking about him during a casual conversation with a neighbour.

'Why didn't you get rid of the brat once you found you was preggers?' the woman asked.

His mother dragged on her cigarette before she replied. 'Didn't have a choice, did I? Too far along.'

The neighbour snorted in derision. 'Stupid bitch. Didn't ya notice you wasn't getting yer monthlies?'

'Nah. They always was hit and miss as to when they'd come.'

'You could have got him adopted once he was born.'

His mother exhaled smoke in a noisy plume. She didn't reply at first, and the silence stretched out in Rick's mind, the implications of *didn't have a choice, did I* reverberating through his brain.

'He's all I have,' his mother said at last. The closest she ever came to saying that she cared.

CHAPTER 6

Drew awoke from a restless doze. The second he opened his eyes and faced the impenetrable blackness, shock and horror crowded his senses once more. Wisps of air continued to caress his cheek; the atmosphere remained breathable. But what if the mechanism delivering his oxygen broke? No, he couldn't—*mustn't*—think that way. He forced himself to breathe the way Holly did when she practised yoga, and the steel band around his ribcage relaxed.

Think, Drew, he chided himself. Whatever was supplying his air, it probably wasn't a pump, given the lack of sounds. A simple vent, then. His breathing close to normal again, Drew lifted his head, and yelled with all his strength: 'Help! Is anyone there?'

His voice bounced off where he thought the ceiling might be. No echo; instead, his words appeared muffled. Drew turned his head to his left, and shouted again. This time the noise stopped much closer, and was, like before, deadened. When he repeated the experiment to his right, the sound travelled further, but not by much. That meant whatever this place was, he was near to one of its walls on his left-hand side, and that sound-proofing existed on them and the ceiling, but not underneath him.

On hands and knees, he explored his prison once more, inch by inch, as far as his restraints permitted. He found only the bucket and the blankets. No clue as to what this place was, or where the door might be.

A whiff of urine lingered in the darkness; together with the pail and vent it sparked hope inside Drew. His captor had provided air and a rudimentary toilet, as well as protection against the cold. Had someone brought him here to die, the vent, bucket and blankets would have been unnecessary. And if his captor had furnished Drew with a toilet, he'd also be getting food and water, surely? That meant his abductor would make an appearance at some point, and the idea caused Drew's stomach to clench in terror.

'Help!' he screamed into the blackness, but silence answered his plea.

******

Alone in bed, Holly awoke from a restless doze. Drew's absence crushed a stone into her heart the second she opened her eyes. She checked the time on her mobile: seven a.m., which meant she'd slept through her six o'clock alarm. Anguish hit her; the notification light wasn't flashing on her phone. Drew hadn't tried to call or text her while she'd been asleep.

Maybe he was snoring off his hangover on the sofa. Holly tugged on her dressing gown, her phone in its pocket, and ran downstairs.

The living room was empty. So, too, was the kitchen. She was alone in the house.

Holly burst into noisy sobs. Wracked by misery, she couldn't ignore the situation any longer. Her finger shaking, she grabbed her mobile and called Todd.

'He's still not home.' Holly's voice shook with fear. 'Something bad's happened. I'm sure of it.'

A pause. Then: 'I'm coming over. Don't do anything until I arrive.'

Holly breathed a sigh of relief. She'd known she could count on Todd. Safe, steady and reliable, he'd know what to do; he always did. Unable to settle, she paced the living room, chewing her fingernails all the while. One thought echoed through her head, over and over: *please let Drew be okay. Please let Drew be okay.*

Her eyes roamed over the eclectic mix of old and new in the room: their ancient bookcase, the handwoven rug, a lamp rescued from a skip. Their home had been furnished with love, not money. But would Drew ever see any of it again?

For that, Holly had no answer.

Within ten minutes Todd's car arrived outside. Before her brother-in-law's finger hit the bell, she wrenched open the door and sank into his arms. He didn't speak, just held her, the way she'd known he would. For a moment his warm body halted the emotional roller-coaster barrelling through her brain.

At last Holly pulled away, wiping a tear from her cheek. 'Where is he, Todd?'

'We'll find him, Hols.' The certainty in his words didn't match the fear in his eyes. He was as worried as she was.

Todd stepped inside, closed the door, then steered Holly into the living room. He'd not bothered to shave, and his hair stuck up at weird angles. She knew he must be concerned about Drew. The brothers had always been close; Todd, at sixteen, had assumed a fatherly role towards five-year-old Drew after their mother's death, and their subsequent adoption by their aunt and uncle. Six feet tall and stocky, Todd stood bigger and heavier than Drew, but with the same blue eyes, dark hair and hooked nose. Few people could doubt they were brothers. How familiar Todd was, how much she'd come to care for him.

Holly slumped on the sofa, unsure whether her legs would support her much longer. Todd sat beside her and took her hand. 'Should I call the police?' she asked.

'Not yet.'

'Why not?'

'It's only seven thirty, Hols. We both know Drew's been at his desk early these past few weeks, given how busy he is, but it's still too soon. We'll leave it until eight, then phone his office. If he's not turned up by then, we'll contact the police. In the meantime—' Todd stood up, pulling her with him. 'Take a shower and put on some clothes. While you're doing that, I'll make you breakfast.'

Holly shook her head. 'I'm too tense to eat.'

'At least have a coffee. I could sure use one.' He walked towards the kitchen.

Holly sat immobile, lost in her thoughts, then administered a mental head slap. Her husband was missing, and she couldn't afford to fall apart. Work could screw itself. She'd call in sick later.

A short while afterwards she'd showered and dressed, and stood in the kitchen, a mug of coffee in her hand. The oven clock showed the time: ten past eight. Time to contact Jonas Software. Holly found her mobile and placed the call.

'Mark Lucas, please,' she said to the woman who answered. 'My name is Holly Blackmore. I'm Drew's wife.'

Seconds later a gruff male voice spoke in her ear. 'Hello, Mrs Blackmore. Is Drew sick today?'

His words scuppered Holly's remaining hopes. 'No. At least... I don't know.' She moistened her dry lips. 'He's gone missing. I've no idea where he is.' How pathetic that sounded. A proper wife should know where her husband was.

Todd walked behind her, his arms squeezing her tight. Their warmth burst a dam inside Holly, the last fourteen hours spilling forth in anguished wails. Todd prised the phone from her fingers and spoke into it while she sobbed. His words reached Holly through a haze of pain: *didn't come home last night... not answering his mobile... she's checked the hospitals.* She sank onto a chair, swiping tears from her cheeks. So much for staying strong. Something terrible had happened to Drew, and she'd prefer it if he'd been with another woman, because then she could hate him, but at least he'd be alive. The not knowing, the dread that he'd suffered some awful accident, or worse—that her husband might be dead—was unbearable.

Holly became conscious of the silence that stretched across the kitchen. She glanced up, noting the ashen hue to Todd's face. 'We need to call the police,' he said.

She nodded. His fingers stabbed at her phone, and she listened while her brother-in-law repeated the words he'd used with Drew's boss: *missing, not been in contact, hospitals*. Followed by Drew's description, his mobile number. Todd's confirmation that his brother had no known physical or mental health issues.

When he finished, his hand rasped over his stubble. Holly glimpsed fear in his eyes.

Todd laid her mobile on the table. 'They're sending a couple of officers round. Should be within the hour.'

Holly nodded, too drained to protest that the police should come *now*, damn it. Todd grabbed her hand, the warmth of his touch welcome. Neither of them spoke. Time ticked by. Nine o'clock came, then went. So much for the police arriving within the hour.

'Where the hell are they, Todd? Don't they understand this is an emergency?' Holly glanced at the kitchen clock: nine thirty, and she'd already received four unanswered calls from her boss. If she didn't phone in sick soon, he'd assume she was missing too.

Todd ran a frustrated hand through his hair. 'They'll be here before long. I hope so, anyway.' Right at that moment, the buzzer sounded.

Two uniformed officers, one male and one female, stood on the step when Holly opened the door. 'Mrs Blackmore?' the woman asked. 'I'm Police Constable Sharon Chapman, and this is my colleague Josh Reid, also a PC. I understand you've reported your husband as missing. Can we come in, please?'

Holly stood aside to let them enter, then led the way into the living room and sat on the sofa. Sharon Chapman took the seat beside her, with Todd and Josh Reid occupying the armchairs. Holly noted the rings on Sharon's wedding finger. This woman was married. She'd understand.

'Please find him,' she said. Her voice rose into the air, high and cracked. 'He's never gone missing before. Something terrible must have happened.'

******

Drew's mouth had turned to cotton wool, and hunger gnawed at his belly. The coffee he'd downed before leaving Jonas Software seemed aeons ago, and he'd slaughter an entire army for a glass of water. Hadn't he read that a human could only survive three days without liquid? If he didn't drink soon, he'd die, leaving behind only a desiccated husk. He'd already had to piss into the bucket; his bowels needed emptying, but Drew ignored their fullness. That was a step too far, at least for the time being.

He'd be rescued soon, surely? By now Holly would have reported him missing. The police would find who'd done this, force the bastard to reveal Drew's location. He just needed to stay calm and wait. Everything would be fine.

Maybe not. His prison could be anywhere, with nothing to indicate his whereabouts. His life depended on his captor, and unless he drank soon, he wouldn't survive. Whichever way Drew looked at it, his situation was dire.

Panic loosened his bowels, and he only just made it to the bucket in time. Seconds later the stench of fear filled the air.

******

'So what did the police say?' Six p.m., and Todd held Holly's hand as they sat on her sofa; he'd called round after work. Holly had texted him once PC Chapman updated her with the progress so far. Which, it turned out, wasn't much.

'That they'd checked the hospitals—I'd already spoken with the main two, so that wasn't any help—and talked to Drew's boss. I feel so helpless, Todd.' Her voice shook. 'You want to know the worst part? When the police asked to look through the house, questioned me as to whether we'd argued. Like they suspected I'd done something awful to Drew.'

'They were only doing their job, Hols.'

'Why didn't they go and search for him instead? Instead of poking around here?'

'It's been twenty-four hours. God, where the hell *is* he?' Holly heard fear in Todd's voice, before he pulled her into a hug. He smelled of citrus and musk, and she breathed in his strength. At times, before this nightmare began, she'd envied Nessa her husband, especially when Drew refused to discuss parenthood. On those occasions, Holly had wondered whether she'd married the wrong Blackmore. She'd once dated Todd. Then she'd met Drew, and fallen madly in love.

Holly shoved her memories aside, ashamed of the direction in which her thoughts had taken her. Her main—her *only*—concern had to be getting Drew back. Alive.

A small voice warned that might not happen. Soon the buzzer might sound from the front door. She'd open it to find police officers, asking to come in. They'd inform her, their faces grave, that her husband's corpse had been discovered. Beaten and bloody after a mugging carried too far. Or how he'd died in an alleyway after a hit-and-run. Yesterday she'd been a wife. Today she suspected she might have become a widow. Hot tears stung her eyes, but Holly brushed them away.

'Drew and me—we just fit together so well, you know?' she said. 'He's not perfect. Grumpy in the mornings, leaves his dirty socks on the floor. None of that matters, because every Saturday he brings me breakfast in bed.' She blushed as she remembered where *that* often led. 'When he hands me the tray, he smiles, and suddenly we're the only two people in the world.'

Todd's arms pressed her closer, before he gently disengaged himself. 'I should go. Nessa will be wondering where I am.'

Holly nodded, albeit with reluctance. She mustn't be selfish, no matter how desperate she felt.

'Let me know the minute you hear anything,' Todd said as he kissed her goodbye.

Once he'd gone, Holly stared at her phone. The time had come to call her parents, tell them the grim news. She willed herself to pick it up, place the call.

Her mother answered straightaway, her trademark cheery greeting soon arrested by her daughter's sobs. 'I don't follow, darling,' Karen Harris said. 'What do you mean, Drew's gone? Gone where?'

'He went missing last night.' The words she'd dreaded saying, because speech made them so real.

A flurry of questions followed. 'Your father and I will fly over as soon as possible,' Karen said, once she'd heard the full story. 'I'll text you once I've booked our flights.'

CHAPTER 7 - Before

As a boy, Rick only ever saw the face of one of his mother's punters; he nicknamed the man Mr Nasty. Unlike the others, he became a regular, settling into a pattern of Saturday nights. Several weeks went by, during which time Rick only heard him. That proved frightening enough.

'Get yerself naked and on yer back, whore. I ain't got all night.' That was his usual greeting to Rick's mother. Once her door had shut behind them, the terrified child listened as curses ricocheted off the walls of the flat.

You want it up yer arse, bitch? Do as you're told, ya fuck-ugly hag.

Sometimes Rick left his bedroom door ajar to peep into the living room after the man arrived. He'd see a big, beefy guy, his features even coarser than his words. Arms like ham hocks. Fists that could split his mother's lip in a second. And often did.

Shut the hell up, whore. Followed by a blow. *Or you'll find out what pain really is.* Her pleas— *I'll do whatever you want… just don't hit me*—only inflamed Mr Nasty further.

Every Saturday Rick listened to the abuse, tears streaking his grubby face, terror gripping his body. As he huddled under his duvet, his mind transformed his puny seven-year-old self into a man. Big, strong and powerful, able to knock Mr Nasty out with one blow. A superhero, no less. He hated the fact he was unable to protect his mother. Often he'd wake on Sunday mornings to urine-soaked pyjamas. He never said anything, just rinsed them in the bathroom, and slept to one side of the wet patch until his mattress dried. His mother rarely entered his room, so there was little chance of her noticing the smell of piss.

One night he disobeyed her orders and crept into the living room, desperate for food. The stink of Mr Nasty's sweat lingered in the air. Rick padded through into the kitchen and found a single slice of white in the bread bin. He stuffed pieces into his mouth, mindful of the need to get back to bed as fast as possible. As Rick slunk through the living room, he spotted the man's shoes and tie on the floor, discarded along with his trousers. In the back pocket was a wallet, the edge of the leather barely visible. Rick hesitated, but the sounds from his mother's room indicated its occupants were busy. The frightened seven-year-old pulled out the wallet, noting the thick wad of notes, the multiple credit cards. He tugged one from its slot, his eyes scanning the embossed letters on it. The real name of his mother's abuser became etched on his memory. As did where he lived, evident from Mr Nasty's driving licence.

After that, Rick often sneaked out of his room on Saturdays, his fingers searching Mr Nasty's clothes, his curiosity about the man rampant. One of those nights imprinted itself on his mind forever.

The night he witnessed his mother's abduction.

CHAPTER 8

Saturday morning, and Vanessa Blackmore was in Holly's kitchen, nursing a mug of coffee. Her caramel-hued hair flowed past gold hoop earrings—almost large enough for a gymnast to swing from, Holly thought—and over the shoulders of her multi-coloured kaftan. Typical of Nessa; she sported a bohemian dress sense coupled with a relaxed attitude. At odds with Holly's business suits and her tendency to over-think. She was Holly's antithesis in other ways too: a stay-at-home mum, eight inches taller and with a body built to last, as Todd had once described his wife's solid frame. Her brother-in-law was catching up with his caseload—the demands of his job as a probation officer were onerous—so Nessa had come instead. She'd arrived on Holly's doorstep along with two-year-old Shane and Jack.

'Drew'll come back, you'll see,' she pronounced, her tone assured, after she parked the twins' buggy by the kitchen table. Both boys were fast asleep. Holly glanced at her nephews, a pang in her heart at her own lack of children. She'd broached the subject several times with Drew, only to run headlong into resistance. His reasons echoed in her head. *No rush, we've plenty of time. Maybe in a couple of years. After we both get promoted.* Every word a slap in the face. Each time she raised the issue, his reluctance grew stronger, his barriers more impenetrable, and Holly's dreams of motherhood faded further.

'Please don't think I'm being flippant,' Nessa continued. 'I love Drew. He's the brother I never had. But I suspect he needs some time for himself. A few days away, and he'll realise he's missing you and walk through the door.'

Holly wished she shared her sister-in-law's confidence. 'What makes you so certain?'

Nessa set down her mug. 'He was talking to Todd last week about how stressed he's been at work. How his boss is a pig, the constant pressure, etc. Well, you hear it often enough, don't you? How people flip and do a runner from their lives.'

Annoyance stabbed at Holly. 'Is that what you think Drew's done?'

'Yes. Seems the most likely explanation, anyway.'

Nessa meant well, but Holly found her sister-in-law's platitudes irritating; yes, of course people sometimes snapped under pressure and walked away from their problems. She had often noticed posters around Bristol, headed *Have you seen this person?* and afforded the photo only a cursory glance. Shame filled her at her casual dismissal of them, because now she understood the pain behind those pleas. Her sister-in-law was being presumptuous, though.

She realised Nessa was expecting a response. 'Okay, so Drew disliked his work. Plenty of jobs involve bad bosses, long hours and tight deadlines. Mine does, yet you don't see me quitting at the drop of a hat, do you?' Bitterness tinged Holly's voice. 'Why not tell me he couldn't cope?

We'd have talked it through. Found a solution. Why would he just up and leave?'

'Perhaps he had issues you don't know about.'

'Like what?' The spectre of another woman flashed across Holly's mind. Followed by Todd's reassurance: *he's not been having an affair, I can tell you that much.*

Nessa released a long breath. 'I've no idea. Could be he had health concerns, or financial problems.'

Holly stayed silent. She knew all about Drew's debts.

'Perhaps no single cause triggered him, but a cocktail of petty stuff that, all together, proved too much,' Nessa said. 'The mind is a funny thing. Mental breakdowns can be a protective measure against stress, as well as a response to it.'

Holly stared at her sister-in-law, considering what she'd said. 'Do you really think Drew's suffered a nervous breakdown?'

'It seems possible. Likely, even.'

'So what do I do? How do I get him back, when I've no idea where he is?'

'You wait. That's all you can do. Until he's ready to deal with whatever's stressing him.'

'But—' Holly could barely bring herself to say the words. 'What if he never returns?'

'That's Drew's call. Not yours.'

Holly's hand itched to slap Nessa. Her plain speaking, however well meaning, grated on her. Every nerve in Holly's body was raw, exposed, unwilling to acknowledge the truth behind the other woman's logic.

'I wish—' She swallowed her anger. 'That he'd trusted me more. That's all.'

******

What little saliva remained in Drew's mouth was thick and sticky, and his lips had grown cracked and sore. He no longer thought about the hollow in his belly, although his hunger persisted unabated. Instead he'd become obsessed with water. Pure, sweet and fresh. Drew pictured himself back home, extracting a bottle of Evian from the fridge, its plastic misted with condensation. He imagined the chilled fluid flowing down his throat, soaking into the parched membranes, and heaved a dry sob.

At times he was certain he'd die in this shithole. Fury would follow despair, though, with Drew screaming his rage into the blackness. 'Don't leave me here! Let me out, you prick!'

Never had he felt so alone. So helpless. His legs, trapped in their restraints, ached to walk, jog, sprint. For a man used to running several miles most days, such imprisonment was torture. At least he wasn't cold, thanks to the pile of blankets. His duvet was thick, and the mattress prevented the chill from the concrete floor striking up into his body. The makeshift sound-proofing didn't muffle all noises, but did provide a degree of insulation. Thank God for that. Drew was under no illusion that his captor cared about his comfort. Whoever had brought him to this place wanted to prevent him dying from hypothermia during the current cold weather. Hence he'd provided basic amenities, although no food and drink, at least not yet. Drew needed to hang on to that sliver of hope. That before long—please, God, make it soon—his abductor would bring him water.

An inkling of the bastard's identity edged its way into his brain once more. He thrust it away, refusing to entertain the memory. Too ugly, too raw.

Wait. What was that noise? Drew yanked himself upwards, as far as his bonds permitted. He held himself still. His ears strained into the silence.

The sound came again. A soft rustle, as though from clothing. Every cell in Drew's body warned him someone was nearby. He sensed, rather than heard, regular breathing. Like the other person was listening out for Drew. Just as much as Drew was for them.

'Hello?' he shouted. Hard to do with his mouth so dry. 'I know you're out there... who are you?' He swallowed, desperate to moisten his throat. 'Why have you done this? Talk to me, for God's sake.'

No response. But his ears detected the whisper of cloth moving. Whoever was outside had shifted their position.

He tried again. 'Fuck it, will you say something? Tell me who you are. Please.'

Silence met his words. Then he heard the rustling again. Followed by footsteps fading into the distance.

******

After Nessa's departure, Holly brooded over her conversation with her sister-in-law. In particular: *You wait. That's all you can do.* She hated feeling helpless. The police, damn them, weren't taking her husband's disappearance seriously enough.

Two cups of coffee later, she'd concocted a plan. Holly reached for her phone.

'I'll come round straightaway,' Todd told her. Guilt bubbled inside her for disturbing his Saturday overtime, but Drew's well-being mattered more.

Fifteen minutes after her call, Todd was sitting in her kitchen, mug in hand. 'So what's this idea of yours? I take it the police haven't found any leads?'

Holly shook her head. 'All that talk about how most missing people turn up within a few days, blah, blah, blah.' Her fist pounded the table. 'You could tell the minute Sharon Chapman lost interest. As soon as I mentioned Drew's under pressure at work, her face got that "I've heard this all before" expression. Well, screw her. What the hell does she know about my husband?'

'Holly.' Todd's voice was calm, although his eyes betrayed his concern. 'The police are just doing their job, hampered by insufficient manpower and resources. I'm not sure what else they can do, to be honest. Drew's only been missing for two days.'

Holly stabbed him with a glare. 'If he's lying somewhere critically injured, every second counts. We've wasted enough time. I'm going to look for my husband, and you're coming with me. We'll start with the woods around Blaise Castle. Perhaps he went for a run there and got hurt somehow. But I'm not sitting here doing nothing. Not while Drew needs me.'

'Wait.' Todd laid a hand on her arm. 'It's too big a job for the two of us.'

His comment echoed her own concerns. 'What did you have in mind?'

'Let's mobilise the local community. Phone radio stations, put up flyers. Post on Facebook. Get Drew's colleagues involved, the guys from the running club, anyone else who wants to pitch in. We'll organise a full search of everywhere Drew frequented. Tomorrow, if possible.'

Part of Holly chafed at the delay, but Todd's strategy made sense. More eyes on the ground. A better chance of finding... what, exactly? Drew lying dead? She repressed a sob.

'Hey.' Concern in Todd's voice. 'Stay strong, Hols.'

She nodded, unable to speak.

'I'll make a start,' Todd continued. 'First step is to inform the police, then slap a post on Facebook. Why don't you knock up some flyers?'

Things moved fast after that. Todd called Radio Bristol, his running club mates, Drew's boss at Jonas Software. He hugged her before he left, three hours later.

'We'll find Drew,' he said, but a hint of fear lingered in his voice, despite his apparent confidence. 'Anything else is not an option.'

Holly trudged through the rest of Saturday in a blur, her heartache doubling once she spotted the first few flakes of snow that fell that afternoon. The house became chilly with the bite of incipient winter, forcing Holly to turn up the heating. By the time she crawled into bed, a sheet of white covered the ground beneath her window. Nessa's theory that Drew had walked out on his life was gaining credibility in Holly's head. Had she pushed him too far with her insistence about babies?

Where are you, Drew? Are you somewhere safe, and above all, warm?

She didn't sleep that night, picturing her husband on the streets. Homeless, scared, and freezing to death.

******

Drew reckoned several hours had passed since he'd heard the rustle of clothing outside his prison. How long had he been there? Thirty hours? Fifty? Or even sixty? The temperature in his cell, always cold, seemed frigid right then, which indicated night-time, and necessitated an extra blanket. He'd left work on Thursday evening, so it was probably Saturday, maybe early Sunday morning. Drew's thirst had multiplied a hundred-fold, his throat a sandpit, his tongue stuck to his teeth. His breath smelled like rotting cabbage whenever it wafted into his nostrils.

A cramp seized Drew's right calf, pulling his ankle tight against his bonds. His leg, unused to so little movement for so long, descended into sheer agony. Drew screamed himself hoarse until the torture subsided. Less than a minute later, his left calf also spasmed; Drew flexed his foot while he hollered into the pain. As the torment eased, his yells tapered into a deluge of gasps: *uuuhhh, uuuhhh, uuuhhh.*

Drew closed his eyes, dragged in a long breath. Try as he might, he couldn't escape self-pity's clutches. Why was this happening to him?

Inside his head, he thought he knew the answer. A voice spoke to him from years before. *Wherever you are, I will find you, and you will suffer.*

CHAPTER 9 - Before

Saturday night. That meant a visit from Mr Nasty. Sure enough, the man arrived at eight p.m., his mood even fouler than normal. Rick waited until the door to his mother's room closed, then crept out from under his duvet. At least he wasn't hungry; his mum had shoved a bowl of soggy pasta under his nose earlier. With his belly full, he could concentrate on Mr Nasty, and what was taking place in the other bedroom. This time no discarded clothing lay strewn across the living room. With nothing to rummage through, and aware of the risk he ran, Rick almost retreated to the comfort of his bed. But he didn't. Okay, so he wasn't the powerful hero of his fantasies, but he could do *something*, right?

He thought of the knife block in the kitchen, of the blades it housed, their metal dull and stained with ancient grime. In his head, Rick saw himself grab the largest one, then pad across the carpet. He'd open the door to his mother's room, then *wham! Take that, Mr Nasty!* He'd stab the blade, hard and deep, into the ogre's belly. The man would sink back with a groan, his hands clutched around the knife handle. He'd die within seconds, although Rick didn't like to think about all the blood there'd be. With him dead, though, everything would be wonderful. Rick pictured his mother, so grateful he'd saved her. She'd press him close, murmuring thanks in his ear. Tell him how much she loved her special boy.

He hesitated amid the darkness, his ears attuned to the fury in Mr Nasty's tone.

'Don't disrespect me, bitch. Or I'll make you regret it.' A fist slammed against flesh.

Fear snaked through Rick's body; his mouth drained of saliva, and his knees trembled. He needed to act—*now*—but the door to his mother's room flew open, the wood banging against the wall. *Find somewhere to hide, Rick, and fast! Over there!* He darted behind an armchair and crouched against the sanctuary it offered. His heart hammered so hard the whole world must surely hear it.

Mr Nasty stormed into the room, fully dressed. He dragged the boy's mother in his wake, her wrists gripped by one huge hand. In his other he held something Rick couldn't identify. His mother's hair was wild; a livid bruise bloomed on one cheek, her bottom lip split and slick with blood. Inarticulate mutterings issued from her mouth. Tears streamed down her face.

'Shut the fuck up, bitch,' Mr Nasty ground out. He took the unidentified object—it was one of her fishnet stockings, Rick realised—and stuffed it between her lips. From his vantage point, Rick watched an expression that terrified him creep over Mr Nasty's face. Even at seven years old, he recognised evil when he saw it. His teeth shook with fear, a rapid *click-clack* that would surely betray him. Wetness flooded his pyjama bottoms and soaked into the carpet. The smell terrified Rick further. Mr Nasty couldn't fail to sniff out the wuss cowering behind the chair.

The man's attention, though, lay elsewhere.

'You need to learn a lesson, whore. You'll get the same treatment I dished out to that slut Rosalie Parker. That'll teach you to respect me.'

A powerful punch knocked his mother unconscious. Rick gave a strangled gasp, his nails driven deep into his palms, but Mr Nasty didn't notice. He slung his victim over his shoulder and stalked out of the flat.

CHAPTER 10

A steady *clump, clump* roused Drew from his sleep. His senses strained for every nuance of noise that reached his ears. Footsteps were what he'd heard, coming closer. Drew jerked himself as upright as his bonds allowed, praying that rescue had arrived at last.

The footsteps stopped outside Drew's prison.

'Hey!' Drew managed to croak, his dry throat straining with the effort. 'Who's there? Help me, please!'

His demand went unanswered. Oh, God. Whoever was outside must be his abductor. Not, as he'd hoped, someone who'd come to save him.

He tried again. 'Get me out of this place right now, you hear me?'

A glimpse of light flashed near to Drew's feet, then vanished. Accompanied by a sound he couldn't place. Then came the thud of plastic hitting concrete inside his cell, followed by a sloshing noise. In that moment Drew forgot all about his captor. All he cared about was getting water.

His left hand scrabbled into the darkness to close around a large plastic bottle. His ecstasy was such he barely registered the soft plop of something else being chucked into his prison. His fingers fumbled with the cap, unable to tilt the container upwards fast enough. He gulped the precious fluid until his throat protested, and he collapsed against the floor amid a welter of coughs. It didn't matter that the water had been stale and tepid; life was returning to his desiccated body. For now, nothing else mattered.

Drew lay in his bonds, gasping, relief flooding his brain.

With infinite care, to preserve the liquid that remained, he screwed the plastic top onto the bottle, then tilted it upside down. By his estimation, a quarter was left in a two-litre container. With no idea when his captor might return, he'd need to eke out his supply.

He listened, but heard nothing. Whoever threw the water into his prison hadn't hung around. Well, when his jailer returned, Drew would be ready. Unwilling to confront his gut instinct, he'd convinced himself mistaken identity must be to blame for his incarceration. He'd yell that he was Drew Blackmore, damn it, followed by: *you've got the wrong guy, you sicko. Get me the hell out of this shit-hole.*

Wait. His abductor would surely kill him to prevent him contacting the police, not release him. Or else he'd abandon Drew to die in the darkness. He'd lose his mind if he spent much longer in this place. Rescue seemed increasingly unlikely; wouldn't the cops have found him by now if they had any clues? No, if he stood any chance of escape, it needed to be through his own efforts.

If his legs still worked. The cramps from earlier reminded Drew his muscles would soon atrophy under his present circumstances.

Maybe he could prevent that. Drew flexed both feet, back and forth several times, wincing at the soreness in his calves, then stretched both legs, pointing his toes. Next a few ankle rotations, followed by bicycling his feet through the air. The discomfort in his lower limbs receded.

He set the water bottle beside him, surprised when it rested against something soft. He recalled the plop he'd heard earlier. His fingers moved through the darkness and closed over a cling-film-wrapped triangle.

Drew ripped off the protective covering, shoving the sandwich into his mouth. The bread was thick, stale, with only a scraping of butter, the two slices bracketing a slice of ham. To Drew, though, his makeshift meal tasted better than the finest fillet steak. His teeth tore off chunks of bread and meat until the food was gone. He slumped back, unfazed by the hard concrete banging against his head wound. He was still terrified and uncomfortable, unable to see anything, but his hunger and thirst had been satisfied. Progress, of sorts.

The sound as his captor delivered the sandwich and water returned to him, along with how it seemed familiar. A cat flap, that was it; Uncle Hal and Aunt Mel had used one for Bandit, their ancient Siamese. What he'd heard hadn't sounded plastic, though. He guessed the door must be wooden and that his abductor had cut a hinged feeding flap into it.

Resolve poured through Drew. Now he knew for certain where the entrance to his prison was located. Soon he'd break free, and when he did, he'd tell Holly he wanted kids, lots of them. He'd do other stuff too. Todd and he had discussed training for the London marathon—time to make good on that goal. As for work, he'd get shot of his boss and set up his own software firm. Never again would he complain about stuff that didn't matter; when he got his life back, he'd treasure every second.

He'd already lost so much that was precious. Uncle Hal and Auntie Mel, who'd raised Drew and Todd after they were orphaned, had died two years ago after a drunk driver rammed their car off a bridge. His parents were long gone. Only the faintest of memories remained of Eloise Blackmore. None at all of Barry Blackmore. Drew's heart hitched when he thought of his father.

His fingers strayed to his right hand, where the man's signet ring had sat for so many years. 'I miss you, Dad,' Drew said aloud. His voice cracked. 'Please, just get me the hell out of here.' A man dead for over two decades couldn't help him, but Drew didn't care. He'd always derived comfort from talking to his father. Love for the man he didn't remember warmed his heart.

Drew touched where his wedding ring had been. Most important, he needed to consider Holly. They had a future as husband and wife. With any luck, one day they'd be parents. He wouldn't let some psycho ruin that.

'Fuck you, you bastard,' he muttered. 'You'll not get the better of me. No way.'

******

One thirty on Sunday afternoon, sixty-seven hours after Drew went missing. More snow had fallen overnight, but Holly remained determined to press ahead with the search. She and Todd were in the main car park at Blaise Castle. Despite her angst, Holly was pleased with the turnout. Her husband's boss and colleagues had shown up, along with Amber and Elaine from her own place of work. Twelve runners from Drew and Todd's club put in an appearance. The rest of the group comprised four people she'd never met, one of whom introduced himself and his cohorts as 'concerned members of the community'.

'Nosy gits, more like,' Todd muttered after the guy moved away. 'Not that it matters. The more eyes we have looking for Drew, the better.' He frowned. 'Where are the police? Shouldn't they be here, along with tracker dogs?'

'Not enough manpower, they said. Blamed recent funding cuts. And they only use dogs if they consider the missing person to be vulnerable, like a child, or someone elderly.'

'Fuck 'em, then. We'll do this ourselves.'

At two o'clock the group split into different factions to conduct the search, with instructions to meet at five for a debriefing at the Bat and Ball Inn. The running club chose to scour the Blaise Castle estate, a herculean task given its six hundred and fifty acres, but Todd instructed them to concentrate on the main walking paths. Drew's workmates would focus on a circle around Jonas Software.

Holly and Todd elected to cover the area near to Drew's home, and the rest of the searchers would check his other running routes.

The weather was dry, crisp and clear, but that didn't help when snow covered the ground they needed to search. Holly didn't hold out much hope.

'At least we can try,' Todd said, his voice pinched, as they turned into the small park behind Drew and Holly's house. A grove of beech trees stood at the far end, sending a flood of memories Holly's way. She'd walked among them so many times with Drew, his fingers entwined with hers. Drained with exhaustion, she lost herself in the past, until the world shifted, and… *yes!* Why hadn't she thought of it before? She knew, without a doubt, where Drew was. Holly sprinted towards the trees, her feet searing a trail through the snow. Her husband lay there, perhaps lying hurt, but alive, still breathing, and she just had to reach him, oh please God…

'Drew! Drew, where are you? Can you hear me?' She ran, panting, amid the trees, her eyes checking around her. The ground was mostly flat, apart from under the nearest tree. That shape— might it be Drew? Holly dropped on all fours, her hands scrabbling through the icy whiteness. She ignored the chill penetrating her knees, too intent on rescuing her husband.

'Hols!' Todd shouted, but his voice sounded very far away. Holly continued to dig until her nails scraped something solid. She'd done it; she'd found Drew. Thank God. Her fingers dug deeper, only to reveal stone instead of flesh. A flat boulder she'd seen many times, but had forgotten in her angst.

Her scream of denial rose high into the afternoon air. A dull pain throbbed through her hands. When she looked down, spots of red stained the boulder. Her nails still tore at it, and she didn't know how to stop them.

Behind her, Todd spoke, his tone gentle. 'Let me hold you, Hols. Please, love.'

He pulled her to her feet to hug her close; her tears soaked his shoulder. Once her sobs tapered off, he took her bloodied hands in his. He cleaned them on his T-shirt, then kissed each finger.

'We'll find him, Hols,' he said. 'It's just a matter of time.'

Holly nodded, too choked to speak. Numb, she allowed Todd to lead her out of the park to continue the search.

Three hours later, the two of them joined the rest of the party at the Bat and Ball Inn. Nobody had found any sign of Drew.

Amber pulled Holly into a hug. 'Don't give up hope, okay?' Over Amber's shoulder she saw Elaine's face, tight with concern.

'We did our best,' Rory Bruce, one of Drew's running mates, said. 'But with snow covering the area—' He shrugged, his eyes sympathetic.

'Aye, and who's to tell what it might be hiding?' Mike Randall, another runner, chipped in. 'Perhaps when we get a thaw—'

In her peripheral vision, Holly saw Adam Scott, the guy beside Mike, elbow him in the ribs, his expression a warning. The man shut up, his face turning red.

Tears came into Holly's eyes. She understood what Adam had stopped Mike from saying. That somewhere, under the snow, might lie Drew's corpse.

******

Footsteps arrived outside the door. Drew's stomach growled with hunger, but other, more important, considerations occupied his mind. Despite his fear, he found his voice, his throat lined with sandpaper.

'My name is Drew Blackmore. I don't know who you are, but I'm not the man you're after.'

The flap opened, lessening the gloom for a second. The subsequent thud told Drew his sandwich had arrived. Seconds later a plastic bottle hit his thigh.

'Did you hear what I said? I'm Drew Blackmore. You took the wrong guy.'

No reply. Whoever stood outside didn't move away, though.

'I won't tell the police, I swear. Just let me go home.'

Still no response. Drew's mouth was so dry he could barely speak.

'You can blindfold me if you want. That way I won't see your face.' Scenarios flashed through his mind: the unlocking of the door, an order to keep his eyes shut. Soft cloth tied over them. Followed by the unfastening of his restraints. Then Drew would attack, using the chains that had bound him. Their metal links crashing against the bastard's nose, or blinding him. A long shot, but it might work.

A stir of clothing, an intake of breath. But no key in the lock, no bolt being drawn back. Perhaps the guy didn't have a suitable blindfold handy.

'For God's sake, do the right thing. You have to let me out of here.' Hysteria pervaded Drew's voice, and he fought to stay calm. He'd never expected this to be easy.

A snort of derision. Then the sound of footsteps in retreat, growing ever quieter.

'Hey!' Drew's vocal cords cracked under the force of his shout. 'Come back! Don't leave me here, you prick!'

His plea met with silence. His jailer had gone.

Fury pounded through Drew's body. He screamed until his voice gave out, terrible yells of rage and denial that filled his makeshift prison. His wrists strained against their bonds as he wrenched himself upright, inflicting savage bruises on his flesh.

Exhausted, he crumpled against his mattress, tears stinging his eyes. His former resolve seemed very distant.

That night Drew slept more deeply than usual. When he awoke, his head felt fuzzy, as though stuffed with cotton wool. He crawled to the bucket, surprised yet relieved to find it empty. Before it had been rank and almost full. The discarded bottles and used cling-film had also gone.

His captor must have drugged him, then cleaned up his cell.

Horror prickled Drew's skin, and sobs choked his throat. While he'd lain unconscious, his captor had been within touching distance. The nightmare had just stepped closer.

CHAPTER 11 - Before

Rick waited in the empty flat, huddled in his bed. His pyjamas were soaked and stinking from when he'd wet himself, but he didn't care. A whiff of stale sweat clung to his duvet; his mother hadn't washed it for months. She'd be home soon, he persuaded himself; she'd never left him alone overnight. It was just a matter of time before he heard her key in the lock.

He wrapped his arms around his pillow, covered in his mother's T-shirt, and held it—*her*—close. The hours ticked by until at last he slipped into a troubled sleep.

When he awoke the morning sun was filtering through his bedroom curtains. He listened, his ears straining for any sound, but heard nothing. Silence wrapped the flat in an uneasy embrace. Rick unfurled himself, threw back the duvet and walked into the living room. His mother's door was open, allowing him a view of her empty bed. He padded towards the bathroom, then the kitchen, but both were deserted. Icy fear clutched his heart.

Rick retreated to his bed, pulling his duvet over his head and the pillow into his arms. He inhaled his mother's scent from the T-shirt, deciding she must have gone straight to work. She'd be back once her shift finished. At least it was the school summer holidays. Instead of fidgeting through lessons, he'd be home, the way a good boy should be, when she returned.

'I want my mummy,' Rick sobbed, his face buried in her T-shirt. Surely she'd come, if he wished hard enough?

Time inched by as the day passed. Rick didn't venture from his room; his empty belly went ignored, and he voided his bladder into an old Fanta bottle. He refused to think about Mr Nasty hauling his mother out of the flat. That way it hadn't happened.

Later, after dark, a fist pounded on the front door. When nobody answered, curses followed in a male voice. Rick recognised its owner: one of his mother's punters. He cowered lower into the depths of the duvet, but the fist hammered on the wood again. After a while, the man's footsteps retreated along the tiles of the communal hallway.

Days passed. Rick continued to wait, only moving from his room if he needed to shit or to grab food from the kitchen. Dry bread eaten straight from the packet. Slices of processed ham rolled up and shoved in his mouth. It didn't take long to empty the fridge and cupboards. Once they were bare, he rummaged through the waste bin. In it he found two chicken bones, both with shreds of skin and flesh clinging to them. Once he'd gnawed them clean, he chewed into the marrow.

Throughout his waking hours Rick lay in bed, replaying in his head the words his mother's abuser had spoken.

You need to learn a lesson, whore. You'll get the same treatment I dished out to that slut Rosalie Parker.

The unknown woman's name became seared on his brain, although he had no idea who she was. Nor did he care. Rick just wanted his mummy to walk through the door, no matter how bruised and battered. She was all he had.

CHAPTER 12

Holly sank into her mother's arms, relief thrumming through her. Around them Bristol Airport buzzed with passengers, baggage handlers, airline staff. The noise crowded Holly's senses, grated her nerves. Despite her joy at seeing her parents, she yearned to be back home. What if Drew returned and she wasn't there?

'No news?' Karen asked.

Holly shook her head. 'He's vanished, Mum. The police don't seem to have any answers.'

Gary Tobin, the detective Holly had spoken to about Drew's case—she winced at the notion of Drew being reduced to a file number—had been friendly, efficient, but non-committal. 'Most people who go missing come home fairly soon,' he'd said, echoing Sharon Chapman's words.

Karen pulled back, tucked a stray wisp of Holly's hair behind her ear. 'Please don't take this the wrong way, darling. But I have to ask. Was everything all right between you two? Before Drew vanished?'

Holly hated the implication: *inadequate wife equals unhappy husband*. From behind gritted teeth, she replied, 'We're fine. Everything was great between us.'

The enormity of the lie smacked her in the face. No, they *hadn't* been fine—far from it. Drew had drifted away from her, flotsam caught in a current, since she'd broached the topic of children.

Not that she intended to mention their argument on the morning he disappeared. The angry words they'd flung at each other were too awful to repeat.

'Our marriage is good,' she reiterated. 'We're happy together.' Her mother didn't say anything, just nodded.

Holly stared at her father over Karen's shoulder. His hair was greyer, the crinkles around his eyes deeper, but the love in them hadn't changed.

'My turn,' Peter Harris said, before wrapping Holly in a tight hug.

'How long can you stay?' she murmured, her voice muffled against his jacket.

'As long as you need us, sweetheart.'

******

Over the course of the next week, Holly was beyond grateful for Karen and Peter's quiet presence. Every day turned into a century, waiting for news that never came. Her husband had been officially listed as missing. Holly had read the statistics countless times; three hundred thousand people disappeared each year in the UK. Ninety-seven per cent, one source claimed, turned up or were found within seven days. Drew had been gone for longer, so she'd married one of the other three per cent; the unlikely odds taunted her with their cruelty. Meanwhile Holly barely slept and struggled to eat, the kilos dropping off her already tiny frame. Her hair was a bird's nest, her skin sallow, her eyes sunken. When she looked in the mirror, an old woman stared back.

On their first evening together she'd told her mother something she'd not revealed to anyone else. Afterwards she felt cleansed, relieved. Karen had held her daughter, and cried, as had Holly. Since then she'd cooked Holly's favourite dishes, coaxed her to eat, and, concerned about her weight loss, begged her to see a doctor. Holly had stood her ground, wary of being prescribed antidepressants, although Karen continued to press the issue.

That morning her parents had gone to the supermarket for groceries. Holly sat in the kitchen, cradling her mug of coffee, her mind on Drew, as always. And money.

She wouldn't be able to take much more time off work. Her boss had made it plain that, while he sympathised with her predicament, he expected her back at her desk before long. The not-so-subtle hint underpinning their conversation had delivered the message: *if you want to make partner level, you need to get your act together.* She snorted inwardly. Yeah, right. As if anyone under forty and minus a penis could reach such hallowed ground. Not that she cared about promotion anymore. Without Drew's salary, she'd struggle to manage the household bills. The mortgage on their three-bedroom detached house in Westbury-on-Trym, one of the smarter areas in Bristol, stretched their finances to breaking point.

Holly stared at the letter in her hand, addressed to Drew, the envelope branded in red: *FINAL DEMAND—OPEN IMMEDIATELY*, the name of a credit card provider on the back. They'd started after Drew burned his way through his inheritance after Hal and Mel died. Afraid of invading his privacy, she'd not questioned him about them. Now she wondered. Had Nessa been right? Might his money worries, along with his job stress, have caused a mental breakdown?

The doorbell buzzed. Holly tossed the letter aside and ran to the door. Please God, let it be Gary Tobin, bringing good news. Instead, Todd stood on the step. Without waiting for her to speak, he pushed past her, an envelope clutched in his hand. Holly, puzzled by his uncharacteristic lack of manners, followed him into the living room. He turned to face her, pumping up and down on his toes, the energy radiating from him almost palpable.

'He's alive, Hols. Drew's definitely not dead.' He thrust the envelope in Holly's face, his breath coming hard and fast.

'What? Oh, my God—how do you *know*? Todd, what's happened?' Holly clutched his sleeve, staring at him. The shadows under his eyes matched hers, as did the red veins threaded through them. He'd not shaved and his skin sported heavy stubble.

'Look at this,' Todd said. Holly took the envelope, blank on the outside and already slit open. Inside lay an object she recognised only too well.

She reached in trembling fingers to extract a gold signet ring. The one that had belonged to Drew's father. It nestled, cool and heavy, in her palm. Her knees shook, and she grabbed Todd's arm to steady herself before she sank onto the sofa.

'I don't understand.' She dragged in a deep breath. 'Where did you get this?'

'Found it this morning, on our doormat. Drew must have delivered it during the night.'

'But why would he do that?'

'I'm not sure.' The anguish in Todd's voice pierced Holly. Her fingers glided over the shank of the ring, traced their way across the initials *BB* engraved on the bezel. As though her skin caressed Drew, not metal, and a jolt of joy shot through her. 'Oh, God, you're right. Drew's alive.' She felt dizzy with relief. 'He's out there somewhere, he might not be able to tell us in words, but that's what this means, don't you see?'

'Hols, please—'

'What else could he have sent to get the message across? That has as much significance as his dad's ring?'

'Will you listen to me—'

'Have you told the police?'

Todd sat beside her, taking her hand in his. 'No.'

She stared at him. 'Why not? They need to know.'

'I agree. And I'll contact them later. But I'm scared, Hols.'

Holly's happiness ebbed away. This was good news, surely?

'Ever since Drew started wearing Dad's ring, I've never known him to take it off. Not once. And he didn't write me a note, Hols. Not even a few words.' Todd sucked in a breath. 'I think he's run out on his life. Why else would he send me the ring?'

'No. You're wrong.' On seeing the scepticism in Todd's face, she elaborated. 'If he'd really walked out on everything, he'd have returned his wedding band to me. But he hasn't.'

Todd was silent for a moment, his expression pensive. 'Because he realised how much that would upset you,' he said at last. 'You might be right.'

'Exactly. He'll be in touch, and soon. I just know he will.'

'I hope so.' Todd prised the ring from Holly's fingers, then replaced it in the envelope. He pressed a kiss into her hair. 'I'll call you later, okay? Once I've spoken to the police.'

******

Nine a.m. the following morning. Holly stared at her alarm clock, fighting the need to roll over and go back to sleep. Her mind was running on Drew's signet ring. What its return meant.

Todd had called the previous evening to update her. 'The police will test the envelope and ring for fingerprints. I'll keep you posted.'

Her mother had agreed with Holly. 'Sending the ring is probably a cry for help,' she told her daughter that night. 'Drew's walked out on his life, but that doesn't mean he doesn't care, sweetheart. He knew Todd would worry, so he wanted to reassure his brother he was still alive. It's his way of getting in touch. That's why he didn't return his wedding ring.'

Holly nodded. 'He'll be home within a few days, Mum. Or at least make contact again. I'm sure of it.'

Now, the morning after, her mood remained buoyant. *In sickness and in health*, she reminded herself. That was what she'd vowed three years ago, and she intended to honour her promise. 'We'll get through this together,' she imagined herself telling Drew. Her arms hugged her body the way his would have, and Holly smiled. Before long she'd be reunited with the man she loved.

Out of habit, she checked her phone for a missed text or call. Nothing. But there would be. Soon.

Holly threw back the duvet and headed for the shower. From the guest room, she heard her father's snores; neither of her parents were early risers. She'd make brunch for them later; time to take her mother's advice and eat more, replace the weight she'd lost. She hummed to herself as she soaped her body.

Once dressed, Holly headed downstairs. A pile of fast-food flyers and junk mail greeted her from the doormat. Another heap had arrived yesterday, which Holly had tossed on the hall table. Time to chuck the whole lot in the recycling bin. She scooped up the latest batch, then grabbed those from the previous day. She stopped, frozen. Something small and hard nestled amid the bunch of paper.

Holly chucked the flyers on the floor, her fingers scrabbling through the junk mail. At last only one envelope remained. Plain white. Nothing written on the outside. A ring-shaped bulge at one end.

Holly tore open the envelope. Seconds later her howl of misery filled the house.

******

'Drink this, darling. It'll help.' Karen Harris offered a steaming mug to Holly.

Holly waved it away. 'I don't want coffee, Mum.' Sobs threatened to choke her. 'I wish I'd found the ring yesterday. But I didn't, because all those bloody flyers annoyed me, and I was worried about the final demand letter for Drew. So I threw everything aside, and never noticed the envelope amongst all the trash.' She wiped her eyes, blew her nose. 'The signet ring gave me hope, don't you see? But Todd was right. Drew's done a runner.'

'He's not the man I thought he was.' Her father's expression was grim, his hands clenched into fists. 'You deserve better, sweetheart.'

'Don't be so quick to judge, Peter,' Karen said. 'Drew may be mentally ill.'

'Why didn't he write me a note?' Holly wailed. 'That's what I don't get.'

'He didn't with me either, remember, Hols.' Todd had arrived ten minutes after Holly's frantic phone call to him. He was sitting opposite her in the living room, his mug of coffee untouched. Behind his head, out of the window, the morning sky looked grey and leaden, the way Holly felt.

'He might not have been able to, darling. Not if he's suffered a breakdown.' Her mother had a point, Holly conceded. Pain still prickled inside her, though. Was it selfish to wish Drew had written a few words to her? Even if they were ones of farewell? The blank envelope, the return of the ring she'd slipped on his finger three years before, seemed cruel in a way she wouldn't have expected.

Within seconds, Karen's arms wound tight around her daughter, rocking her like a child. 'Don't you worry. It'll be okay, my love.'

'But how? Drew doesn't want me, Mum. That's what this means, don't you see? Our marriage doesn't matter to him anymore. He's left me, and I've no idea where he is, and—'

'Shhh, darling. We'll make this right. You'll see.' Karen hugged her daughter tighter. Holly cried for a long time, until exhaustion took over. Still her mother rocked her, one hand stroking Holly's hair.

Eventually Holly pushed her away. 'I need to inform the police.'

'I'll do it,' Todd said, extracting his phone from his jacket. 'You've been through enough, Hols.'

She smiled her gratitude at him. Thank goodness for Todd. As her life continued to implode, his support meant the world to her.

CHAPTER 13 - Before

Rick found out later that it took a week before their neighbour, the one who'd asked why his mother hadn't aborted him, realised she'd not seen either of them around. By then he'd not eaten for two days. The toilet had blocked, and he'd used all the available paper. Part of him knew he should summon help, but he didn't dare to move. The terror that Mr Nasty might return proved too great, despite the hunger that gnawed at his guts. Instead, he listened to their neighbour knock on the door, then prise open the letterbox.

'Anyone home?' Her forty-a-day cigarettes voice rasped through the gap.

Rick held his breath. He heard the woman yell his mother's name, then his. Again, but louder. After a while, her footsteps moved away. The door to her flat opened and shut, and silence reigned once more.

She returned the next day, her knock more insistent this time.

'Fuck! What the hell's that stink?' Her voice reeked of disgust. The stench from the blocked toilet must have reached her nostrils.

Rick heaved a sigh of relief after she'd gone, but the reprieve proved temporary. Shortly afterwards, multiple voices, male and female, sounded outside the door. A thunderous crash followed. Rick screamed, then stopped, ashamed of his weakness. He wrapped his arms around the T-shirt-covered pillow, then slid beneath his filthy bedclothes, leaving a small gap for air. If he kept very, very still, then maybe—

But no. 'Hey there, sweetheart,' a female voice said. 'Can you tell me your name?'

Rick cracked open an eye. A bowler hat and uniform, both dark navy, with white squares bordering the hat's brim. A lady from the police, then. Hot urine flooded Rick's legs and soaked the mattress. Of course he was in trouble; he'd been a bad boy, hadn't he? He'd failed to protect his mother from Mr Nasty, and now the police would arrest him. In his peripheral vision, he saw men, also in uniforms, searching the flat. He burrowed deeper under his filthy duvet.

'Where's your mummy, darling?' the lady said. Still Rick said nothing. She didn't sound angry, but...

She squatted beside his bed. 'I'd love it if you came out and said hello.'

Rick shut his eyes. *Go away*, he willed her. *Please.* He opened them again, but she was still there.

'You're safe now.' The police lady smiled at him, but her face looked as though she might cry. 'There's nothing to be afraid of.'

How wrong she was. Sobs filled Rick's throat. 'I don't wanna go to jail,' he wailed. Then he leapt from the bed, and into her arms.

What happened next became a blur. He remembered a hot bath, fresh clothes and pizza—cheesy, delicious and wonderful. Somewhere new to live—*just for now, sweetheart, while we get things sorted*—with a clean bed, a toilet that worked. Along with a promise from the nice police lady.

'You won't go to prison, my love.' Despite her assurances, Rick remained silent, too scared to say anything. His seven-year-old brain figured that, were he to speak, Mr Nasty would *know*, and retribution would quickly follow. Both for himself and his mother, should she still be alive. Even the police couldn't protect them from Mr Nasty.

In the next few days, another lady came to talk to him. 'Hello, young man,' she said. 'My name's Lisa and my job is to help children like you. Is it all right if we chat for a while?'

Rick shook his head. He hadn't spoken since leaving the flat.

'Maybe you could draw me a picture, then. Does that sound like fun?'

Paper and wax crayons appeared. Rick picked up the black one. He poised it above the paper, then began. A stick woman took shape, being dragged by a monstrous blob, her mouth an 'O' of terror. The blob had fangs but no face. All the while the fury inside Rick grew until it burst forth in a riot of black. His fingers scrawled over the paper, harder and harder, covering what he'd drawn, until the crayon snapped.

Rick threw the two halves on the table and folded his arms, his expression sullen. He wouldn't say another word until the questions about his mother stopped.

It took a long time before they did, but Rick didn't waver. He never revealed to anyone how he'd witnessed Mr Nasty hauling his victim, bloodied and unconscious, from her home.

Instead the memory festered, growing more putrid as the years went by.

CHAPTER 14

Two weeks had passed since Drew's disappearance, and so far all enquiries had drawn a blank. The presumption was that Drew had snapped under the stress of his job and financial worries, and had run, full pelt, from life's pressures. None of the NHS psychiatric facilities had admitted him, so Holly assumed he must be coping with his mental meltdown by himself. She hated to think of him alone and distraught, afraid to return home and face a multitude of questions. The weather forecast had predicted more heavy snow for most of the UK, including Bristol, for the coming weekend. She shivered, despite the heat in the kitchen. Wherever Drew was, she hoped he was warm, at the very least. Safe, too. Her heart ached for her husband, even though he'd walked out on their marriage and left her to muddle through alone.

Holly pushed away her plate. She'd not managed more than a mouthful of food. Karen had cooked lasagne that evening, and the smell of fried onions still hung heavy in the air. Across the table her father eyed her with concern, as worried as his wife about Holly's lack of appetite. Beside him sat Todd. He'd called in on his way home from work.

'Have you spoken to Gary Tobin today?' Her brother-in-law's question startled Holly from the darkness of her thoughts; her nerves were shot to pieces. Every time her mobile rang, she jumped as though she'd sat on hot coals; each ring of the doorbell scraped fingernails over her mind.

'Still no news,' she said. 'Every time I call, it gets harder to hear him say there are no fresh leads. I've phoned so often I worry that I'm pestering the guy.'

'That's what he's there for, Hols. All part of his job.'

Holly grimaced. 'I think you're right. Drew's done a runner.'

'It looks that way, yeah.'

'Have the police located his mobile?' Peter Harris asked. 'I thought they could track his whereabouts through that?'

'Not if it's turned off,' Todd said.

'You know what worries me?' Karen set down her coffee mug, her expression grim. 'He's not used his credit cards. How on earth is he living?'

Holly didn't reply. That fact, relayed by Gary Tobin early in the search for Drew, had kept her awake at night.

'It's not like he's surviving on cash,' Todd replied, when Holly stayed silent. 'Remember what Gary said? How his last withdrawal was fifty pounds, three days before he disappeared. Unless he's got a secret stash, or he sold something valuable before he left, I can't understand how he's getting by.'

Holly had already discounted that notion. Drew hadn't sold anything, or if he had, it was an item she knew nothing about. Besides, such action suggested premeditation. That he'd not cracked under work pressures but had planned to leave. Had chosen not to tell anyone. She couldn't bear to consider such a possibility.

She shuddered. 'But where *is* he? If he's mentally sick, he needs medical care. Instead he might be living on the streets, sleeping in doorways. In this awful weather. I can't bear to think of it.'

'Perhaps he's rented somewhere,' Peter said.

'How? He's got no money, remember.'

'Unless he has access to funds nobody knows about,' Todd said.

'But how does that fit with him having a breakdown?' Karen asked. 'Finding a place to live, providing references, sorting utility suppliers. None of that stacks up with a man who's so fragile he walks out on his life.'

'I guess not.' Todd glanced at his watch, and stood up. 'I should get going. Nessa's expecting me.'

Holly also got to her feet. 'Thanks for coming over. I'll see you out.'

They walked into the hallway. Out of sight of Karen and Peter, Todd held out his arms, and Holly slipped into their warmth. The steady *one-two* of his heartbeat allowed her to forget, for a few seconds, her fears.

'You've been a tower of strength since Drew left,' she murmured. A faint trace of his aftershave wafted into her nostrils.

His lips pressed a kiss into her hair. 'He's my brother. Without him, I'm not complete.'

'I need him back, Todd.'

'Me too.' His mobile pinged in his pocket. He pulled it out, his expression rueful. 'Nessa,' he said. 'Annoyed I'm not home yet.' He ran a finger down her cheek. 'I'll talk to you soon.'

After he'd gone, a pang of regret stabbed Holly. She'd been so damned lonely, and Todd helped her feel less isolated.

As she walked back into the kitchen, she overheard Karen talking. The words she'd used— *our sweet girl needs to be careful*—puzzled Holly. When she spotted her daughter, Karen fell silent.

'Of what?' Holly asked.

Her mother didn't answer at first. Then: 'Todd still carries a torch for you, darling. I know you're hurting. But maybe you shouldn't lean too heavily on him.'

Heat flushed Holly's face. 'He's been really good to me. And he's in pain too.'

'I know, but—' Karen didn't get to finish her sentence. Holly walked from the kitchen, and up the stairs, into her bedroom. She didn't want to hear any more.

Her parents meant well, and her mother did her best, but Todd understood Holly's pain in a way Karen couldn't. Drew and her mum weren't related by blood, whereas Todd was. Holly couldn't think how she'd cope without his support. What that boded for the future, she wasn't sure.

CHAPTER 15 - Before

Eleven years of life in various foster homes followed for Rick; he repelled the women's attempts at affection and the men's at male bonding. He was starving emotionally, desperate for the mother he'd lost, despite her inadequacies. Strangers, however well meaning, could never take her place.

On the outside he appeared normal, albeit moody and withdrawn. 'A typical teenager,' he heard his current foster father tell a social worker. 'Always playing video games or with his nose in a comic book. He's a good kid, though. Never gives us any trouble.'

Nobody knew about the rage that boiled inside Rick like a volcano. To release it, he set fire to things: rubbish bins, garden sheds, park benches. When that didn't help, he tried a different cure.

One day a local girl, aged ten and with learning disabilities, went missing. Rick, sixteen by then and with his appearance disguised, lured her into a disused factory. He held her captive for two hours, then released the terrified child. Disappointment followed. He'd expected to feel cleansed emotionally; he'd rescued a female in distress, hadn't he? But he didn't. He simply felt like shit.

One of his foster fathers was a devout Christian. For a brief time, Rick flirted with religion. It didn't help either.

He had no idea how to purge his inner fury; nor did he want to, he realised. All he craved was revenge on the man who'd stolen his mother.

No trace of her had ever been found. In his heart, he accepted she was dead. What other reason could there be for her failure to return home?

She'd never loved him, not the way he'd wanted. But she'd been his mother, despite her flaws, and her loss cut him in two. When the pain grew unbearable, he'd slip her T-shirt over his pillow, and hug it tight. The fabric was grubby and stained, the smell of her perfume long gone, but still evocative. Still poignant.

He's all I have. In her way, she'd loved him too.

Rick had nothing left in his life that meant anything. Except his hunger for retribution.

CHAPTER 16

Drew had given up trying to guess what day it was. Either he'd die in this place, in which case time was irrelevant, or he'd break free and reacquaint himself with calendars and clocks then. He refused to contemplate the former option, determined to stay positive. Soon he'd breathe fresh air once more, go running, drink beer with Todd and the guys from the club. Most of all he yearned to kiss Holly, hold her close.

'Your name suits you,' he'd once told her early in their relationship. 'Holly, all shiny and pretty, but with a sharp prickle when you're annoyed.' From then on he'd called her Prickle every time she got angry. Ah, his tiny, gorgeous firecracker of a wife; he'd never stopped loving her, despite their marital problems. They could rediscover the magic, right? All Drew needed to do was escape this hell-hole.

But what if it took a while for him to break free? Holly was so pretty, what with her dark hair cut in a glossy bob, her soft smile, those chocolate eyes. Men would fight for a chance to be with her. How long might his wife wait before she moved on?

More to the point, how long could he himself endure? Months, or God forbid years, in total darkness and silence would fuck up his brain beyond redemption.

Enough with the negativity. He mustn't think that way. He'd survive this shit-hole; all he needed was a plan.

If he could break free from his shackles, then escape might be possible; he just had to solve the problem of the locked door. He felt the chains around his wrists. Solid metal, half a centimetre in diameter, and double-wrapped; Drew stood no chance of pulling his hands free, or breaking his bonds. He gave another experimental tug on both sides; the metal was fastened tight to the ring bolted to the floor.

Don't despair, he told himself. A different plan formed in his mind. He needed to keep himself strong, ready for escape. He'd use the chains for resistance training to boost his upper-body strength. He could place both hands behind his head, so sit-ups were achievable. He lay back, preparing to try one. A deep breath in, and then Drew hauled himself upright, pleased that his restraints were long enough to allow a full sit-up. Yeah, this was the way to go, although he'd need to be mindful of the chains around his wrists. The skin under them was already chafed and angry. He'd begin with thirty and aim to increase his score. Later, though. When he possessed more energy.

A cramp seized his left calf, causing him to howl in agony. Harsh gasps ripped from his throat, and sweat pearled his brow. Drew clenched his teeth, flexing his foot and stretching against the pain. Gradually the contraction eased its iron grip. God, that hurt. If he didn't take action, he'd lose muscle mass from his legs and the ability to walk.

Or escape. At least he could turn over, and move his body enough to avoid pressure sores. Small mercies, and all that.

He tensed and relaxed both feet, repeating the motion twenty times. Next he scissored them outward, then inward once more. Thirty of those. Then he circled his ankles in both directions. It felt good to get movement, albeit not much, back into his lower limbs. Next he bicycled his legs through the air. His final manoeuvre was to stretch each one in turn, over and over.

Now that he'd sorted his basic exercise programme, he'd do as many repetitions as possible whenever he was awake. Rest, then repeat.

Drew needed exercises for his mind, too. He'd always been good at maths, so why not mental arithmetic?

'Fifty-five multiplied by thirteen,' he said aloud, his brain whirring.

'Seven hundred and fifteen,' he pronounced not long afterwards. That had to be around half a minute, right?

'Twenty-four cubed.' He continued for a while, until a headache throbbed at his temple. Enough for now, he decided. He needed a distraction. Okay, so he couldn't escape physically, not yet, but mentally? That was a different story. His eyes closed, and his mind drifted to a happier time. Within seconds he'd become a child, laughing as a teenage Todd kicked a football at him in Uncle Hal and Auntie Mel's garden. Somehow, although he was dead, his father watched, one arm around a ghostly Eloise Blackmore, his smile filled with love. Safe in the cocoon of his imagination, Drew slipped into a doze.

******

Eight. Nine. Sweat coating his body, Drew hauled himself into his tenth sit-up, then collapsed against the concrete. He dragged air into his lungs like a man surfacing from near-drowning, then took a gulp of water. He might have to abandon his exercise programme, thanks to the chains rubbing his wrists and ankles raw. Not to mention the lethargy that pervaded his limbs; his sparse diet meant his energy levels were depleted. Hardly surprising, given that his meals comprised a sandwich and a small bottle of water brought, he estimated, once a day.

He had other concerns too. The deterioration in his brain bothered him. Mental arithmetic grew more difficult every time he tried, and his efforts occurred less often. And the long spell of enforced darkness had affected his vision. He'd glimpse flashes of colour amid the blackness, vivid streaks of red, yellow and blue, the occasional stripe of green. They'd first appeared after one of his exercise sessions, causing him to wonder if he'd pushed himself too far. A headache had pulsed behind his eyes, and Drew had rubbed them, willing the colours to vanish. They receded, but soon returned even brighter. Drew's prison now came complete with his own version of the Northern Lights, forcing him to examine some grim possibilities. Either he was losing his eyesight or his mind. Or both.

He'd read about people hallucinating through lack of sleep. Maybe it could happen through an absence of light too.

Every few days Drew would sleep deeply and awake to find his cell had been cleaned. As to who did that, his instinct told him his abductor was male. So did the evidence; the heavy tread he heard when his meals were delivered indicated masculinity. Drew renewed his attempts at communication every time the footsteps stopped outside his door, but without success. However much he begged or screamed, silence met his efforts.

His captor often lingered, though, the occasional rasp of his breath or a rustle of clothing reaching Drew's ears. As if his abductor relished his victim's frantic pleas. The guy was a cat, Drew decided, himself the hapless mouse with which the man toyed.

That could only mean one thing. Drew wasn't a victim of mistaken identity. He'd fallen prey to a psychopath.

Well, screw the fucker. With that, Drew heard footsteps. Time to put into action the plan he'd hatched. A shaky one, but better than staying helpless. His options were few, and he'd be damned if he didn't try every avenue. He sucked in a deep breath, then lay rigid in his bonds.

The flap opened, and a bottle of water landed next to him, followed by his sandwich. Drew didn't react. Play dead, get the bastard worried. When he unlocked the door to check on his victim, he'd get the shock of his life.

Drew sensed his captor outside, listening, waiting. The silence stretched between them, each second a century. Drew's heart hammered in his chest, blood pulsing through his eardrums, so loud his jailer must surely hear it. He sucked in a deep breath, then released it, long and slow.

Time hung suspended, ceased to matter. Then a scraping sound reached his ears, that of a bolt being drawn back. The rasp of wood on concrete as the door opened. A shaft of light appeared, swiftly blocked by the bulk of his captor. Impossible to see his face, given the darkness. Drew caught a whiff of stale breath laden with old garlic. The man was close, so close, and Drew lunged forward, his aim to sink teeth into flesh, his hands striking upwards to rifle the guy's pockets for a knife, his keys, anything to serve as a weapon.

His wrists yanked against their chains, jerking Drew back to the fact he was alone. His captor had vanished, leaving confusion in his wake. Drew's fingers scrabbled over the floor, searching for his water, his sandwich, but found nothing.

Fuck, fuck, FUCK. He was losing his mind. It had all seemed so *real*. What the hell was happening to his head?

Drew fought for breath, struggled to calm himself. First the weird lights; now he was imagining sounds. Smells, too. The thought terrified Drew.

'Help me,' he begged his dead father.

'Hang in there, son,' Barry Blackmore said. 'Can you do that for me?'

Could he? Maybe, if he wasn't already insane. 'Don't leave me, Dad. Please.'

'Love you, kiddo. You'll find a way out, I promise.' With that, Barry's voice faded away.

The pressure on Drew's lungs eased. That was what he needed—reassurance that his nightmare would end. Okay, so he'd imagined the scenario with his captor, but who was to say it couldn't happen for real? Besides, having a plan, no matter how sketchy, helped stave off madness.

Think positive, he told himself. Easier said than done. If only he had someone to talk to other than his father. As though in response, Holly's face arose before his mind's eye, her smile filled with love. Such comfort lay in imagining the two of them reunited. For Drew, no other woman matched Holly. Ah, his little Prickle. He'd never pinpointed what made her so special. She was pretty, and smart, but so were lots of women. If pushed, he'd have said that she just *fitted* with him. Over time they'd entwined around each other, become one person.

Yes, Holly was the answer. The arguments of the last few months melted away, and they were newlyweds again. Drew heard his wife's voice in his head, all laughter and light, the sound wonderful beyond belief.

'I don't care if money's tight for a while. So long as we're together, that's all that matters.' Her words to him on their wedding night. She'd kissed him, all warm and inviting, her perfume strong in his nostrils, and Drew floated away on a tide of remembrance. They'd talked for hours after making love: plans for decorating their house, visiting Holly's parents, weekends away. By the time he returned to cold, dark reality, Drew's cheeks were wet with tears.

He knew the solution he'd found wasn't healthy, but didn't care. Like an addict hooked on crack after the first hit, he craved the comfort of those bittersweet memories. Hadn't he always talked to his dead father? This, he reasoned, was no different.

Somehow he'd force his captor into unlocking his prison door. With that thought in mind, he shut his eyes, hopeful for a few hours of sleep.

******

True to his plan, Drew didn't move or speak when the flap next opened. His daily bottle of water landed beside him. Followed by his sandwich. His fingers reached out, skimmed over cling film and plastic. Too solid to be unreal, surely? No trick of his imagination, this, which emboldened him. He stayed rigid, mute, despite his thirst, the hunger in his belly. Every nerve in his body sensed his captor outside the door. The cat was waiting to pounce.

The minutes ticked by. Drew remained silent.

He had no idea how much time passed before he heard a muttered curse. The flap opened, and pain shot through his foot, provoking an agonised scream. The bastard had prodded his sole with something sharp. Definitely not imaginary, given how it throbbed. Well, that scuppered his plan of playing dead.

A soft chuckle reached Drew's ears. Fury poured through him.

'You fucker!' he yelled. 'Damn you to hell and back! Let me out of here, or else I'll—' His anger morphed into sobs. He heard his captor snicker a second time. Defeated, Drew cried himself dry. A third snigger, and then the footsteps padded away.

******

After that, Drew made no attempt to converse with his abductor. He seemed out of options. Over the next few days, he came to realise how close he hovered to madness. His mind had buckled under the constant hunger and thirst, the darkness and the fear. Worse, though, was the isolation. He'd never been fond of his own company, had always been a sociable guy. He'd enjoyed drinks with Todd and his mates from the running club—Adam, Rory, Mike. Time spent with Holly. Social chit-chat with his neighbours. After not having spoken with anyone for so long, he yearned for five minutes of connection. He didn't care with whom.

His abductor didn't count. The freakish silences outside his door terrified Drew.

To relieve his loneliness, he continued to talk to the people he loved. 'Let's go to Paris for a week, then drive to Bordeaux,' he told Holly one time.

'That's a great idea. We can relive our honeymoon.'

'I'll water the plants while you're away,' Nessa said.

'Make sure you do a trip on the Seine,' Todd suggested.

Drew smiled. He was so lucky. Then a rainbow of light filled his cell, sweeping his family from his head. He sobbed at the loss; they'd seemed so *real*. As for the rainbow, his private Northern Lights show plagued him more frequently nowadays, he'd noticed. A near-constant headache pounded at his temples to accompany it.

'What's nine cubed?' he muttered into the blackness. Drew did his best to keep up with his mental arithmetic exercises, but his mind failed to grasp numbers anymore. They slithered around in his brain, resisting all attempts at coercion. Nine times nine was eighty-one, but eighty-one multiplied by nine proved more difficult. No matter how hard he tried, the answer wouldn't come.

CHAPTER 17 - Before

You'll get the same treatment I dished out to that slut Rosalie Parker. By the time Rick learned Rosalie's fate he'd grown into a man. One who kept himself to himself, his home a cramped bedsit in one of the poorer areas of Bristol. He earned his living from cash-in-hand labouring jobs that never lasted long. Sex consisted of an occasional one-night stand or a visit to a whorehouse. He persuaded himself he didn't feel lonely. Why would he? At twenty-nine years of age, he'd been alone his whole life. Apart from the Watchman.

One evening Rick watched the six o'clock news, forking curry into his mouth between swigs of Coke. The camera zoomed in on the reporter, a disused building behind her, crime-scene tape fluttering in the breeze.

'Police have revealed that the body found earlier in this abandoned warehouse is that of Rosalie Parker, who disappeared twenty-three years ago from her home in Greenbank. Workers discovered her remains after they began preparing the building for demolition. No further information is available at this stage, but her family has been notified. A police spokesperson has confirmed they are treating the case as a murder enquiry.'

Rick slumped in his seat, his curry forgotten, the dead woman's name hammering through his brain. He swept his plate of food onto the floor, tears wetting his face. Realisation dawned. Rosalie

Parker, whose name he'd had stuck in his head since the age of seven, had been murdered. That meant his mother must have suffered the same fate. No other explanation existed, given Mr Nasty's threat. *You'll get the same treatment I dished out to that slut Rosalie Parker.*

'The bastard killed her,' the Watchman told him. 'Just like you suspected.'

The words jolted Rick from his thoughts. He didn't answer, too distraught.

'I doubt he stopped there. He must have murdered other women too.' The Watchman, as Rick was well aware, also believed he'd lost his mum to Rosalie's killer.

'Yeah. But there's fuck all anyone can do about it.' In his late teens, Rick had searched for Mr Nasty. He'd forgotten most of the address on the man's driving licence, but recalled the suburb: St George. It proved sufficient. He tracked down Mr Nasty easily enough. After that, things turned difficult. What he'd discovered had forced Rick to shelve his quest for revenge.

'You've always been weak.' Followed by a sneer from the Watchman. 'Lacking the balls to do what's needed. Looks like it's up to me.'

Rick blanked him out, too wrung out by the news about Rosalie. In bed that night, he huddled against his mother's T-shirt, her loss still raw.

He devoured every local bulletin during the subsequent week, but Rosalie Parker wasn't mentioned again. The details revealed by the newscast had been scant, which led him to suspect the cops must have suppressed information.

'They said the Parker family had been informed,' Rick said to the Watchman. 'I wonder if Rosalie had kids.'

'Easy enough to find out. She might have had a son. One keen to exact revenge.'

Rick shifted in his seat, uncomfortable at the notion. 'Maybe I should go to the police. Tell them what I know.'

'You're a fucking wuss. What good would that do?'

Later Rick considered the idea further, but decided against it. He knew her killer's name, but little else, and he doubted an investigation would lead to his mother's body. That could be anywhere. Justice for Rosalie, and Rick's mother, seemed impossible.

Rick had reckoned without the Watchman, though.

CHAPTER 18

'Two and a half weeks, Todd. Not one text, email or phone call. Just those damn rings. Where the hell is he?' Holly paced the carpet. Her emotions had ricocheted throughout the last eighteen days: hope, despair, grief, anger. At that particular moment fury prevailed. Why hadn't Drew confided in her about his money worries? If work had proved too stressful, why not change jobs? Why abandon his wife?

It was the job he hated, she told herself. Not her. Although the return of his wedding ring told a different story.

Perhaps the catalyst had been her biological clock. Why had she been so insistent on a baby?

Or maybe they'd built their marriage on quicksand. Both of them impulsive, but too young, too naïve, to make such a life changing commitment.

Every day Holly phoned the police to ask if any fresh leads had emerged, only to be disappointed. One bright light shone in her world: Todd. He checked on her every night after work; he never stayed long, too drained by dealing with ex-offenders all day, but she welcomed the company. She suspected Nessa might not react well if she realised how tightly Todd hugged Holly each time. How his lips pressed a kiss into her hair. Her sister-in-law was no fool; she must realise her husband still carried a torch for Holly. Did it matter? Todd would never cheat on Nessa and she'd never betray

Drew. Surely Nessa couldn't begrudge her a shred of comfort during such dark times?

Her parents' visit had been brief; Holly still needed them, but felt guilty at disrupting their lives. After a while, she'd urged them to go home.

'I'll be fine,' she told her mother, as she hugged her before Karen and Peter left for Spain. 'I have Todd, remember?'

Karen's lips pursed, but she didn't comment. 'Love you, darling,' she said. 'Call me any time, you hear?'

Holly made a mental note: *phone Mum tonight.* The thought calmed her. She ceased pacing and sat beside her brother-in-law.

'Give him a break, Hols. Drew disappeared because he's mentally ill. That's the most likely explanation, anyway. The stress of all *this*.' Todd waved the latest 'Final Demand' letter that had arrived on Holly's mat. 'Which won't resolve itself overnight. He'll need time. And space.'

'I can't help but wonder. About other families in which someone goes missing. Does everyone react like me?' Holly shook her head. 'Sometimes I'm so angry at Drew I want to smash his face in. Other times I'd gladly die if I could hug him one more time.'

'He'll be in touch, Hols. When he's ready.'

'Will he? Maybe he's not mentally ill. What if he's—' She couldn't bring herself to say 'dead'.

Shock filled Todd's face. 'You can't think that way. Drew's out there somewhere, I know he is. Remember the rings.' Only the tremor in his voice betrayed his doubt. Like her, he must worry that Drew's body lay undiscovered, his brother a victim of an attack or accident.

Or, as she dreaded, suicide. 'I'm scared he might have killed himself,' Holly said.

The idea had tortured her for a while. What if the two rings were her husband's farewell note? Appalled, she thrust the thought away.

'Don't go there. Please.' Todd's face was shuttered. 'I'll make us coffee.'

Todd was right, Holly decided, after he'd left the room. She had to stay positive. Despite her resolve, her thoughts spiralled towards Drew's wedding ring. If suicide wasn't his intention, he'd been callous to return it under cover of darkness. Her mother might judge it a cry for help, but perhaps a simpler explanation existed. She'd married a coward. Too chicken to tell her he no longer loved her. Had Drew tired of her? Yearned to break free from their marriage?

The more Holly thought about it, the more convinced she became. Fury rose inside her, hot and strong, until it boiled over. Filled with rage, she grabbed their wedding photo from the windowsill and hurled it on the ground.

'Bastard!' she screamed, as her heel slammed down on the glass.

Todd rushed into the room. 'For God's sake, Hols! What are you doing?' He pulled her away, then eased her onto the sofa. He tugged off her sock. 'Your foot's bleeding. Where's your first-aid kit?'

Pain throbbed through Holly's heel. 'Downstairs toilet. In the cabinet.'

Todd soon returned with it, his fingers working the zip on the case. He extracted tweezers, antiseptic wipes, plasters, before examining her foot. 'You've been lucky. Just one small piece of glass.' With infinite care, he removed it and dressed the wound. He swept up the remaining shards and replaced the photo on the windowsill. Only then did he sit next to Holly, taking her hand. Hot tears slid down her face and she collapsed, sobbing, against his shoulder. Her anger had fled, leaving only exhaustion. Coupled with a fierce need for Drew. What she wouldn't give to hear him call her Prickle again, the way he always did when she lost her temper.

She'd not really been mad at Drew. Fury had merely been a vent for fear.

Todd pulled her close. 'What was all that about?'

Much as she trusted him, she couldn't say the words. 'Nothing. Just finding it hard to cope.'

Todd's hand stroked Holly's hair. Had she a choice, she'd have stayed in his arms for ever. She felt bereft without Drew, her anguish worsened by her parents' return to Spain. Why had she urged them to leave? Stupid of her. Perhaps she should give Amber or Elaine a call. But she didn't know them well enough, she realised. Their friendship hadn't reached the stage where Holly felt free to unburden her soul, even if both women had shown her sympathy.

So there she was, with nobody to confide in, only this man. Even with him, she'd not been honest. Holly harboured a secret she needed to tell

Todd, yet hadn't. Words would make everything real; Holly wasn't sure she could handle the consequences.

She mustn't be selfish. He had his own grief to cope with. A family who needed him.

'You should get back to Nessa and the kids,' she murmured.

'She's staying with Shane and Jack at her parents' place in Bridgwater tonight.' Relief flooded Holly. Maybe...

'There's only so much I can take of my father-in-law,' Todd continued. 'Cantankerous doesn't begin to describe the old git.'

'I'm glad you're here,' Holly said. 'I need you. More than you know.'

Over his shoulder, she watched the snow flurries outside the window intensify. Blizzard warnings had already been issued for the South-West. She should get up, close the curtains, but that required effort. Her eyes closed while Todd's hand stroked her hair.

Holly made plans. The roads might soon be impassable; it wouldn't be wise for him to drive home. She'd dig out a supermarket curry from the freezer and open a bottle of beer for Todd. By morning the streets would have been gritted, hence safer to travel on. What harm could it do? Right then they needed each other.

'Stay,' she whispered.

Todd pulled back, stared into her eyes. Panic shot through Holly. She hadn't meant *that*.

How could she be angry, though? People behaved in strange ways when hurt. As demonstrated by her throbbing foot. Besides, perhaps she'd misinterpreted his reaction.

'The bed in the guest room's made up,' she said.

He nodded. 'Do you have a spare toothbrush?'

'We always keep a few for visitors.' Holly's smile trembled with relief. She wouldn't be alone that night, even if Todd slept in a different room.

He took her hand, and they went upstairs, all thoughts of curry and beer gone from Holly's head. Outside her door, he leaned in, his fingers cupping her cheek. His lips brushed her skin before he stepped back. 'Goodnight,' he called over his shoulder as he walked away.

Loneliness swamped Holly. Rational thought fled, to be replaced by need, raw and urgent. 'Can I sleep beside you? Please?'

Todd turned, then headed towards her, and Holly swallowed hard. 'Hold me. That's all I ask.'

He smiled at her, and joined their hands again. They walked in silence towards the open door of the guest room. To the double bed beyond.

CHAPTER 19 - Before

One year prior to Drew's abduction, and a week after Rosalie Parker's murder aired on television, the Watchman decided on his plan for revenge. First, though, he needed more information. Easily gained through flattery, his prey a data entry clerk at Bridewell police station. Single, mousy, badly dressed—every inch of the woman oozed low self-esteem.

'Be careful,' Rick warned him. 'She's from the police, remember.'

'Shut the fuck up,' the Watchman growled. 'She's not a copper. And I know what I'm doing.' He'd given her a false name, of course.

'Must be fascinating to discover what goes on in the high-profile cases,' he told the woman one night in bed. They'd been dating for a month by then, and had managed clumsy sex—she was all angles and inhibitions—a few times. 'Like that poor woman whose body was found after she'd been missing for over twenty years. Do you know much about that one?'

She nodded. 'Made my skin crawl, it did.' Horror filled her bony face.

With care, he drew her out. In time, she revealed who the police's main suspect had been. Just as he, and Rick, had always known. Mr Nasty.

'Sickens me to think of it,' he told her. 'The bastard chained the poor cow up, you say?'

She nodded. 'With her legs forced open. So he could—' A shudder passed through her. 'I'm not supposed to tell you any of this. I could lose my job.'

'You can trust me.' His finger stroked over her cheek. 'In case you haven't realised...' He smiled. 'I'm falling in love with you.'

After that, she didn't hold back. The Watchman heard about the darkness, the sound-proofing, the isolation. His anger doubled, tripled.

He remembered Rick's comment about Rosalie's family. 'Did she have any children?'

'Yes. A son. Ethan. He's a man now, of course.'

Ethan Parker might prove useful, the Watchman decided. Very useful. He made a mental note to uncover the whereabouts of Rosalie's son. The two of them needed to talk. Chances were he might persuade Ethan Parker to come on board with his plan.

'Someone will pay for that bastard's crimes,' he told Rick later. 'First, I'll ditch the bitch. Then I'll wait before I make my next move.'

'For how long?'

'A year at least. Until the trail's gone cold. I don't want that dozy cow putting two and two together.'

CHAPTER 20

A car horn in the street woke Holly. At first she was disorientated, aware something was different but unsure what. A soft snore catapulted her into reality. Oh, God—Drew had come home, and she'd missed his return. Then she turned over, and her eyes rested on Todd's sleeping form.

He looked younger in repose, the worry added by Drew's disappearance gone. Dark stubble framed a slightly open mouth, and one arm, thatched with hair, lay on top of the duvet. He was still fully dressed, as was Holly.

Nothing happened, she consoled herself. She'd been so angry at Drew yesterday. Furious, and hurt, and every emotion in between. And Todd had been there, solid and real, whereas Drew had abandoned her, and…

Last night Todd had shut the door of the guest bedroom behind them. Holly slid under the duvet; Todd tugged off his shoes and joined her. His arms closed around her, and he pulled her against him.

For a while Todd did as she'd asked, and simply held her. Then his fingers shifted, ever so slightly, towards her breast. Maybe he'd meant nothing by it. Nonetheless, Holly felt it best to set some boundaries. She pushed him away, breaking the spell.

'I need to make something clear,' she said. 'We can't—'

'Yeah, I get that.' Regret flared in Todd's face. He ran an agitated hand through his hair. 'I'd never fuck up things up between you and Drew. But—'

'Don't.' Holly moved away to curl into a ball on the far side of the bed. Tension arced through the air.

He let out a long sigh. 'Please, Hols. Just let me hug you.' Raw need in his voice. 'Nothing else, I promise.'

His plea undid her. She unfurled, turning over to press against Todd's body, and he slung an arm around her shoulders. Holly knew they'd crossed a boundary, but couldn't bring herself to care. Before long, Todd's rhythmic breathing indicated he'd fallen asleep. Holly's eyes closed, and she also drifted away.

Now, in the cold light of day, she regretted their folly. Unwise to have shared a bed with Todd, however innocently. They were both married to other people, for God's sake.

She pushed away her instinct that warned Todd still cared for her. That he'd wed Nessa on the rebound. Oh, God, what about her sister-in-law? How could she look her in the eye when they next met?

Todd shifted position, flinging his other arm outside the duvet. His wristwatch told her the time was six twenty. She stared at his face, the dark lashes that fringed his eyes, the freckles dusted over his nose. He was an attractive man. But her heart belonged to Drew, not Todd. It always would.

Out of habit, she checked her phone. Still no text or email from her husband.

Holly tossed back the duvet and stepped out of bed, heading for the shower. Once dressed, she went downstairs to fix breakfast for the two of them. Thank God she'd booked the day off; she wouldn't have to struggle through the snow to work. Outside the kitchen window a white blanket covered the world. A gritting lorry edged along the road beyond their garden, its curved top barely visible above the fence. At least the roads wouldn't be so dangerous for Todd's drive home.

Half an hour later, she heard his footsteps on the stairs.

His eyes met hers after he entered the kitchen, then slid away. 'Hey,' he said. 'That coffee smells good. You sleep well?'

She nodded. Awkwardness, so different from their normal easy familiarity, stretched between them.

'About last night.' He cleared his throat, and Holly seized her chance.

'We needed each other. That was all.'

'Right.' He gazed at her, his expression inscrutable.

'Remember what you said. About not fucking things up between Drew and me.'

Todd pulled out the chair opposite Holly and sat down. He didn't speak, just stared at her. Was that anger in his face? Hurt, maybe?

A little of both, she decided. The weight of the secret she'd nursed for the last few weeks threatened to crush her. Time to be honest. 'There's something I need to tell you.'

Todd's fingers toyed with the salt cruet, his lips pressed tight. 'Spit it out.'

'I didn't get a chance to speak to Drew. Before he—well, you know. I wanted to, but we'd been arguing, and he looked so desperate when he left that morning, like he couldn't wait to get away from me. And it wasn't the right time, not with him half out the door, anyway. I told Mum and Dad, though, when they were here. Oh, God, I'm babbling—'

'Holly.' Todd's voice sliced through her torrent of words. 'Cut the crap. Just tell me.'

'I'm pregnant.' Shock flitted across Todd's face. He dropped his gaze to the salt pot, his teeth worrying his lower lip.

Holly couldn't bear the tension in the air. 'Say something. Please.'

'Sorry.' He smiled, but it appeared to take effort. 'Well, congratulations, I suppose. It'll be great to have a niece or nephew to spoil. Nessa will be in her element.'

'Don't tell her. Please.' She couldn't cope with people other than Todd and her parents knowing, not yet.

'Okay. If that's what you want. She'll realise once you start to show, anyway. She'll be happy for you. So am I.'

'Are you? Really?'

'Yes.' He exhaled a long breath. 'It's just that—well, you can't deny the timing isn't great. With Drew missing.'

Holly willed away tears. 'Sometimes I think I hate him. He's walked out, left me to deal with parenthood on my own, and I'm scared, Todd. Really scared. Suppose Drew doesn't come back? What if I have to cope with a baby by myself, because the bastard's too much of a coward to face his responsibilities?'

'But he didn't know, Hols. How could he run from you being pregnant, when you hadn't told him?'

'He ran from the *prospect* of it.' The words sat like ashes in her mouth. 'We argued about it the day he disappeared. That morning he told me he still wasn't ready, and I got so mad. I yelled at him that he'd failed as a husband. How, if he didn't want kids, I'd have to reconsider our marriage.' She swallowed a sob. 'He looked so hurt. Like I'd stuck a knife in his chest. Then he left. And didn't come back.'

Todd sucked in a breath. 'You blame yourself. For his disappearance.'

'Yes. No. I'm so confused, Todd.'

'How far along are you?'

'Only a few weeks. I did the test the day before he went missing. I was tempted to break the news straightaway, but we'd argued yet again, and he insisted we should wait before becoming parents. How could I tell him? Knowing he didn't want this baby'—Holly patted her belly—'when being its mother was all I could think about?'

'I love my brother,' Todd said. 'But at times he's an idiot.'

'I feel so alone.' The tears flowed freely then. 'How will I ever cope?'

'You have Nessa and me.' Todd gripped her hand, squeezed it tight. Holly saw determination in his eyes. 'We're here for you. Even if Drew isn't.'

CHAPTER 21 - Before

The Watchman stood across the road from the block of flats where Ethan Parker lived. Waiting, observing. Armed with the information he'd gleaned from the police data clerk, he'd found the guy easily enough. Had spent time tracking his movements. The Watchman knew all about Ethan's weekly appointments at a group session for anxiety and depression. Not surprising, given his mother's murder.

He considered his options. Ethan's issues might mean he was pliable. Easily directed, which was good. On the other hand, he might prove unpredictable. Either way, the Watchman would need to keep Ethan—and Rick—on a tight leash. He intended to retain full control at all times. Anyone else he included would be a mere minion.

He should definitely talk to Ethan. The guy had to be hurt, angry, about Rosalie's death. The Watchman could divert his ire into more constructive channels. Such as revenge. *Justice.*

He pushed away from the wall he'd been leaning against and crossed the street.

CHAPTER 22

Uncle Hal wiped sweat from his brow, damp patches blooming under his arms. 'The Premier League clubs will soon be fighting over you!' He laughed, but his breath came in harsh pants; they'd been kicking a football in the back garden for over an hour, on the hottest day of the year. Hal had elected to guard the makeshift goal while Drew practised his penalty shoot-outs. Auntie Mel watched from the kitchen window, a fond smile on her face.

Drew grinned, keen to convince his adoptive father they were having a great time. That Drew was happy. But he wasn't. On the periphery of his mind lurked a memory. Rank and unpleasant, ready to smear its filth over him. Ten-year-old Drew froze, his senses screaming at him: *it's behind you!* Uncle Hal, Aunt Mel and the garden faded away, leaving him at the monster's mercy. A clawed hand, huge and hairy, landed on his shoulder.

Drew jolted upright, sweat on his brow, his breath frantic gasps. Still half awake, he found the dream clutched him tightly, refused to let go. As his awareness returned, the monster that had pounced after his tenth birthday faded away, inch by inch. Drew knew, though, with every fibre of his being, that sixteen years later, it was waiting, jaws slavering, to pounce again.

Wherever you are, I will find you, and you will suffer.

He shuddered. He couldn't allow his mind to go there. Madness would surely follow.

Footsteps sounded outside his room, heading towards his door. Drew didn't think, just acted. Fully awake by then, he leaned forward, stretching his arms until they were at full length. A minute later the flap slapped open, and Drew seized the moment. His fingers swooped as soon as his bottle of water landed beside him, and for an instant they closed around flesh. Drew clutched his captor's wrist, tugging it so hard the man's shoulder banged against the door. The next second its owner wrenched the hand away with a snarl. The footsteps strode off, leaving him with water but no sandwich.

Drew slumped back in his restraints, satisfied. Brief though it had been, he'd connected with another human being; it didn't matter that the hand had belonged to his captor. And he now had confirmation that his abductor was male.

Drew replayed in his head the moment he'd touched the other man. His fingers had bumped over the dial of a watch, then skin. The back of a hand, then a wrist, and both had sported a mat of hair.

'Knowledge is power,' he muttered. In addition, he'd shown the bastard that inside this dank hell-hole lay a human being, not a *thing* to be abused.

Drew became aware of footsteps stomping above where he lay. Then a sound reached him that he couldn't quite identify, before the footsteps returned outside Drew's door. A rustle of clothing followed, as though his captor had sat down.

Seconds passed, and then minutes. Nothing happened.

Fear shivered through Drew's body. His former impression, of a cat toying with a mouse, returned full force. Time ticked away. The man was waiting, but for what?

Panic gripped his chest, and he struggled to drag in a breath. Then he realised. The usual faint stir of air around his nose had gone.

That sound he'd heard? Cloth being stuffed into a hole. His captor had blocked his air vent. As Drew's scream, high-pitched and filled with terror, bounced off the walls, the man outside laughed.

Drew pulled in what breath he could, licked his dry lips. 'Please,' he managed. If he was right, and his captor took pleasure in toying with him, then maybe he'd let him live. 'You don't have to do this.' He waited. Nothing.

Sweat prickled on Drew's brow. The temperature seemed less frigid, almost warm, but that must be his imagination. He reckoned enough oxygen remained for several hours yet, but in his head the atmosphere had already become thicker. Staler. He had no way of knowing how airtight the area around the door, or the feeding flap, might be.

Drew understood the man's message, delivered via the blocked air vent. *Attempt to defy me and you will suffer the consequences. I can snuff out your miserable life whenever I choose.*

He tried again. 'I'll do whatever you want. Just don't kill me.' That earned him a throaty chuckle.

'It was because I touched you, right? You're punishing me.'

Still no response. Drew thought of Holly, and the kids he wanted. His plans—the London marathon, his own software consultancy. None of that mattered, only survival. Because if his captor didn't unblock his air vent, he'd never be a father, cross the finish line or set up a business. Faced with death, he yearned beyond all else to live.

Despair took hold, forcing a sob from Drew. Then another. They multiplied until he could hardly speak. 'Please. I'm sorry. I won't do it again.' His fists pounded the floor, over and over. 'I'm begging you. Don't do this.' His voice petered out amid a riot of whimpers.

Drew slumped back, exhausted. Footsteps sounded in his ears. They moved across the ceiling of his cell. He waited.

Was it his imagination, or did air stir against his nostrils? No, it wasn't in his mind, it was real, and Drew gulped in several deep breaths. His lungs swelled with gratitude.

He heard his captor approach his prison again. 'Thank you,' Drew whispered. Another raspy laugh, then the man left, taking with him Drew's sandwich. At least he had water, although his stomach growled at the thought of hours without food. His condition had weakened, both physically and mentally. The demons in his head shouted at him how he'd die, alone and cold. That nobody would ever find his corpse.

Not a single person would miss him. Not Holly, not Todd, or his nephews. He was nothing, forgettable.

'Fuck off!' Drew yelled into the darkness, the stench of his breath wafting into his nostrils. Without toothpaste or a brush, his teeth had become rough with plaque, rotten food wedged between them. His body stank too. Sometimes he no longer felt human. He found it hard to remember how he'd once lived. His life had narrowed to a routine regulated by his captor, and to three key components: sleep, sustenance and his memories. Time had ceased to exist; the notion of daytime, of light, seemed absurd in a place where no sun ever shone. In Drew's prison all was blackness, for eternity and beyond.

Apart from the hallucinations. As Drew sank back in his restraints, a rainbow arced before his eyes. A symphony of shades that stretched, twisted and wrapped itself around the enclosed space. Drew no longer knew where he ended and the colours began. In the few seconds he stared into its glory, the arc grew fainter, smaller, until only a patch of indigo remained. An anguished moan escaped his lips. Although the rainbow had been imaginary, its absence left Drew bereft. Who said company had to come in human form?

Tears of self-pity pricked his eyes. Had he sunk so low he craved something that wasn't real?

'Come back... don't leave me...' he whispered, uncertain if he was addressing his captor or the rainbow. Silence and blackness met his pleas. Alone in the dark, he attempted to doze.

CHAPTER 23

Drew shifted in his sleep, his nightmare filled with the monster he'd sensed in his earlier dreams. This time, though, the creature wasn't an *it*. Instead the thing was human, and male. How Drew knew that, he couldn't fathom, but the fact was as incontrovertible as the sky being blue. A link existed with Uncle Hal, although its nature remained elusive. Right when realisation seemed within his grasp, Drew awoke. And found himself staring at a man's face.

One he'd hoped never to see again. The monster now had a name. Fear pounded through Drew's veins. He screamed, long and loud.

Ian Morrison appeared unfazed by his captive's frenzied shrieks. He didn't speak, but his expression was smug, triumphant. A gust of stale breath, heavy with garlic, wafted into Drew's nostrils. His gaze fastened on Morrison's hair, dark and thick; the eyes, so pale they looked lifeless. The tiny scar that bisected his top lip, his yellowed teeth. Every nuance familiar, despite the fourteen years that had passed since he'd last seen the man.

Drew's instinct about his abductor's identity, which he'd worked so hard to suppress, had been right. Only one person hated him enough to inflict such torment.

Morrison had left the door open and in the half-light his captor stared at his victim. Still no words, unlike years ago. Back then he'd done all the talking, whereas Drew had mostly stayed silent. Too afraid to speak. Unlike now.

'Let me go.' A sob choked his voice. 'For God's sake, didn't you torture me enough before?'

He shut his eyes, lost in memories. When he opened them, Ian Morrison had gone. Absorbed in the past, Drew hadn't heard him leave.

A shiver ran through his body, followed by another, and not from the cold. All he could think about was the threat Ian Morrison had made to the younger Drew.

I will make your life hell. Wherever you are, I will find you, and you will suffer.

Followed by worse. In Drew's head, beefy hands seized his throat. Squeezed hard enough to make spots dance before his eyes. *Oh, God, he couldn't breathe, the pressure on his windpipe was too great, he was about to pass out…*

In the past, fourteen years ago, Morrison brought his mouth close to Drew's ear. His victim had turned twelve by then. 'If you tell anyone, boy, I'll strangle you. First I'll have my fun, and then you'll die.'

******

Over the next few days Drew tensed every time he heard Morrison's footsteps outside his prison, but his captor didn't enter Drew's room again. Instead, he continued to deliver his food and water, then left, still drugging Drew every so often to clean his cell. Drew concluded the reason for Morrison's visit must have been to gloat. To enjoy the *thing* to which he'd reduced his captive.

Even pondering that much took effort. Drew was aware he was deteriorating, both mentally and physically, but lacked the wherewithal to care.

He hadn't exercised in a long time. As for mental arithmetic, that proved impossible; he couldn't have added two and two together. His brain was jelly, his grasp on sanity hair-thin. As evidenced by the hallucinations.

The first time one struck he'd been chatting to Holly in his head. 'Might enter a half-marathon next year,' he'd told her. A second later Holly appeared before his eyes.

The shock rendered Drew breathless. He stared at his wife, too stunned to speak. Her face floated, disembodied, in front of his. She seemed so *real*, despite the lack of arms and legs. If he chose, he could reach out a hand and touch her cheek. Run his fingers through her hair, so sleek and glossy. The scent of her coconut shampoo teased his nostrils. Tears stung Drew's eyes.

Holly smiled at him. 'Sounds a great idea,' she said. How he'd missed her soft voice, the curve of her lips. Drew lost himself in his wife, entranced by each line, every nuance of her. She might have stayed with him for hours, or a few seconds. When she faded from view, a trace of coconut lingered in the air. Drew sobbed, stunned by the depth of his loss.

Sane people didn't imagine heads without bodies. Drew knew madness lurked, waiting to pounce, but lacked the energy to fight it.

Holly visited often after that. On another occasion Auntie Mel came. She didn't say anything, just stared at him, her expression filled with compassion. Her face was hazier, more insubstantial, than that of Holly. Drew no longer cared that he was hallucinating. All that mattered was that he wasn't alone anymore.

One time Uncle Hal appeared. The second of Drew's visitors to speak. 'I'm sorry, lad. I should have protected you better.'

'It's okay. You weren't to know.'

Todd came next. Drew stared at the face of the brother he adored. 'Don't worry,' Todd said. 'I'll look after Holly.'

With that, his wife's face took shape out of the darkness, floating beside Todd's.

'Goodbye, Drew,' Holly said. Then she vanished, taking Todd with her.

'Stop! Don't leave me!' Drew shouted, but she'd already gone.

******

In the days that followed, Drew no longer thought about escape. Why torture himself with something that could never happen? Instead, in his darkest moments, he flirted with the possibility of suicide.

Such a seductive idea. Sweet oblivion, if he could kill himself. He'd already planned how he'd do it. No more darkness, hunger, captivity.

Holly materialised before him. 'Don't worry about me, Drew,' she said. Her disembodied voice sounded very distant. 'I'm happy now.' Then she vanished.

Yeah. He was going to do this. He no longer wanted to live. The people he loved would be better off without him. The world would continue to turn, the sun to shine. He wasn't needed, never had been. Besides, Morrison was going to strangle him anyway, once he'd had his fun. This way Drew got to choose how and when he died.

He unwrapped his cheese sandwich and ate it, eking out his food. The customary last meal of a condemned prisoner, he thought, with a grimace.

Drew inhaled, then released the contents of his lungs in a measured breath. He covered his lips and nose with the cling-film from the sandwich. Then he clamped both hands over his face.

CHAPTER 24

Since telling Todd about her pregnancy, Holly's impending motherhood had become all too real. Before that she'd stuck her head in the sand, the only proof the blue lines on the plastic stick from the test kit. Too wrapped up in Drew's disappearance, Holly hadn't even consulted her doctor.

'You need to tell your GP,' Karen urged her daughter whenever they spoke on the phone. 'Promise me, darling. Don't leave it any longer.'

Her mother's nagging won out; Holly made an appointment, and kept it. She found it hard to believe a baby was growing inside her. Apart from tender breasts she didn't feel pregnant; no morning sickness, constipation or fatigue. Holly would stare at the leaflets, full of advice for expectant mothers, that she'd brought home, hoping to experience a surge of joy. She didn't.

If only Mel and Hal were still alive. She'd been close to Drew's aunt and uncle, had loved them fiercely. Their sudden deaths had been the catalyst for her desperate urge for a baby. She'd always wanted kids, but later, in her thirties, once she'd established her career. After the joint funeral, all that changed; she yearned to fill the void Hal and Mel left with new life. Tiny hands to clutch hers, a baby at her breast. Drew, the loving father, at her side.

Instead single motherhood beckoned. Holly knew she shouldn't burden Todd with her loneliness. His family was his priority, not her. As proof of that, his daily visits had tapered off, as though he, too, had moved beyond the initial shock of losing his brother. *Life goes on*, thought Holly. A cliché, sure, but one she'd do well to heed.

At times she felt ancient. Ninety-six, not twenty-six.

I need a friend, Holly decided one day at work, as she stared at the stack of files on her desk. She'd been too isolated, and it didn't help. Her office landline sat to her left; she gazed at it, willing herself to pick up the receiver. When she did, her fingers shook. *Say yes*, she pleaded in her head.

'I'd love to do lunch,' Amber said, to Holly's relief. 'Shall I ask Elaine too?'

The pub meal that followed delivered a measure of comfort. The inevitable questions about Drew didn't hurt as much as Holly had feared. She confirmed he was still missing, but didn't mention the rings. Their return had hurt her too much.

Besides, other news seemed more important. Holly had informed her boss earlier, so why not Amber and Elaine?

She took a deep breath. 'I'm pregnant. Seems Drew left me a little present before he disappeared.' She tried to smile, but couldn't.

Amber clapped her hands, a huge grin on her face, then frowned. 'How do you feel about that? With him gone?'

'I've no idea.' Holly picked at her salad, her gaze on her plate. She'd just have to make the best of a crap situation. What choice did she have?

'We're here for you,' Elaine said. 'Don't be a stranger. Please.'

Tears tickled Holly's eyes. 'I won't.' She sensed in these two women a quiet compassion, a willingness to help.

The three of them went out for lunch again the following week. Both Amber and Elaine avoided any mention of Christmas, which was fast approaching. Holly didn't bother with tinsel or a tree; there seemed no point without her husband. Her parents had urged her to stay with them until New Year, but she'd refused. What if Drew returned and found her gone?

Fat chance of that happening. A few days before Christmas, Holly stared at the envelope in her lap. It had mocked her from the hallway when she'd come down for breakfast that morning.

As the hours slipped by, her hurt hardened into steel. To hell with Drew. His behaviour smacked of cruelty, not mental illness. She sat, immobile, on the sofa, her lips a thin line of anger.

Todd came round that evening, the first time he'd done so that week. His expression, when she pulled open the door, was grim. Holly stared at what he held in his hand.

'You got one too,' she said, her tone dull.

Todd pushed past her, brandishing the card. On it Holly glimpsed two cartoon reindeer, antlers entwined, tinsel around their necks. The caption read 'Happy Christmas To A Dear Brother.'

'Blank inside. Same as the envelope. Not a single word.' He snorted, tossing the card on the sofa. 'Where's yours?'

Holly pointed to the coffee table. Todd picked up the Christmas card, his fingers running over the embossed letters. 'Season's Greetings To My Darling Wife,' they said, on a mistletoe-festooned background. Like Todd's, the card, and its plain white envelope, was devoid of any message.

'I had to take the day off work,' Holly said. 'I cried most of the morning. Then I got angry. Mad as hell, in fact.'

Todd shook his head. 'I thought I knew my brother. Clearly I don't.'

'I did wonder if the card was some cruel practical joke. Sent by someone else.'

He frowned. 'Who, though? I can't think of anyone that spiteful.'

'Me neither.' She shook her head. 'Unlike the rings, this isn't a cry for help. Drew's taking the piss.'

'Hard not to see it that way. Why didn't he write us a message?' Todd frowned. 'At least we know he's alive. And close enough to hand deliver the cards, which is good. I'm still furious, though.'

'Will you take yours to the police?' She supposed DC Tobin needed to know.

'Yes. Although I suspect they'll only find Drew's prints on the envelope and the card. Besides ours, that is. Like they did with the rings.' His gaze swept over Holly, took in her red-rimmed eyes. 'I never thought Drew could be so heartless.'

Fury seized Holly. She grabbed the card from Todd's hand. Seconds later it lay in pieces in the waste basket. She took special care to rip through 'My Darling Wife.'

When she'd finished, she felt purged, lighter. Screw her husband. She had no idea who he was anymore.

'Oh, Hols. Come here, love.' The empathy in Todd's tone broke Holly. His arms wrapped around her.

Safe against his solid warmth, she gathered the courage to voice her fears. 'I'm scared, Todd. About having this baby on my own.'

His hands moved to her neck. Strong fingers massaged her flesh, caressed her skin. 'Don't be,' he murmured against her hair. 'You're stronger than you realise.'

For a minute, Holly allowed herself the joy of being held, touched. 'It's good to see you,' she said, once she disengaged herself. 'I'll get the kettle on.'

Over coffee, Holly learned Nessa had taken the boys overnight to her parents' house in Bridgwater. Todd's expression seemed awkward, and Holly found herself unable to meet his eyes. The memory of his body against hers when he stayed over had got her through many a long night. Neither of them ever mentioned it, though.

Nothing happened, she reminded herself, while Todd rambled on about Nessa's Christmas preparations. *We took comfort from each other, that's all.*

'Christ, I'm sorry, Hols.' Todd's voice shattered her introspection. 'I'm being thoughtless, banging on about Christmas.' He glanced around Holly's living room, at the lack of decorations. 'Must be rough on you, this time of year.'

She nodded. 'It is. At work people talk about turkey or gammon. A real tree versus artificial. Who'll be there and who won't. Then they see me, and the conversation stops.'

'That must hurt. You'll come to us, of course. Shane and Jack will be over the moon.'

A rumble sounded from his stomach. Todd laughed. 'Someone's hungry, it seems. I should go.' He didn't move, however.

Holly remembered Nessa was in Bridgwater with the boys. 'Shall I rustle up some dinner? Or order something in?'

He cleared his throat. 'I'd like that.'

******

Holly glanced at her watch: ten to midnight. She'd enjoyed the evening: the Chinese takeaway she'd eaten with Todd, the crime drama they'd watched, the easy conversation they'd shared. Now, though, exhaustion, engendered by the fierce emotions of earlier, had caught up with Holly. Half of her longed for her bed, the other part to soak up more of the comfort Todd offered.

He shifted position beside her. 'About time I got going,' he said, the hint obvious. He didn't move, though.

Holly nodded, but didn't reply. To her relief, he stood up. She heard the rustle of cloth as he put on his jacket. Followed by the jangle of car keys.

'Shall I come over again tomorrow?' he asked. Only the faintest *please* sounded in his voice.

Holly's resolve broke. Her sense of isolation won out over her need for sleep, driving her into Todd's arms. He hugged her tight, blocking out her loneliness.

She found her voice. 'Stay. I don't want to be alone.'

'Neither do I.'

She couldn't risk another night together in the guest bedroom. That would send all the wrong signals. Holly knew it would happen, if she didn't speak. Yet she stayed silent.

Just a cuddle, then sleep. Like before, she told herself, the voice in her head silky, persuasive. *What harm can it do?*

Plenty, it seemed. Without warning, Todd pulled her closer. His mouth found hers, his lips insistent, one palm on Holly's left breast. His erection pressed against her as his other hand caressed her neck. Appalled, Holly tore her lips from his. She stepped back, shame heating her cheeks.

'No,' she said. 'This can't happen.' She was furious with her husband—the card had bitten deep with its hurt—but she still wore her wedding ring. Inside her belly she carried Drew's child. Bedding his brother was a no-no.

Todd clearly thought otherwise. 'We need each other, Hols.' His voice was rough with lust. 'Sex was always good between us, right?'

She couldn't deny that. When she didn't speak, he pulled her in for another kiss. With all her strength, Holly shoved him away.

'I'd like you to leave. Now, please.' She wouldn't—*couldn't*—look at Todd.

Silence. Then: 'This isn't over. Not by a long way. You and me—we belong together.'

With that, Todd strode from the room. Seconds later the front door banged behind him.

CHAPTER 25

The next morning, Holly sipped her orange juice, her stomach too knotted for food. Her relationship with Todd was heading towards dangerous waters, and it was time to steer it to safety. Establish some boundaries, clarify things. They'd long been affectionate with each other: the occasional touch, a glance accompanied by a smile. Drew had never seemed to mind. Nessa's reaction had always been harder to gauge.

A harmless flirtation, nothing more, Holly had always thought. Except Todd's hand on her breast the previous evening proved otherwise. He was her brother-in-law, a man she loved and respected, but she needed to set him straight. Her marriage was sacrosanct, at least until she decided what to do about Drew. Even then she wouldn't steal another woman's husband.

Decision made. She'd address the situation with Todd, and soon. She didn't think she'd have to wait long.

That evening, her buzzer sounded at six o'clock. She peered through the spy-hole. As she'd expected, Todd stood on the step.

Holly opened the door. His expression told her the reason for his visit. Need for her was etched into every line of his face.

'You shouldn't have come,' Holly said.

'Please, Hols.' When she made no move to let him pass, he continued, 'Just five minutes. That's all I ask.'

She stood aside. Once they were both seated in separate armchairs in the living room, she waited. Todd gazed at her; his eyes revealed what his mouth didn't. This was madness. She had to convince him to leave.

'I love you,' he said eventually. Holly tried to interrupt, but he held up his hand. 'Just hear me out, please. There's always only been you. From the first time we met.'

'Don't do this, Todd.'

'I hoped you'd feel the same one day, even though I was so much older. When you ditched me for Drew, you ripped my heart out. I told myself you'd get tired of him, see how immature he was, and come back to me. You didn't, though. You married *him*.'

'I'm sorry.' Holly's voice was a mere whisper.

'I had to watch the woman I love build a life with my brother. That sucked, Hols.'

'I never meant to hurt you.'

He continued as if she'd not spoken. 'When I met Nessa I persuaded myself I could be happy with her. And I have been—mostly.'

'Remember Shane and Jack. Don't forget your sons.'

'I don't. My boys mean the world to me. And Nessa—she's a good wife.'

'Do you love her?' Of course he did. He was that kind of man.

'Yes. Just not the same way I do you.'

Holly didn't reply. The words had frozen in her mouth.

'She knows how I feel about you.' Confirming what Holly had always suspected. 'And still she wants me, sees us sharing a future.' He shook his head. 'She's a wonderful woman. I don't deserve her.'

Holly remained silent. She bit her lip, unsure how to handle the situation.

'Whenever I saw you with Drew, it was like a knife through my heart. Over the years, it's got harder to bear. We'd share a glance, a moment, and I'd wonder'—he sucked in a deep breath—'whether you had regrets. If you ever thought you'd married the wrong brother.'

From somewhere Holly found her voice. 'It was just flirting. None of it meant anything.'

Anger flashed into his eyes. 'It did to me.'

'I'm sorry.' It was all Holly could offer.

'When Drew went missing, I was frantic with worry. He stole the woman I love, but he's still my brother. At first I thought he'd be back within a week. Then, as time passed, I began to hope. That you and I—'

'Don't!' Holly's fury took Todd, and her, by surprise. 'We should never have slept together, however innocently. It's best we pretend it never happened.'

'We needed each other.'

'I was lonely and frightened.'

'You don't have to be. I'll take care of you.'

Her anger burned hotter. 'Drew is missing. He's out there, mentally ill, maybe freezing and scared, and you're exploiting the situation.' Her voice cracked on the final syllable.

'I don't know why Drew left. He did, though. He walked out on you without a word. Those blank Christmas cards, the return of his rings—his behaviour sucks.' Todd's voice was tight with anger.

'I still think you're taking advantage of him being gone.'

'That's not how I see it. If you'd married me, I'd never have deserted you.'

'You hypocrite.' Holly spat out the words. 'You'd leave Nessa for me, though, wouldn't you? Isn't that what this is about?'

Shame crossed Todd's face. He didn't reply.

'I'll remind you again. You have Shane and Jack, as well as your wife, to consider. Not to mention Drew. You want him to come back and find his wife and his brother living together? And what about his child? I'm pregnant, in case you'd forgotten.'

'No, of course I haven't. But—'

'You're planning to wreck two marriages. Desert your children. You're worse than Drew.' She ran out of breath.

'Holly.' His voice was firm. 'Drew isn't coming back.'

'You're wrong. When he's ready, he'll get in touch.'

'You need to face reality. He left without even a goodbye.'

'He wasn't well. He had financial problems—'

'I'd treat you so much better than he has.'

'I love him. Not you.' She held his gaze. 'It will never be you.'

Anger snaked into his eyes again and stayed there. She'd cared so much for this man, but he'd turned into a stranger.

'I think you should leave,' Holly said. 'Don't come back.'

He walked past her to the front door. Seconds later she heard it slam, and his footsteps crunched over the gravel path.

Holly stumbled into the kitchen, her anger making her unsteady. She filled the kettle, her brain replaying the conversation with Todd. When her coffee was ready, she sat at the table, her hands clasped around Drew's favourite mug, as if to draw her husband closer. And repel the fear edging into her mind.

Holly considered the facts. She'd met Todd after she got dragged to a singles' night by a colleague, and his dark good looks had drawn her to him. They'd discussed novels, travel and politics; when he'd suggested a second date, she'd agreed straightaway. He seemed so solid, so stable, so suitable. More evenings together followed.

'I love you,' he'd announced, his voice thick with desire, two months later. Startled, she hadn't been sure how to respond. She liked him, the sex was good, but love? Too soon, by far.

It'll come, she persuaded herself. *Give the guy a chance.*

Drew, at the time, had been backpacking in Asia. A week after Todd's declaration, he returned to the UK, and Holly met him for the first time. Her gaze locked on her future husband's eyes; their soft blue ignited a spark in her belly. From that moment, Todd ceased to exist.

To his credit, he'd yielded Holly to Drew with grace; he'd said that, at eleven years her senior, he was maybe too old for her. How he wished them well. Things were awkward for a while; Holly sensed his hurt, but she pushed her guilt aside, thrilled to have found Drew. Their wedding had quickly followed, as did Todd's; he met Nessa a scant two weeks after Holly's rejection. A rebound relationship, most likely, but she'd been too crazy over Drew to care. The four of them fell into an easy routine of shared Sunday lunches most weekends. Todd and Drew started running together, and any tension between them seemed long gone.

Holly replayed Todd's words. *I had to watch the woman I love build a life with my brother. That sucked, Hols.*

Did Todd still harbour a grudge against Drew? Had his resentment grown into hatred? Enough to—?

No. She couldn't believe Todd capable of *that*. Besides, there were the rings, the Christmas cards. The fact they'd been hand delivered testified to Drew being alive, and still in the Bristol area.

She refused to consider the alternative. That Todd had harmed his brother in some way, then used the rings and cards as red herrings.

******

Christmas came, and almost broke Holly. She regretted having agreed to spend the day with Todd, Nessa and the boys, but to back out might arouse suspicion. Besides, she'd persuaded herself Todd would never hurt Drew. She'd been angry and confused; he deserved better, despite the way he'd acted. Even so, she backed away from Todd's attempt to hug her after she arrived. Nessa glanced between her husband and sister-in-law, her expression shuttered, but didn't comment. Holly pasted a smile on her face for her nephews' sake, all the while fighting the urge to flee.

Shane threw chubby arms around his aunt's legs. 'Auntie! Look what Santa got me!'

'Not now, darling. Lunch is almost ready,' Nessa said, before hurrying into the kitchen, from where the aroma of roast turkey wafted. Holly walked into the dining room, the table awash with decorations and party hats. In one corner stood a Christmas tree, decked with tinsel and baubles. Festive cards lined the windowsill. 'With Love To My Wife At Christmas' proclaimed one. Holly thought of how she'd ripped Drew's card into pieces, and turned away. The contrast to her barren home sliced through her heart.

'Uncle Drew!' Jack screeched once they'd sat down to eat. 'Wanna see Uncle Drew!'

Nessa spooned roast potatoes onto his plate. 'We all do, sweetie,' she replied, with a side glance at Holly. Holly stared at her food, willing tears from her eyes, aware of Todd's gaze on her. She sensed he had things he wanted to say, given the opportunity. Not that he'd get the chance.

She should have known she wouldn't escape so easily. After they'd eaten, he accosted her in the kitchen while Holly loaded the dishwasher.

'Can we talk?' Todd's voice was low, furtive.

'No.' She refused to look at him. 'Not here. Not now.'

He fell silent for a few seconds. Then: 'I regret—well, you know. What I said. The last time we met.'

When she didn't respond, he elaborated. 'How I feel about you, I mean.'

'You betrayed Drew.' Holly became acutely aware of Nessa, laughing with her sons, only metres away. She didn't think her sister-in-law could hear, but even so...

'I crossed a line,' Todd said. 'I'm aware of that.'

'Yes, you did. What the hell were you thinking?'

'I got carried away. Said stupid stuff that I regret. You don't have to worry. I'd never put my boys through the trauma of divorce.'

'We shouldn't be having this conversation. I made myself very clear.' Holly's voice was as cold as the snow outside.

Todd blew out a breath. 'I wish I could stop loving you, but I can't. Anyway, I'm sorry. It won't happen again.'

'Make sure it doesn't.' Holly turned back to the dishwasher. When she looked up, he had gone. In his place stood Nessa.

Holly's stomach knotted. How much had her sister-in-law overheard?

Nessa didn't speak, just slotted a stray plate into the dishwasher. For a moment her gaze met Holly's, her lips pressed tight. Then she walked from the room.

As soon as she could, Holly made her excuses and left.

******

By the time New Year's Eve arrived, Holly's anger had melted. Todd had suffered a moment of frailty, all part of being human. To her relief, he didn't contact her; not once did he visit, call or text. Once she'd thought things through, Holly found it easy to forgive him. Hadn't she also been weak?

Besides, she had other stuff on her mind. Her husband had left, but life carried on, bringing a surprise for Holly: love for her baby. *Must be my hormones kicking in*, she decided, one hand on her belly. A surge of nest-building had followed, even though her pregnancy was still in its early stages. Holly tracked down a second-hand cot, found a pram in a charity shop, bought tiny romper suits. When the time came, she wanted to be ready.

By now, according to what she'd read, her child would be the size of a fig; Holly pictured tiny fingers on starfish hands, and tears flooded her eyes.

She hadn't realised she could experience love so pure, so all encompassing.

'We'll be all right, my darling,' she reassured her baby, as the evening's fireworks exploded through the sky. 'Even without your daddy.'

'A new year, a fresh start,' she told Amber and Elaine over lunch, once back at work the following week. 'Other women manage alone. Why can't I?'

'You go, girl,' Elaine said. 'That's the attitude.'

Despite her brave words, Holly's evenings stretched before her, long and lonely. She loved the baby growing in her belly, but craved adult companionship. Reluctant to put pressure on Amber and Elaine, she spent her free time alone, firm in her resolve not to contact Todd. To do so would send mixed signals. Most nights she cried herself to sleep, in a bed that seemed too big without Drew.

Her husband still held her heart, despite the fact he'd abandoned her. Britain remained in the clutches of the worst winter on record; snow had gripped the country since November, and January showed no sign of a let-up. Temperatures stayed freezing for days on end, with only a brief respite before further snowfalls. Holly prayed that, wherever Drew was, he had food, clothes, bedding.

February came, and the weather turned milder, although still chilly. By the time mid-March arrived, her husband had been missing for four months.

And Holly's pregnancy had begun to show.

CHAPTER 26

Following his failed suicide attempt, Drew no longer contemplated death. It had been a stupid idea; the urge to breathe had proved too strong. Besides, what the hell had he been thinking? If he'd lost consciousness through lack of oxygen, he couldn't have maintained an air-tight seal anyway. Not with a flimsy piece of cling-film and senseless limbs.

Drew didn't do much of anything anymore. The darkness and silence, the confinement, the monotonous food, had whittled his spirit into passive acceptance; he didn't care whether he lived or died. Hour after silent hour he lay in his shackles, hallucinations dancing before his eyes. Holly still visited, as did Todd, his father and Uncle Hal. Once Nessa put in an appearance. Drew welcomed their company, but as time passed, he couldn't remember their names. Or who they were in relation to him.

Ian Morrison still stopped by every so often to check up on Drew. The man would gaze at him in the half-light from the open door, then withdraw when satisfied his prisoner still lived, never saying a word. Drew would endure his stale breath, stare at his scarred lip and think: *who is this?* He remembered his jailer was a monster from his past, someone to fear, but the guy's identity had slipped from his mind. As had his own. Drew Blackmore no longer existed. His captor had transformed his prisoner from a human being into a *thing*.

Other torments plagued him too. His anus itched from the faeces that lined his unwashed crease; try as he might, he couldn't stop scratching himself. His legs had long since ceased to cramp and lay wasted in their bonds. His mouth often bled; his gums were sore, his teeth loose, and his skin had turned scaly and dry. The stench from his body, his breath, along with that of the bucket, fouled the air, but he didn't notice. His discomfort seemed one step closer to the road to death.

'You will suffer,' he'd mutter sometimes, then wonder what the words meant. 'I will make your life hell.'

In many ways Drew was already there.

He had no idea his ordeal was almost over.

CHAPTER 27 – Present Day

The Watchman took a slurp of beer, then settled into his armchair. Beside him, on the chipped melamine table, lay a box of pizza, its sausage and garlic odours filling the cramped bedsit. He'd not long returned from his daily food delivery to the abandoned abattoir and had spent a satisfying half hour listening to the sounds coming from his victim. Or, as the Watchman preferred to think of him, his *guest.*

He selected a triangle of pizza and shoved it in his mouth. God, how he was enjoying their game. He had every intention of playing it for years to come. He just needed to keep Rick on board. That little runt could be too soft at times.

The Watchman brought to mind the horrors Rosalie Parker had endured. How her son Ethan had been left motherless. As had the Watchman and Rick. His resolve strengthened.

The shriek of his door buzzer interrupted his thoughts. With a curse, he threw the half-eaten slice into the box, and stomped towards the door, gluing an eye to the peep-hole.

Two police officers stood on his doorstep. One male, the other female. Shit, a thousand times over.

Only one possibility existed. His guest at the abattoir, and the Watchman's connection to him, had been discovered. The police were there to arrest him.

He was trapped; his tiny bedsit offered no chance of flight. The bathroom lacked natural light, and the only other room, the one in which he lived and slept, had windows that gave onto the passageway where the police officers stood. Impossible to pretend he wasn't at home; the floorboards, ancient and creaky, must have betrayed his approach to the door. The two of them must be wondering why he hadn't opened it.

His only hope was to deny everything and pray whatever evidence they possessed was weak.

The doorbell buzzed again. The Watchman remained frozen. His letterbox flipped open. The woman called into the hallway. 'Sir? It's the police. Can you let us in, please?'

The Watchman dragged in a steadying breath. His fingers released the chain to the door, then pulled it open.

He grinned at the two police officers, his expression rueful. 'Sorry. Not every day coppers appear at my door.'

She laughed. 'No problem, sir. We get that reaction a lot.' After he confirmed his identity, she stepped closer. 'We have some information for you. If we could come inside, please?'

Her manner confused him. It didn't fit with his imminent arrest.

'Of course.' He allowed them to pass. Perspiration rendered his palms clammy, his neck damp. He prayed they wouldn't notice.

He observed the male officer glance around the cramped space, then position himself with his back to the door. 'Do you have some ID we can check?' the man said.

The Watchman retrieved his wallet, extracted his bank cards and handed them over. He stood awkwardly next to his box of pizza, his arms crossed.

'Is it all right if I sit?' The woman gestured towards the sole armchair. He nodded.

'Let me introduce ourselves properly,' she said, once seated. 'I'm PC Keri Donaldson, from Avon and Somerset Police. This is PC Steve Johns. Like I said, we have some news.' She cleared her throat. 'We received a call from our colleagues in London. Croydon, to be exact.'

What the hell? He had no connection with Croydon. Where the fuck was this going?

'We're here about your mother.' She paused. 'I'm delighted to tell you she's been found. Alive.'

The world fell away from the Watchman. Keri's words repeated themselves in his head, but made no sense. *Mother. Found. Alive.*

Impossible. The police data clerk's information had pretty much confirmed her death at the hands of Rosalie Parker's killer, hadn't it? The same way Rick's mother had met her end.

When he tried to speak, every drop of saliva had drained from his mouth. He stared at Keri Donaldson, aware of a roaring in his ears. If he wasn't careful, he'd embarrass himself by fainting.

From somewhere he found the words. 'Are you sure it's her? I've always believed—' He scrubbed a hand over his jaw. 'That she must have died.'

'We're certain. Although—' She gave him a tentative smile. Then told him what else she knew.

'This changes everything,' Rick told him later.

The Watchman didn't reply. The little runt was right.

CHAPTER 28

Drew dragged open his eyes, his brain fuzzy with sleep. Something felt different. Then he realised what had changed, disappointed to find he was still dreaming. If only it were true. His freedom felt so real. Might as well enjoy it while it lasted, though.

Slowly, with infinite care, Drew raised his hand into the air. Moved it from side to side. Stretched his arm as far as his weak muscles permitted. He didn't hear the chink of the chain, or feel its weight. He switched his attention to his legs. Shuffled his left ankle forward. Lifted his right calf. The shackles were gone from all four of his limbs.

Inarticulate sounds bubbled from Drew's lips as he moved back and forth, stunned by the realisation this was no dream. His arms flailed; one hand collided with something solid. A plastic bottle full of liquid. Drew's fingers groped further, located a cling-film-wrapped triangle. He must have slept so deeply he'd missed his daily food delivery. That didn't explain the lack of restraints, though.

Hope surged within Drew, sparking his brain back to life. He seized the sandwich, tearing off the wrapping and stuffing bread and cheese into his mouth. Blood from his rotting gums leaked, sharp and coppery, into his food but he didn't care. He gulped the water, not stopping until he'd drained the bottle. Once he'd finished, he sat up further, gasping for breath.

As though warning him his new-found freedom might not be real, a woman's face appeared before his eyes. Young, pretty, dark-haired, her edges blurred; his favourite hallucination. Drew stretched out his arm, but his fingers only met air. He reached down to touch his calf and encountered skin. He searched for the chains around his ankles, but brushed flesh instead. Unlike the hallucination, his legs, and the lack of restraints around them, were real. The face disappeared.

What if this was some fresh mental torture? To offer hope, only to snatch it away? Perhaps his captor—what *was* his name?—expected him to try to open the door. He might be hovering, anticipating Drew's despair on finding it locked.

Escape. A miracle that had once seemed impossible. Dare he risk it?

He listened, every sense alert for a sound to show he wasn't alone. Nothing.

With infinite care, Drew positioned himself on all fours. Stripped of flesh, his knees grated, bony and painful, against the floor. He braced himself with his right hand and placed his left foot down. With all the effort he could muster, he attempted to stand.

He collapsed straightaway, his howl of frustration filling the blackness. He tried on his other side, but failed a second time. His withered legs could no longer support him.

He could crawl, though.

Drew reached out an arm, followed by a knee, then repeated on the other side, hauling himself forward. Within seconds pain thudded through his skull; his head had hit the door, causing him to collapse to the floor. Not onto concrete, though. Something soft lay under his emaciated frame.

He raised himself on one elbow, his hand examining the item. His fingers touched cloth, a zipper, press studs, belt loops. His brain flashed a word into his mind: *jeans.*

An excited whimper burst from Drew. His hands groped further, discovering a sweatshirt. Then a thicker garment: a fleece jacket, soft and warm. Socks. Underpants. Shoes.

Drew didn't stop to question their appearance. Muscle memory guided him to drag on the clothes. His fingers fumbled with the fly of the jeans, baulked at the zip on the fleece, but before long he'd accomplished his task. Instinct told him freedom lay within his grasp. All he had to do was open the door.

He reached up a hand. His palms roamed over its wood until they touched something cold, metallic. A handle. Drew pushed down, then pulled. The door didn't budge.

He tugged again. Still nothing.

Drew seized the handle, wrenching it with all his strength as his howls of frustration split the darkness. Then the door gave way and crashed into his head, knocking him backwards.

The movement slammed his head against the floor, unleashing a sea of pain. Gasping for breath, he rode out the shock waves. Once the discomfort eased, Drew stared at the door, aware he was no

longer surrounded by pitch black. Light was
diluting the gloom into a thick grey, shaped by the
aperture he'd created. His captor—no, his *saviour*—
hadn't tricked him. He loved the man, whoever he
was. A name nagged at him—Morris, perhaps?—
before it slipped away.

Drew crawled towards the greyness. He
eased the door further ajar, then pulled a deep
breath into his lungs. 'You can do this,' he told
himself.

Once Drew had dragged himself through the
gap, he lay panting and sweaty on the floor outside
his prison. The greyness seemed less dense to his
right, but his eyes hurt too much to glance at it for
more than a fraction of a second. Panic sized him.
His legs no longer worked. What if the blackness
had robbed him of his sight? But no, that wasn't
possible. He'd seen his captor enough times, hadn't
he?

Determined, he crawled towards the not-so-
grey, his eyes shut tight. Then his hand slammed
against an obstacle. His fingers explored its surface
until his brain recognised it as a step, the bottom
one of several.

A saying he'd once heard floated into his
brain. *Yard by yard, it's hard, but inch by inch it's a
cinch.* He reached out an arm, placed it on the
second step, and hauled his body upward.

'Inch by inch,' he muttered, as he dragged
himself up further. Onwards and upwards. His
muscles, unused to exertion, screamed for mercy,
and twice Drew collapsed, panting and close to
exhaustion. Driven by dogged determination, he

managed to pull himself forward each time. Towards the greyness. A cold breeze assailed him every so often, indicating a broken window; the reason, he guessed, for the air that used to stir around his nose while he'd been a captive.

Without warning, his ordeal was over. His hands met flatness, and Drew pulled himself over the last step. He edged forward, guided by the torment behind his eyelids. The pain was good. It confirmed a window lay ahead. That meant escape. Freedom.

Inch by inch...

The agony in his eyes proved too great after a few feet. Drew wrapped his right arm over them, then crawled using only his left. Before long he crashed into something solid and wooden. He opened his eyes, scanning for a door handle, but quickly covered them once pain stabbed his irises. Panic seized him; in that small window of time, he'd seen nothing. Perhaps he really had gone blind.

Drew hauled himself against the door to rest. Once his breathing returned to normal, he reached up an arm, and pulled on the handle with what remained of his strength. The door opened, and Drew howled with pain. The agony came from the intense whiteness that burned his retinas. Even clamping both hands over them didn't help.

For a moment, Drew wondered whether he'd died. The brilliant light—was it part of a near-death experience? If so, he'd soon be reunited with the loved ones he'd lost. Even if he couldn't remember their names.

But no. The bone-biting chill that seized his body persuaded him he was very much alive. Wind gusted through the open door, and Drew shivered. With one hand still pressed over his eyes, he reached the other into the gap. His fingers met icy-cold powder. The world outside his prison lay carpeted in a late frost, thick and glistening, with a full moon bright in the sky.

All he had to do to achieve freedom was to crawl into the whiteness.

'Inch by inch,' he muttered, and dragged himself forward.

Within seconds melted frost soaked his jeans, and the bitter chill gnawed his flesh. Exhausted, Drew realised he might soon die from exposure. He had to turn around while he still had the strength. His decision made, he hauled himself back inside and shoved the door shut, his limbs frozen with cold. Uncontrollable shudders racked his body.

Drew lay on the floor, chilled and defeated, certain that death was close. Well, there were worse ways to go. With that thought, Drew shut his eyes. The world drifted away in a haze of whiteness.

******

Voices. Noise, bustle, people. Too much, and too many: Drew's eyes shot open, only to meet an explosion of searing light. He slammed them shut, amid a scream of agony.

Hands seized his body, pulled at his wet clothing. He was conscious of an icy chill that pervaded his bones, before somebody wrapped a foil-type blanket around him. The urge to drift back to sleep proved strong, but Drew overrode it. A ball of terror grew in his gut. Who were these people? This cold, God-forsaken place—how had he got here, wherever *here* was? One thing was clear. He needed to escape, and fast.

'Sir, can you tell me your name?' A female voice, close by, shouting at him. Words sounded in his ears: *hypothermic, blood pressure dropping, appears drowsy…*

He cracked open an eye, before pain forced it shut again. In that split second he saw a face. Young, pretty, framed by dark hair. She reminded Drew of someone he'd once known and loved. He tried to conjure up her features, but failed. Couldn't be her, though. This woman had a mole on her neck.

'My name is—' Drew stopped. He had no idea. The realisation terrified him.

He tried again, without success. He sounded like he had treacle in his throat. Why couldn't he talk properly? And how come he didn't know his own identity?

More words. *Slurred speech… confusion… weak pulse…*

Danger surrounded him on all sides. Time to act.

'Get the hell away from me!' Drew thrashed the air, arms flailing, hitting whatever he could reach. Too late, he saw the needle approaching his arm, felt its sting as it slid home. After that, nothing.

Part Two

Hospital

CHAPTER 29

The Watchman had spotted the police presence near the abattoir, and known he needed to leave, fast. Once home, he'd turned on his television, his impatience growing all the while. At last six thirty arrived, and with it the local news. The screen showed a reporter, crime scene tape stretched behind her, a microphone held close to her mouth. A derelict building stood in the background. 'Police say that the man had been held captive in this disused abattoir near Chew Magna. His identity is— as far as we can gather—still unknown. The circumstances of his confinement and subsequent rescue are unclear, but he is now recovering in hospital. We'll bring you more on this story as we get it.' The broadcast cut back to the studio presenter.

He closed his eyes, struggling to control his emotions. So Drew Blackmore had escaped. No, been *released*. Anger pounded through the Watchman's veins. Mistakes had been made. Time to rectify them.

With an effort, he recalled how it had all started, over a year ago. Rick's horror at learning of Rosalie Parker's murder. The Watchman's scheme to recruit her son Ethan. In hindsight, that had been a bad idea.

Actions have consequences, he thought. Rick had been right. Everything had changed, which meant the Watchman's plans needed to as well.

No problem. He was nothing if not adaptable. One thing was for sure: he'd need a new place to live. Somewhere the cops would never find him, where he'd pay cash and the landlord wouldn't ask too many questions. No way could he afford for the police to connect him with the disused abattoir.

CHAPTER 30

'You ever seen anything like this before?'

Matthew Thomas, senior psychotherapist at Bristol's Southmead Hospital, shook his head. 'I'm not sure what we're dealing with here. We'll know more after the police talk to him.'

Shauna Sutherland, chief staff nurse, nodded. 'That won't be possible just yet. He's malnourished, dehydrated, and disorientated. Not to mention the fact he can't walk. His muscles are too wasted. He'll need extensive physiotherapy.'

'Any other injuries?'

Shauna shook her head. 'Nothing significant. His eyes are hypersensitive to light, which is the reason they're bandaged. His teeth and gums require attention. He has infected skin around his anus.'

'Wouldn't the bacteria from that have killed him once in his bloodstream? Given his weakened state?'

'You're right. I suspect he's been fed antibiotics.'

'What else?' Matthew asked.

'There's damage to his wrists and ankles— looks like he's been chained up, hence the muscle wastage—but his mental state concerns me the most.'

'Which is why I'm here, right?'

'Yep. He's exhibiting confusion. Doesn't know his own name. Even worse, he's experiencing hallucinations.'

Matthew frowned. 'What sort? Visual? Auditory?'

'Visual. People, mostly. This morning he seemed convinced a man was threatening him. He kept gesticulating wildly, while mumbling about a man with hairy hands.'

'That's a little... offbeat.'

'Then he started shrieking in terror, pointing and yelling, "I won't tell anyone, I swear! Please don't make me suffer!"'

'Jesus Christ.' The psychotherapist shook his head. 'Anything else?'

Shauna frowned. 'He often screams out, "For God's sake, don't leave me! Come back, please!" Oh, and he's muttered a name a few times. Morris, Morrison, something like that.'

'How long until the police can interview him?'

'Hard to say. He's reacting well to intravenous vitamins and anti-psychotic medication. Once he starts responding to the ward staff, we can judge whether he's recovered enough to stand questioning.'

'And he came in with no ID? Nothing to indicate who he might be?'

Shauna shook her head. 'From what I've been told, he was found with no wallet, credit cards or mobile phone anywhere in sight. That's all I know.'

******

Drew huddled under his bedclothes, his body a foetal ball. Inside his head swirled a maelstrom of fear. All that remained of his memory was a black hole, deep, dark and awful, into which his life had vanished. He remembered fragments: fear, hunger, despair. Nothing else. Drew shuddered. He had no wish to glimpse hell, but did he have a choice? He sensed the truth was inching closer hour by hour, minute by minute. Soon he'd remember the horror his brain had suppressed, and then…

'You will suffer,' he mumbled into his pillow.

******

'It would help us enormously if we could ask him some questions,' Detective Sergeant Alison Tucker told Matthew the next day. 'That's where you come in.'

'I'll talk to him later this morning. Check whether he's well enough. What can you tell me about him?'

'About him, not a lot. About how we found him? Plenty.'

'Don't hold back. It's stuff I need to know if I'm to help the poor bastard.'

DS Tucker leaned forward. 'Someone shackled him to the floor and kept him a captive. From the degree of muscle wastage he's suffered, we estimate he'd been there three to four months.'

'What, all throughout the winter? With the weather we've been having, I'm surprised he didn't freeze to death.'

'He'd been supplied with blankets and a duvet. His abductor clearly wanted to ensure he didn't die. There's more. He'd been kept in total darkness, the reason for his eye issues. Fed the bare minimum to keep him alive.'

'Shit.' Matthew scrubbed a hand over his jaw. Whoever had done this was one sick bastard.

'The room had also been soundproofed. Not the work of a professional, but enough to muffle a fair bit of noise. When you factor in the remote location, the poor sod could have screamed for England and nobody would have heard.' Tucker picked up her coffee cup. 'I'm going for a refill. You want another?'

'Nah, I'm good, thanks.'

After she'd gone, Matthew blew out a breath, his brain whirring. Memories of his university days, of one particular research study, came back to haunt him. At the time he'd found the subject harrowing, albeit fascinating. Now he wondered. Should he mention the similarities to Tucker?

Seconds later she returned, a steaming coffee cup in her hand. Once she'd sat down, Matthew spoke. 'Perhaps his captor had another motive for the sound-proofing. Noises from outside wouldn't have reached him either. It would have worked both ways.'

'I'm not sure I get your point.'

'You said he'd been kept in complete darkness. No light, coupled with an absence of most sound. That all adds up to an extreme form of sensory deprivation.'

'You're saying his abductor wanted to torture this guy?'

'Maybe.'

Tucker exhaled a long breath. 'You're the psychotherapist, Dr Thomas. What kind of person would do that?'

Matthew grimaced. 'One hell of an evil bastard. Whoever took him intended to keep him alive, but ensure he suffered horribly. Humans are social animals; even the most introverted don't do well in isolation. Solitary confinement inflicts terrible psychological wounds. Researchers have abandoned many studies into its effects for that reason, and much sooner than you'd expect.'

'Really?'

'Yes. After only a few hours in some cases. The human guinea pigs involved became restless, craving mental stimulation. They'd sing or talk to themselves, anything to break the monotony. When you consider our brain is the most sophisticated computer ever created, that's not surprising. Mental acuity deteriorates rapidly under such circumstances.'

'In what way?'

'The participants struggled with mathematical and word association tests. Their sense of time worsened too. Many insisted they'd been in isolation for far less time than they actually had. Hallucinations were an issue too. All the test subjects suffered them in one form or another. Our man's also experiencing them.'

'Hallucinations? Really?'

'Once he can bear light entering his eyes, they should stop. His brain won't be attempting to fill a void any longer.'

'So is he wearing protective bandages?' When Matthew nodded, Tucker's lips pursed. 'Damn. That means we can't photograph him, not yet anyway.'

'I'll let you know when he's ready to face some questions. It might take a while. He's lived with an altered sense of reality for months, remember. Not something that'll resolve itself overnight.'

******

Matthew surveyed the man in the bed. Two days after his conversation with Shauna Sutherland, she'd told him her patient had begun to interact with his nurses. A nod on receiving his breakfast, a muted *yes* when asked if he required the bedpan. Matthew needed to decide whether he was well enough for police questioning. He dragged a chair close to the bed and sat down.

The man looked pale and gaunt, his face a skin-covered skull. His age could have been anywhere between late twenties and mid-thirties; he appeared closer to thirty-five, but the trauma he'd suffered had probably aged him beyond his years, Matthew thought. His hair was brown, thinning a little on top and cropped short, thanks to a nurse.

He'd sported a full beard on admission, which had been shaved off to reveal chapped, crusty lips. Dark wraparound glasses had replaced his bandages; Matthew guessed his eyes must still be sensitive to light. Restless hands played with the blanket covering him, the man's fingers rubbing the fabric. He ignored Matthew's approach.

'Hello,' Matthew said. 'I'll pull the privacy curtain around us. I'd like to chat to you, if that's okay?'

No response. Matthew reached out a hand, tugging the blue material along the runner rails. A petrified howl stopped him. The man's expression had filled with terror. A scream issued from his mouth. 'No! No! No!'

Too late, Matthew realised his mistake. Someone had confined this man to a small room for months. The curtain encircling his bed must have panicked him; he'd probably developed a fear of closed spaces. Matthew pulled it open. The screaming stopped.

'I'm sorry if I startled you.' Seating himself next to the bed, Matthew introduced himself. 'What can I call you?' he asked.

A blank stare met his question. Followed by a look of distress. 'I don't know,' the man said.

'You can't remember?'

A shake of his head. 'Sometimes a name comes to me, but before I can say it, it vanishes.' A tear slid down his cheek. 'Where am I? In hospital, right?'

'Yes. Don't worry, you're getting the best possible care. Everyone is keen to help you.'

Matthew leaned forward. 'Do you feel well enough to answer a few questions?'

A defensive look crept over the man's face. 'What sort of questions?'

'Ones that might establish who you are.'

'I don't know.' The man's voice was hoarse. More tears edged down his cheeks. 'Why can't I remember?'

Because you've been stripped of your identity, Matthew replied in his head. *Whoever did this dehumanised you.*

'Try not to get agitated.' He adopted his most soothing tone. 'Is it all right if we talk again? Soon?'

******

Matthew visited the nameless man again the next day. The morning after that he told Shauna Sutherland she could contact the police.

They didn't delay. DS Tucker arrived with DC Gary Tobin at Southmead that afternoon.

'I'll stop the questions if I deem he can't cope,' Matthew told DS Tucker. 'His mental state is still fragile, but he hasn't experienced any hallucinations—or none that we're aware of—over the last twenty-four hours. You'll need to go easy on him, though.'

The detective nodded. 'I'll bear that in mind. Shall we get going?'

Matthew led them to a side room off the ward, to where nurses had moved the patient before Tucker and Tobin's arrival. When DS Tucker tried to shut the door, a frantic howl came from the room's occupant.

'You won't achieve anything with it closed,' Matthew said. 'If anyone has a right to suffer claustrophobia, it's this guy.'

DS Tucker nodded, and left the door open. She seated herself to the left of the bed, with DC Tobin and Matthew the other side.

'Good afternoon,' she said to the figure under the blankets, her warrant card visible in one hand. 'I'm DS Alison Tucker from Avon and Somerset Police. This is my colleague DC Gary Tobin. We're here to ask you some questions.'

The man in the bed didn't respond. He'd improved a lot physically—his skin less pasty, his lips not so dry—and he no longer wore protective glasses. His eyes told a different story, though. The bleakness in them hinted at terrible suffering. Matthew tried to imagine what being chained to the floor in total darkness must have been like. To lose the use of one's legs, to develop scurvy. Minimal food and water. No meaningful human contact. For God alone knew how long.

He shuddered. Had that been him, he didn't think he'd have emerged even one per cent sane.

'We need to record our session today,' Tucker informed Matthew and the man in the bed. She waved a hand towards Tobin, who was setting up the equipment. 'Standard procedure.' She pulled out three chairs and sat on one, with Matthew taking another. Once Tobin had the audio and visuals ready, Tucker gave an introductory spiel for their benefit, then began proceedings.

'Can you tell us your name?' she asked.

A shake of the man's head.

'Or where you live?'

Another denial.

Tucker leaned forward, her expression sympathetic. 'I appreciate you've suffered a terrible ordeal. We're keen to catch whoever did this, so they can't hurt anyone else. Anything you can tell us would be an enormous help. Was your captor male or female?'

A long pause, during which Matthew considered whether to halt the interview. Then the man spoke. 'Male.'

'How can you be sure?'

'His wrists. They were hairy.'

Tucker exchanged glances with Matthew. 'You touched him?'

'He wore a watch. And he brought me food. Water.'

'Excellent. That's very good,' Tucker responded, her tone soothing, as though to a frightened child. 'What else can you tell us? Young, old? Black, white?'

'Too many questions at once,' Matthew warned.

Tucker acknowledged his comment with a nod. She turned back to the figure in the bed. 'Do you have any idea who might have done this to you?'

Tears pooled in the man's eyes. 'I've no idea. At least... there's a name. But I can't remember it.'

'You think it belonged to the man who abducted you?' Tobin asked.

'I don't know, I tell you!' His voice rose into a scream.

'Time to wrap up,' Matthew said, his tone crisp. 'We're done here.'

Tobin and Tucker stood up; the latter's expression betrayed her frustration. Then the man in the bed sat upright.

'Holly!' he pronounced. Excitement filled every line of his face. 'I remember that name. But I don't know where from.'

DS Tucker glanced at Matthew. He nodded briefly, upon which she, and Tobin, resumed their seats. 'Who is Holly?' she asked.

'Holly,' the man repeated. 'Where is she?'

'Is she your wife? Girlfriend, maybe?' From DC Tobin.

The figure in the bed chewed his lower lip, his brow furrowed. He shook his head. 'I can't remember.'

Tobin pulled Tucker aside. 'I think I know who this is.'

CHAPTER 31

The Watchman's fingers drummed a steady beat against his thigh as the train headed towards London, and the hospital in Croydon where his mother was a patient. Rain hammered against the window, mirroring his thoughts, which were a mess. For so long he'd been convinced she'd died, shackled and alone, captured and imprisoned. The way Rick's mother had done. Ethan Parker's as well. How had he got it so wrong?

Hurt throbbed through the Watchman, followed by fury. Instead of dying, the bitch had simply abandoned him, but why? And how the fuck had she ended up in London?

Keri Donaldson and Steve Johns hadn't told him much. Their Croydon colleagues had arrested his mother for shoplifting, it seemed. At first they'd attributed her odd behaviour to alcohol, until they realised something more sinister was at work. She'd told them her name was Crystal but had no idea of her surname. Further enquiries led Croydon police to a filthy squat in a local Victorian terraced house. Along with Eddie Shriver, a man who claimed to be Crystal's boyfriend but who was obviously more of a pimp. When they asked him her real name, instead of her whore one, he merely shrugged. The empty beer cans and wine bottles that littered the floor told their own story. A search of the national missing persons records, together with Crystal's accent, a tell-tale burn mark on her arm, the mole by her mouth, outed her as the Watchman's mother.

So there he was, on a journey to meet the woman he'd long believed dead. The two of them needed to talk; she might harbour vital information. Details he and Rick could use when it came to sorting the situation with Drew Blackmore.

The Watchman could imagine what Rick would say about all this. The fucker was too malleable, too weak. Needed a good slap at times.

******

After he arrived at the hospital, he asked to speak with the ward sister responsible for his mother's care.

'Tests revealed she's suffering from cirrhosis of the liver, consistent with chronic alcoholism,' Luna Gonzalez told him. 'We believe that's the reason for her confusion. Long-term alcoholics can develop dementia through lack of nutrients.'

'But she's only...' The Watchman struggled to remember; how old was his mother? 'In her early fifties,' he ended.

'Alcohol-related dementia commonly reveals itself between the ages of fifty and seventy. Your mother's symptoms aren't advanced, but she's muddled about certain things. Her name, where she lives. Sometimes she's lucid, others not.'

Crunch time, the Watchman decided. 'Can I see her?'

'Of course.' Luna motioned for him to follow, then led him into the ward, towards the windows at the end. She stopped at the last bed on the right.

'Let me know if you have any other questions.' With that, she left him with his mother.

The Watchman sat on a blue plastic chair. He took a deep breath, then stared at the occupant of the bed.

He would never have known her. His initial impulse was to run after Luna Gonzalez, insist she'd made a terrible mistake. The woman before him appeared in her sixties, not her fifties. Matted grey hair framed skin that sagged, yellow and unhealthy, around alcohol-coarsened features. Thread veins carpeted her cheeks, criss-crossed her nose. Her arms lay flaccid on the bedspread. A soft snore rumbled past her lips. Her open mouth offered a glimpse of brown teeth, some missing. Whoever Crystal was, she wasn't his mother.

Then he noticed the small mole by her mouth. The familiar chip-fat burn on her left arm. The Watchman dropped his head into his hands and groaned.

CHAPTER 32

Holly wished she'd taken a day's sick leave, but her divorce caseload dictated otherwise. Now five months pregnant, her breasts were sore, her back ached, and exhaustion dogged her every step. She wasn't coping, despite the bravado of *new year, fresh start*. That had been weeks ago anyway; it was now March. Her friendship with Amber and Elaine helped, as did her mother's phone calls, but loneliness still gnawed at Holly. She missed the easy familiarity she'd once shared with Todd. He'd been in her thoughts a lot lately.

Should she contact him, make it clear she'd forgiven his gaffe? What must Nessa be thinking? Her sister-in-law had noticed the tension between them on Christmas Day. What if Drew returned and found his wife estranged from his family?

Holly's eyes filled with tears. She blinked them away, angry at herself for being so weak. *He's not coming back. Deal with it.*

The mountain of paperwork on her desk mocked her. A career as a divorce lawyer held no interest anymore. She needed the money, though. But how would she manage once the baby arrived?

Todd. She was desperate for him to convince her single motherhood wouldn't be so terrible. He'd always known the right thing to say. But was it fair to ask him?

You created this rift, she reminded herself. Shouldn't she be the one to mend it? Todd was hardly likely to spurn her. Still she remained unsure.

The afternoon ticked by, Holly's indecision a constant buzz in her head. She caved in at four o'clock and texted Todd, asking him to call round after he finished work. He answered with a simple 'Fine.'

At six fifteen he arrived on her doorstep. 'It's good to see you, Hols,' he said. He glanced away, biting his lip.

'You too.' She stood aside to let him pass. He wore dark grey chinos, topped with a blue shirt and a leather jacket she'd not seen before. Faint stubble darkened his jawline. A whiff of his aftershave reached Holly, and she breathed in its musky aroma, glad she'd contacted him. Todd represented safety, security, reassurance.

He didn't try to hug her, she noted. A pang of regret shot through Holly, but it was for the best. Giving out mixed messages, even if unintentionally, wasn't fair on Todd. She could, however, attempt to salvage their friendship.

Minutes later he was sitting opposite her in the living room, a mug of coffee in one hand.

'Thanks for coming,' Holly said. She took a deep breath, then plunged in. 'I've missed you. Can't we get back to how we were? Before Drew went missing?'

He studied the steam rising from his coffee, and for a moment she was afraid he'd say no. But then he looked at her, and smiled. 'I'd like that.'

Before Holly could reply, Todd continued, 'I love my brother. I'd never hurt him. That night I spent here, though, and that other time, I was mad as hell at Drew. He should have talked to me about his problems, not just disappeared.'

'I get that. I was angry with him too.'

'I'm ashamed of my behaviour. Can you forgive me?'

Holly smiled. 'Consider it done.'

Todd took a sip of coffee. 'Thank you.' The relief on his face was clear.

'What did you tell Nessa?'

'That you needed time alone.'

'Did she believe you?'

He shrugged. 'She seemed to.'

Holly recalled Nessa's stiff bearing at Christmas, her suspicion that the other woman didn't trust her. Todd's relaxed attitude, though, indicated otherwise.

Her phone rang, making them both jump. When she picked it up, she saw the caller was Gary Tobin.

Panic swamped her. But if Drew was dead, why hadn't the police come to the house?

Maybe someone had reported seeing him. Please, *please*, let that be why Tobin was calling.

Her fingers shook so hard she was barely able to hold the phone. 'Yes?'

Holly listened to the voice on the other end. Tears ran down her cheeks, clogged her nose with snot. 'We'll leave right away,' she told Tobin, before ending the call. She hid her face in her hands, too overcome to speak.

Todd grabbed her wrist. 'Is it Drew? Have they found him? Is he...' He sucked in a breath. 'Alive?'

Holly peeled her palms off her cheeks, which threatened to split if her grin grew any wider. How was it possible to experience such happiness and not die?

'They reckon so, yes.' Her smile faded. 'He's in hospital, though. Gary wouldn't tell me why.' Had Drew attempted suicide? Was that why he'd needed medical care?

'You'll find out more when you get here,' Tobin had said. He'd refused to elaborate.

'He'd inform you if Drew's life was in danger.' Todd's cheeks were flushed with emotion, his eyes shiny with tears. He scrubbed a palm over his jaw. 'Drew's been found. Thank fuck for that. *YESSSSSS!!!!*' Todd punched the air, a huge grin on his face. He stood up, one hand pulling Holly with him. His hands on her waist, he whirled her off her feet and through the air. 'I can't believe it! This is the best news ever. Oh, my God.' He spun her faster, until the room became a spiral of joy, blurred with a million emotions. Holly threw back her head and laughed, the sound a deep whoop of delight, her former concern gone. Todd was right. The world was a glorious place.

At last he set her down, and they collapsed against each other, panting and grinning. Todd wiped his eyes. 'Where is he? We're going there now, yeah?'

'Southmead Hospital. Gary said he'll meet us in the main lobby. Says he needs to talk with us first.'

'I'll call Nessa. She'll be delighted, as will the boys. Drew's alive. He's *alive*, Hols!'

******

Drew stared around the hospital room, unaccustomed to getting his sight back. Once his eye dressings had been removed, his pupils had taken time to adjust to light; dark glasses had helped during the transition period. His depth perception was still off, but the colours around him were a delight: the blue bedspread, the yellow of a magazine cover, the red of a plastic beaker. How could he have forgotten such magnificence existed?

Drew had asked for a mirror, but hadn't received one. He guessed he must look rough. He ran his hand over his face and scalp; his head was bone covered by a thin layer of flesh, his fist fitting into the hollow of each cheek. His hair felt coarse, and dry, too short for him to gauge its colour after the shave and drastic crop he'd been given. Like so much else, he couldn't recall if he'd been dark, blond or something in between. Not that he was able to check. A frustrating reminder of the Black Hole—his name for his former prison—was that he couldn't walk to the bathroom to use the mirror there. His physiotherapist had told him his legs should work again, but only after extensive treatment.

On the physical front, he'd heal. Mentally, though? A different story. Matthew Thomas, his psychotherapist with the fierce dark eyes, had informed him that his name was Drew Blackmore. He was twenty-six and had been married to Holly for three years. Matthew also told him he had an older brother called Todd. Drew found himself unable to process the man's words. The guy must be talking about some passing acquaintances of Drew's. He recalled Holly's name, how she was his wife, that he loved her, but little else. How come he didn't remember? And try as he might, he couldn't recall his brother's features.

Matthew had also told him about the Black Hole.

'You've been through a highly traumatic experience,' he'd said. He'd already explained the hallucinations, how solitary confinement affected the mind. 'Your brain needs time to recover. You've suffered what's known as a mental fugue.'

Drew stared at him. 'What's that?'

'When the police and paramedics arrived to rescue you, your brain shut down. Light, sounds, people, after so long alone in the dark—it must have been terrifying. Too much to cope with. You didn't forget your incarceration. Instead, you blocked it out.'

His memory was seeping back, though. Drew recalled the shackles, the bucket, but hazily, as though such horrors had happened to a stranger. His mind had also clamped down on the subject of Ian Morrison. He'd told Matthew, and the police, that he had no idea of his captor's identity, which was partly true. At night, as he lay awake, Morrison's name bubbled to the surface, but he shoved it away. He dared not allow his thoughts to go there. Not yet.

Other times a face crept into his mind. A woman, dark hair curling towards her shoulders. Drew knew this must be Holly, his wife, but marriage? An alien concept. Being a husband was for men who hadn't been dehumanised the way he had. He was broken, and he didn't think Matthew Thomas could fix him.

CHAPTER 33

By the time the Watchman glanced up, his mother was awake. Bloodshot eyes stared at him. Yellow lurked among the red. Jaundice, he supposed, the result of her ruined liver.

'It's me,' he said. When she didn't respond, he tried again. 'Your son.'

Stupid, of course. Rick had warned this might happen. The Watchman had been a child when he last saw his mother. How could he hope she'd recognise him as a man?

Confusion washed over her face. Then she seized his hand, her skin dry and cold against his. 'You're another bloody john, right?' The words wheezed past her lips. 'Come to fuck me, yeah?'

'I'm your son.' He stared at his mother, willing her to remember.

Instead, a sneer twisted her face. 'Oh. *That* little fucker. Left him behind long ago.'

In that moment, he could have strangled her. The bitch. Whore. Hatred filled his soul, and he pulled his hand away. He stared at her, a battle for self-control raging in his brain. Then her eyes dropped closed, and she began to snore.

The Watchman stayed by her bed for what remained of visiting hours, but she didn't wake up.

No matter. He had plenty of time. It would be best all round if he returned tomorrow. He had questions, and needed answers.

CHAPTER 34

Holly and Todd were sitting in a side room for visitors next to Drew's ward. Heat blasted from the radiator, and a faint tang of disinfectant hung in the air. Gary Tobin sat opposite them, his expression unreadable. Beside him sat a woman he'd introduced as DS Alison Tucker. 'I have both good and bad news,' he said.

'Spit it out, for God's sake.' Strain showed in every line of Todd's face. 'You've found my brother, right? Why can't we see him?'

Holly laid a hand on his arm. 'Gary's only doing his job. There's no need for rudeness.' She readied herself for what was to come.

Tobin fixed his gaze on Holly. 'We have identified a man undergoing treatment here as your husband. The photographs you provided when he went missing indicate a match. As does the little he's been able to tell us.'

Holly released the breath she'd been holding. Thank God. She'd dreaded hearing there'd been some terrible mistake. That her husband was still missing. Or worse.

Beside her, Todd shifted restlessly. 'So how come we're with you, not him? Haven't we already waited four months?' He was shouting now.

Holly gritted her teeth. 'Don't. This is hard enough, without you going off the deep end.' She turned to Tobin. 'Was he in an accident? What happened?'

Tobin shook his head. 'I need to warn you that Drew is suffering a degree of confusion. On admission to Southmead he didn't even know his own name. He remembers you, though.'

Happiness seared Holly's heart. Followed by sadness. Like everyone had believed, Drew must be mentally ill. 'Who found him?' she asked. 'Took him to hospital?'

'The emergency services received a tip-off,' Tucker said. 'A man phoned, giving Drew's location. Saying he needed an ambulance, and urgently.'

'Who made the call?' Todd asked.

Tucker shook her head. 'He didn't give his name.' She leaned forward. 'There's no easy way of saying this. It appears Drew was abducted. Held captive throughout the winter.'

'*What?*' Todd shot to his feet, fury in his face.

Shock filled Holly, gluing her to her seat. Despite the overheated room, she shivered. She must have misheard DS Tucker. The woman hadn't said Drew had been held prisoner. Impossible.

'Sit down, please, Mr Blackmore,' Tucker said. 'There's more. A lot more.'

As Tucker spoke, Holly's happiness shattered into fragments so small she had no hope she'd ever be whole again. She heard how Drew had spent the last four months chained to the floor in the dark, his prison a deserted abattoir. The egg cartons and blankets on the walls that had provided partial sound-proofing. A plastic bucket for a toilet, the feeding flap cut into the door. How, apparently, someone eventually unchained him, then unlocked the door. Holly barely registered Todd's fist pounding the table when Tucker revealed Drew couldn't walk. She listened, but Tucker's words made no sense. She felt frozen, numb; her mind recoiled from such evil. She'd go mad in such circumstances. And who was to say his ordeal *hadn't* rendered Drew insane? He didn't know his own name, for God's sake.

Her poor husband. Shame filled Holly when she recalled how she'd stamped on their wedding photo. All the while she'd been angry, he'd been suffering hell. The thought choked her.

A low moaning sounded into the room. Holly realised it came from her. DS Tucker thrust a tissue into Holly's hand. She wiped her eyes, blew her nose. She needed to stay strong for Drew's sake. Todd's too.

Holly sensed the fury in her brother-in-law. He'd become a snake ready to strike.

'What about Drew's rings? Those Christmas cards we received?' he demanded, his face flushed.

'Odds are whoever abducted him did that,' Tobin said. 'Hand delivered them to make everyone think Drew had done a runner, but was still in the area.'

'But his prints were on the envelopes. And the cards,' Holly said.

'Easily obtained anytime Drew was unconscious. Which he almost certainly was at first.'

Such calculating behaviour stunned Holly. Her husband's captor had planned his captivity in great detail. Not caring about the hurt he'd cause. All that mattered was throwing the police off the scent.

'I'd like to kill whoever did this,' Todd spat out. His fist banged the table again.

'I need to prepare you both for how Drew looks,' DS Tucker said. 'He's lost a lot of weight and is suffering the effects of malnutrition. The hospital needed to extract several teeth. His attention span is short, and he gets stressed easily. And don't close the door to his room. He'll panic if you do.'

'Who did this to my husband?' Cold fury filled Holly's voice. She'd never thought of herself as capable of murder. Now, given the chance, she'd strangle Drew's abductor, then spit on his corpse.

Tucker grimaced. 'We don't have much to go on. Once you've seen Drew, I need to talk to you both again. Discuss the day he disappeared.'

'Haven't we been through that a hundred times already?' Irritation spiked Todd's tone.

'Your brother was held captive for four months,' Tucker replied. 'If we're to catch whoever's responsible, we'll have to turn Drew's life inside out. We need to arrest the man who did this, and fast. Because, speaking off the record, he's one sick bastard.'

'Then why did he release Drew?' Holly asked. 'He didn't escape, right? You indicated earlier that his captor unchained him, unlocked the door, then called an ambulance. After four months. It makes no sense.'

'Someone else may have done that. We can only speculate at this stage,' Tucker said. 'I appreciate this is a difficult time for all concerned. With that in mind, I'll ensure that a Family Liaison Officer is assigned to the investigation. He or she will be your point of contact and is there to keep Drew and everyone related to him informed.'

Holly nodded, mute.

Tucker stood up. 'Go see your husband. Visiting hours finish at nine tonight. Let's meet outside the cafeteria afterwards. I'll find somewhere we can talk in private.'

After she'd gone, Todd turned to Holly. 'You ready?'

She sucked in a breath. 'Yes. No. Let's just do this, okay?' With that she ran, Todd close behind. Within seconds they reached the separate rooms at the end of the ward. The door to the middle one was open.

Holly hurtled through the gap, followed by Todd. She stifled a gasp on seeing the figure in the bed. Beside her, she sensed Todd stiffen.

******

The man was Drew, and yet not. His face was gaunt, his hair cropped short, his skin dry and sallow. He'd lost weight, his shoulders bony under his pyjama top. Holly almost screamed that this wasn't her husband, damn it. Then the man in the bed turned his gaze her way, and their eyes met. His blue irises appeared haunted, bleak. They lingered on her, before shifting to Todd. Then back.

Recognition crept into his face. 'Holly,' Drew whispered, his voice a thin quaver.

The man was no longer a stranger. He was her husband. Holly launched herself at Drew, crushing him tight. His body was little more than a skeleton, or so it felt. She held him close, so his head rested near to their baby, one hand stroking his hair. Drew was weak, he was ill, but he was alive. She drank him in, intoxicated by the feel of him in her arms. Tears slid down her face, dripped onto Drew's hospital gown. She'd never loved him more.

After a few seconds, he pushed Holly away. The loss of physical contact with him pierced her with regret.

'Is it really you?' Doubt hovered in her husband's eyes. She spotted a gap where the dentist had extracted a tooth.

'Yes.' Her voice was hoarse with emotion. 'It's me, sweetheart. Holly, your wife.'

He stared at her, clearly uncertain. His hand took hers, his touch tentative. As though sight alone wasn't enough. His gaze turned towards his brother, but he didn't speak, just stared.

'Hey, Drew,' Todd said. 'How are you doing, mate?'

Drew didn't respond. Todd shifted from foot to foot, his hands thrust in the pockets of his chinos. Holly realised he was holding back, giving brother time to process things.

'Todd?' Drew said at last, wonder in his voice. At that, Todd rushed to seize him in a fierce hug. Holly saw dismay flit over his face, despite his joy. He must also have been horrified at Drew's emaciated frame.

Thank God she'd mended the rift with Todd. Drew had never needed his brother more. Same with her.

Holly became conscious of her swollen belly, concealed by her coat. Her husband had fathered her child, a fact he needed to know. Right then wasn't the time to tell him, though.

Once Todd stepped back, Holly kissed Drew. 'You remember me,' she said. Her heart sang with happiness.

CHAPTER 35

The following day the Watchman's mother seemed more lucid. He approached her bed, noting how her skin looked less sallow, the whites of her eyes not so jaundiced, although she still appeared a decade older than her age.

'You came back,' she whispered. Was it his imagination, or had her eyes grown teary?

He pulled out the blue plastic chair and sat on it. His mother stared at him, reminding him of when he was a kid and she could cow him with a look.

'You want chips or mash with yer sausages?' she asked, and he knew she'd also travelled back in time.

That was good. All he had to do was to keep her firmly in the past.

'Tell me what happened,' he said. 'The night you left Bristol.' *And me*, he thought but didn't say.

Fear stole into her eyes. A tear hovered under one lid, then slid over her cheek. 'Dunno what you're talking about.'

'Sure you do. You were with—' He couldn't bring himself to say the bastard's name. The ogre whom Rick, as a child, had called Mr Nasty.

A sob, before fury replaced the fear. His mother hauled herself off her pillow, her sour breath hitting his face. 'That fucker. Wished I'd killed him.'

'But you didn't.' The Watchman already knew that. 'What happened?'

'That bastard assaulted me. Punched me, kicked me.'

No surprise there. Like Rick, the Watchman had witnessed his mother, also a whore, being abused. Then abducted.

'He shoved me in the boot of his car. Told me I'd never see daylight again.' Spittle ran down her chin.

The Watchman waited. Her hands plucked at the bedspread, but she didn't continue. 'But you got the better of him, right? How did you escape?'

He watched her fingers tear at the material. Angry. Punishing.

'We went for a drive. Then he dragged me out of the boot,' she mumbled. 'Said I was nothing but a worthless whore.'

'Then what?'

'I fucked him up good and proper.' Satisfaction leered from his mother's voice. Her face was a mask of hate.

'How?'

She sagged back in the bed. Her eyes closed, and he feared he'd lost her. Before long a soft snore sounded out. He shook her shoulder, hard, and the roughness worked. Awake again, she stared at him.

'What did you do to him?' he said, but she'd drifted away once more, into a world he couldn't reach.

The Watchman remained by her bed, the plastic of the chair biting into his buttocks. The minutes ticked by, and still his mother slept.

CHAPTER 36

'I love you so much,' Holly said. Remorse stabbed Drew. How could he have forgotten his wife? Or his brother?

He hadn't, not really. She'd always been in the Black Hole with him, as had Todd, in one way or another.

'It's all a muddle in my head,' he replied. 'I've no idea what's real and what isn't.' Pain flashed over Holly's face, and guilt pierced his heart.

'You've suffered one hell of an ordeal, mate.' Todd pulled his chair closer. 'It'll take time to come to terms with it. But we're all rooting for you. Nessa's over the moon you've been found.'

Nessa? The name was familiar, but...

'My wife,' Todd clarified, and Drew glimpsed the same hurt in his expression he'd spotted in Holly's. A memory crept into Drew's head. Himself as Todd's best man, the pair of them top-hatted and tailed to within an inch of their lives. Next to Todd stood a bulky woman, resplendent in white, a garland of baby's breath woven into her toffee-coloured hair. He zeroed in on her face. The dusting of freckles across her nose, the brown eyes, her pale skin, the radiant smile. Nessa, his sister-in-law. And behind her memory, something else.

'Jack,' Drew said. 'Shane.' God, he'd forgotten his own nephews.

Matthew Thomas chose that moment to enter the room. The man never seemed to go home. 'Hello, Drew,' he said, a professional smile clipped to his face. He nodded at Holly and Todd, his expression curious. 'Good evening. I'm Matthew Thomas, consultant psychotherapist here at Southmead. And you are—?'

Holly stepped forward, proffered her hand. 'Holly Blackmore. Drew's wife.'

Todd also introduced himself. 'How soon before Drew can go home, doctor?'

Matthew shook his head. 'That will depend on how quickly he regains the use of his legs. Has your physiotherapist given you any indication, Drew?'

Drew struggled to remember. A tall guy came to mind, his bony fingers massaging Drew's calves with excruciating firmness. A metal walking frame, the man's hands under Drew's armpits to help him stand. Drew's legs had collapsed like a building under demolition; he'd crumpled to the ground, cursing. He didn't recall whether that had been today, yesterday or last century. His brain didn't work so well anymore.

He realised Dr Thomas was waiting for an answer. 'It'll take time.'

'Now that you've regained parts of your memory, Drew, the police are eager to talk to you again,' Matthew said. 'Tomorrow, if you're up to it.'

'Will you be there?' Drew felt safe with this man. To his relief, Matthew nodded.

'Well, I'll leave you to it,' he said before turning towards the door.

'Wait!' The urgency in Holly's voice startled Drew. 'Can I talk to you?' she asked Matthew. 'Outside?'

'Don't leave me.' Drew's plea emerged a hoarse whisper.

Holly smiled at him. 'I won't be long. I just want to ask Dr Thomas a few questions.'

'I'll stay with you, mate,' Todd said. 'Holly will only be a few minutes, won't you, Hols?' Drew saw his brother shoot her a look of warning.

******

Once they left the ward, Holly grabbed Matthew's arm. 'Talk to me, please. I need to understand what the prognosis is for Drew. How come he forgot his family? His own name?'

Matthew guided her to a row of plastic chairs set against the wall. 'The brain requires constant stimulation,' he said, once they'd sat down. 'Without input it deteriorates rapidly. Denied human contact, your husband lost his sense of identity.'

'Will he recover? Mentally?'

'Hard to say. Drew's suffered horrors most of us never have to endure. He's suffering from post-traumatic stress disorder.'

Holly had heard of PTSD, but knew little about the condition. She made a mental note to bone up on it. 'What does that mean for him?'

'Flashbacks, panic attacks. Triggered by any reminders of his ordeal. Paranoia may well feature too.'

'But he'll get better, right? Given enough time?'

Matthew grimaced. 'PTSD can be very tenacious. Your husband might experience lifelong effects.'

Holly's chest grew tight with fear. Would the man she'd married ever return? *Stop it*, she chided herself. *This is about Drew, not you.*

'How can you best treat it?' she asked.

'Various talking therapies are available. Medication too. Drew will need a lot of support, both from us and those close to him.'

'I'll be there for him. I won't let him down.'

Sympathy flickered over Matthew's face. 'It won't be a walk in the park, Holly.'

'Maybe not. But I have to try.' She thanked him and walked back into the ward, her mood sombre. This would be easier if she weren't so exhausted all the damn time.

For the next hour, Holly allowed Todd to monopolise Drew. Meanwhile, her thoughts ran on how best to support him. She loved her husband, but was out of her depth. Drew had suffered hell; she had no idea how that might change him. Whether they could rebuild their marriage, reclaim what Drew's abductor had stolen. Thank goodness she had Todd. Now, more than ever, she needed his strength. She couldn't do this alone.

The evening wore on; nine o'clock came around, but Holly didn't move. Drew's face, gaunt yet so beloved, was a sight she'd feared she'd never see again. How could she abandon him, even if only for a few hours?

A nurse approached. 'Visiting time is up, I'm afraid.'

Holly wanted to scream at the woman. *He needs me. Don't make me leave him*. Instead, she leaned over and kissed Drew. 'I'll be back tomorrow morning, darling.'

Panic settled over her husband's features. 'You promise?'

'Yes.' Holly exchanged a glance with Todd. He must be thinking the same thing: *when did Drew get so clingy?*

Once outside the ward, she turned to her brother-in-law. 'Let's go grab that coffee with DS Tucker. I have a boatload of questions I need answered.'

******

Outside the cafeteria, DS Tucker awaited them, a cup of vending machine coffee cradled between her palms. She acknowledged Holly and Todd's arrival, then stood up. 'I've found somewhere we can talk. Follow me.' She led the way to a small room along the corridor and flipped the sign on the door so it read 'Occupied'. Inside were two sofas either side of a low table. Tucker motioned Holly and Todd towards one.

'How is he?' she asked.

Holly seated herself opposite Tucker, with Todd beside her. 'Who did this to him?' She fought back her anger. 'Tell me you have some leads.'

DS Tucker shook her head. 'I hope to obtain more information when I next speak with Drew. Meanwhile, I need to revisit the time when he was kidnapped. Can you run through again what happened that day?'

Holly sighed inwardly. As Todd had pointed out, they'd been over this several times already. 'Drew went to work that morning, the same as always. He left just after seven. I didn't hear from him during the day, but that's not unusual. Both of us normally get back around six o'clock. When six thirty came, I assumed he must be working late and hadn't bothered to text or phone.'

'Did Drew ever call at your house on his way home from work?' Tucker asked Todd.

'Sometimes during the week if we went running together. Other than that, no.'

'Did he mention any worries in the weeks leading up to his disappearance?' Tucker directed her question at both of them.

Holly grimaced. 'He was concerned about our finances. And he had credit card debts.' She told Tucker about the final demands. 'But the police already know that, from before.'

'Just trying to get a picture of the man and the life he led,' Tucker countered. 'Did he seem worried to you, Todd? Did he hint at anything when you went running?'

Todd shook his head. 'No. We're both members of our local club. So a bunch of us run

185

together, not just the two of us. We don't get much chance to talk privately. Drew did say he had some serious money issues.' He threw his sister-in-law a glance. 'Might explain his reluctance to become a father.'

'You were trying for a baby?' Tucker stared at Holly. 'You didn't mention that before.'

Holly's face flushed. 'More than trying. I'm five months pregnant.'

'Congratulations. I take it Drew doesn't know?'

'Not yet.' Holly shook her head. 'I've no idea when I should break the news.'

'Can either of you think of anyone who'd want to hurt Drew? Who might have done this to him?'

'No,' Holly and Todd said in the same instant.

'It doesn't need an expert in psychology to understand the kidnapper intended him to suffer,' Tucker continued. 'What Drew endured betrays a shocking level of cruelty.'

'I should have asked before. Was he—' Holly swallowed hard. 'Molested in any way?'

'The hospital reported no signs of sexual assault,' Tucker said. 'That means his abductor had other motives for keeping him alive. We're hoping Drew can shed light on them.'

'He's not said anything?' Todd asked.

Tucker frowned. 'Not to us. And very little to Matthew Thomas. We do have one clue, though. Drew mentioned a name several times. Morris,

Morrison, or something similar. Does that signify anything to either of you?'

It didn't to Holly. She glanced at Todd. His face had turned thunderous.

CHAPTER 37

The Watchman stayed by his mother's bedside while she continued to snore. After half an hour, her eyelids opened, and she muttered something he couldn't catch.

He leaned closer, mindful of her foul breath. 'What did you say?'

A cackled laugh wheezed from her. 'Whacked him hard, I did. Across his legs. Fuck, did he ever yell. Then I ran.' She grinned, all brown teeth and inflamed gums.

'You hit the bastard?'

She didn't reply, her fists clenching an imaginary weapon. Seconds later she pounded it repeatedly into the mattress. A chant of *'nnnnngggghhhhh....'* issued from her mouth.

He feigned pulling the pretend baton from her grasp. 'What's this?'

She frowned. 'Dunno. Long. Metal. Hard.'

A crowbar, the Watchman decided, or a tyre lever. Snatched from the boot of her abuser's car.

He dragged his tongue over dry lips. 'You didn't come home afterwards.' She made no response.

'I have to know. Why did you abandon me?' But she was lost to him, her eyes vacant.

'Crystal,' she whispered. 'That's what my Eddie calls me. Such a pretty name, don't you think?'

He'd probably never find out. Maybe she'd considered it too risky to return home, given her abuser's violent streak. Or, more likely, she hadn't cared enough. Instead, she'd escaped to London, where she drank and whored her life away. His mother had died years ago, just not in the way he'd always believed.

Rage seized him. He leaned over the bed, staring at her ruined face. So easy to end her miserable existence. Pinch her nose shut, clamp a hand over her mouth. He'd be doing the sad cow a favour.

He could imagine what Rick would say. The little runt's whiny voice sounded in his head. 'Don't kill her. Please.'

'Fuck off, you wuss.' The Watchman's hands reached towards his mother. *Do it, just do it....*

The sound of the drugs trolley's wheels scraping the floor snapped him back to reality. A busy hospital ward, people all around him. Not the best place to commit murder. Better for the bitch to rot in some care home, end her life incontinent and bedridden. Alone and friendless, the way her son had always been. He was done with her.

The Watchman was halfway to the exit before he remembered. He was far from finished with his mother. He strode back to her bed, yanked out the chair and sat down.

CHAPTER 38

Drew screamed. Around him the blackness closed in, ready to suffocate him with inky fingers. The stench of urine and faeces assaulted his nostrils, along with the whiff of that day's sandwich. Crumbs of bread and cheese were stuck to the cling-film he clutched in his hand. The taste of the stale water he'd drunk lingered in his mouth. Around his wrists and ankles his shackles lay heavy and cold. He'd been abandoned; he was alone, and would be forever. No hope of escape existed. His solitude gnawed into his soul until terror filled his skull. He shrieked even louder.

Strong hands held him down. He'd been wrong, it seemed. He wasn't by himself in the Black Hole. But who was with him? Why hadn't he heard them enter?

'Easy, Drew,' a voice said. Warm breath drifted against his ear. 'You're safe now.'

The flashback receded. Drew found himself staring into the face of John, one of his nurses. He grew aware of the harsh panting that burst from his chest, the sweat that trickled down his forehead. Behind John, he saw the open door to his room, the colours and shapes around him, and the tension drained from his body. He was in hospital. Safe. No more Black Hole.

'Sorry,' he gasped, ashamed of his weakness.

'Bad dream?' John enquired, his tone sympathetic, and Drew nodded. Close enough.

John offered him sleeping medication, asked whether he needed his bedpan. Drew shook his head to both. Once the man had left, he lay back against his pillows, questions throbbing through his brain. In his flashback, who had brought him the sandwich? The musty-tasting water? A memory teased him, yet remained out of reach. A man he'd feared, who'd promised he'd make Drew suffer.

Don't dwell on him, he told himself. *Think of your wife. Your brother.*

Except that Holly also seemed elusive. She'd kissed him, said she loved him, yet he sensed his wife was concealing something. But what?

Todd, then. Drew searched his memory. His brother's visit had dredged Nessa from its depths, along with Shane and Jack, but did he have any other family?

Two names surfaced. Melody and Hal Reynolds. Drew knew they'd raised him, that he'd loved them. That they'd met a tragic end, although the details were hazy. Something didn't fit, though. His surname was Blackmore. Then he remembered. Auntie Mel was his mother's sister, Uncle Hal her husband. So where were his parents?

Drew dug way down into his brain, summoned up a woman, frail and gaunt, her face betraying the ravages of cancer. His father proved more difficult. Drew couldn't recall his features, or even his name. He knew one thing: he had adored the man.

He buried his face into the pillow, fear deep in his gut. What if he never remembered?

Todd would know. Todd could tell him everything tomorrow.

******

Holly sat rigid with disbelief at what Todd had said, once DS Tucker had left. 'Why am I only hearing this now?' she asked.

Her brother-in-law spread his palms wide in appeasement. 'Drew buried the abuse Ian Morrison inflicted on him deep inside. He made me swear never to tell anyone. If it hadn't been for DS Tucker's insistence, I'd have kept that promise.'

Hurt filled Holly. What else had her husband concealed?

'Either you or Drew should have told me.' Her mouth compressed itself into a thin line of anger. 'I'm his wife, for God's sake. Didn't I have a right to know?'

'No.'

The vehemence in Todd's tone startled Holly. She stared at him in shock.

'It wasn't my story to tell. Only Drew's.'

'But—'

'You ever been sexually abused?'

She shook her head, unable to speak.

'Then you have no right to judge him.'

A tear slipped down Holly's cheek. 'I guess not.'

'You weren't there. I was. When he turned ten Drew spent hours in his room, wouldn't talk to anyone. Nobody knew why.' Todd's eyes were stones of anger. 'Eventually he told me, and I spoke to Auntie Mel. She called the police. They found horrible photos on Morrison's computer. Dozens of different boys, including Drew, all suffering unspeakable things. The cops never identified some of them.' Fury filled his voice.

'How long did the abuse go on?'

'Two years. My brother endured hell at that man's hands. The bastard said he'd track him down, make him suffer, if he told anyone.'

'What happened to Morrison?'

'He got a twelve-year jail sentence. As well as his come-uppance.'

'What do you mean?'

'A gang attacked him in the showers. Kiddy-fiddlers don't do great in prison, remember. The fucker lost a testicle, but the surgeon managed to save his dick. Shouldn't have bothered, in my opinion.'

Holly did the maths. Drew's abuser had completed his prison term two years ago. Ian Morrison must have been the guy who abducted Drew, made him suffer, the way he'd once threatened.

'How did Drew cope with Morrison's release?' she asked.

'He told me he felt pretty safe, despite his fear of the man. Bristol's big enough to ensure anonymity, and Drew as an adult looks very different to how he did as a twelve-year-old.' Todd shook his head. 'I suspected he wasn't as unconcerned as he made out, though.'

Holly agreed. Drew had needed to pretend, because he'd chosen not to confide in her, right? The realisation hurt, but she thrust aside her pain. Drew mattered more.

'I can't bear to think of what he's suffered.' A sob choked Holly's throat. Todd pushed back his chair, walking round beside her. He wrapped his arms around her, and that simple gesture, so missed during their estrangement, brought tears to her eyes.

'It's okay, Hols,' he whispered into her hair. 'We'll get Drew through this, don't you worry.'

Later that evening, after she'd returned home, Holly called her mother. In between sobs, she'd outlined the horrors Drew had endured. By the time she'd finished, Karen was also in tears.

'We'll fly over on the next available flight,' she informed her daughter.

Holly wasn't sure how to respond. 'I need time alone with Drew,' she managed at last.

Her mother understood, as Holly had known she would. 'If that's what you want, sweetheart. Drew will require a lot of support, though. If I can help, just call.'

'I will, Mum.' Somehow the burden on Holly's shoulders weighed lighter after their conversation.

Afterwards she lay in bed, unable to sleep. Drew's wounds might never heal, and if they did, the scars would run deep.

She adored her husband. But would her love be sufficient to pull him through?

As though in answer, Drew's child stirred within her for the first time, and Holly gasped in awe. She'd felt a soft flutter of tiny limbs, wonderful beyond words. Tenderness for her unborn baby flooded her, along with resolve.

Everything will be all right, she reassured herself. *It has to be.*

******

The next morning Holly sat beside Drew's bed, gathering her courage for what she needed to tell him. Her husband hadn't spoken since her arrival, just stared at her with dull eyes, then glanced away. Undeterred, she reached for his hand and squeezed it tight. *Oh, darling*, she longed to say. *You've endured hell, and more than once. I wish you'd told me about the man who abused you. Don't shut me out. Please.*

Holly trailed her fingers down his cheek, saddened by how dry and old his skin felt. Still he didn't look at her. She leaned in, pressed a kiss on his temple. 'I love you.'

He looked at her then, with his dead gaze, and Holly's gut clenched with fear. How could she burden him further with the news he'd soon be a father? Drew could barely cope with being alive. The added pressure might break him. How she wished she'd asked her mother's advice about this.

For a second, his hand pressed hers, and hope replaced fear in her heart. He had a right to know she was pregnant, and besides, Holly reasoned, he might even be pleased. A baby could offer the fresh start he needed. She pictured Drew cradling their child, love in his face as he rocked it in his arms. The way he'd been with Shane and Jack. What a great dad he'd make. Fatherhood would force Drew to confront his demons, which would be good, right? She had only to open her mouth and speak.

She planned to say nothing about Ian Morrison. Drew's silence on the subject hurt her, but Todd had helped her understand his reasons. Once DS Tucker arrested Morrison, Drew's abuse would no longer be a secret anyway. That particular can of worms could remain unopened for a while.

Meanwhile she needed to stop procrastinating. The time would never be right to inform Drew he'd soon be a father, so she'd better get it over with. As though offering reassurance, the baby kicked inside her.

She sucked in a breath. He'd shifted away from her again.

'Drew.' Holly's voice came out hoarse. 'Look at me. Please.'

He turned his dead eyes on her. Hope shrivelled within Holly, but she steeled herself.

'I have something to tell you,' she said. He didn't respond. Disappointment pooled in her gut.

Sometimes actions spoke better than words. Holly stood up, slipping her coat from her shoulders. Underneath she wore a sweatshirt and yoga trousers, their fabric stretched over her bulge, making her pregnancy obvious. She waited, assessing his reaction.

Holly watched Drew's eyes travel over her belly. Realisation flooded his face, but his expression remained inscrutable. Beyond the open door the ward rumbled with life, with voices, yet Drew stayed silent. Anguish swept over Holly. He didn't want their baby.

'Drew,' she said, her voice barely a whisper. 'I'm pregnant with your child. Don't you care?'

'How many months?' She shrank at his hard tone.

'Five.' She watched him do the maths.

'Did you know?' he said. 'At the time I went missing?'

Holly nodded, a stone heavy in her heart. 'I couldn't tell you, not back then. You were so adamant that we should wait, but the truth is different, isn't it? You just don't want children.' Maybe she should mention Morrison. If the abuse had damaged Drew's desire for kids, help was available. Books, support groups, counselling…

'You were on the pill.' Was that accusation in his voice?

'It's not a hundred per cent effective.' She stumbled over the words. Did he suspect her of deceit? 'Not if you're sick. Remember that time I got ill after eating those prawns? I never planned this, Drew.'

'I wish I'd known.' Sadness filled his tone. 'I'd have fought harder. Against the blackness. The silence.'

'What are you saying?'

Drew closed his eyes, shutting her out. 'You're wrong. I want children, always have.'

'Then why—?'

'Some things I remember, although a lot's still a blank.' He released a long breath, pain in his expression. 'We argued, didn't we? Before I left for work, on the day I was abducted.'

Holly couldn't respond. The words she'd flung at him had been shameful. *If you won't have kids with me, I need to reconsider our marriage.*

'All that day at work I thought about what you'd said. I planned to tell you I was ready to be a father. The night I got abducted.' He shook his head. 'Not anymore, though.'

Holly's throat closed over with hurt. Inside her, the baby lay still, perhaps sensing its father's rejection.

'I've seen twice over how fucked up the world can be. Bringing a child into it is a bad idea.'

'Twice over? What do you mean?' Was Drew about to open up about Morrison?

Panic crept into her husband's face. 'Nothing. Forget I said that.'

A cocktail of emotions swirled inside Holly. Sadness, anger, but most of all disappointment. Then Todd's words—*you have no right to judge him*—floated back to her. *Stop being selfish*, she chided herself. Time, and patience, would heal Drew. All she had to do was love him. And she did—so very much.

'I should go,' she said. Visiting hours had ended five minutes ago. When he didn't respond, Holly walked towards the door, her eyes awash with tears.

CHAPTER 39

Back in Bristol, the Watchman slumped in his chair, his gaze roaming around the unfamiliar room. As planned, he'd moved address before visiting his mother, his new home secured with cash and by using a false ID and fake references. It was, he reflected, extraordinarily easy to buy a different identity. He was sure the police wouldn't find him a second time.

He closed his eyes, mentally drained. So much had happened since he'd concocted his scheme for revenge. The way he'd found Ethan Parker. Followed by Drew's abduction. Then his release.

'Didn't I warn you?' Rick said, unusually defiant. 'If you'd let me talk to the cops, like I suggested, you wouldn't be in this mess.'

For once the Watchman didn't tell him to shut his mouth. The little bastard was right. Actions had consequences, after all.

'What are you going to do about Drew Blackmore?' Rick asked.

Good question. The Watchman intended to keep a close eye on his former captive while he recovered. Once the hospital discharged Drew, the Watchman would make his move. No rush; instead, he'd bide his time. What was that weird old saying? *Softly, softly, catchee monkey.* He intended to proceed very softly indeed.

Like before, Drew would never see him coming. The outcome, though, would be very different.

The Watchman grinned. 'I've unfinished business with him. And this time around my plans include Todd.'

CHAPTER 40

Holly's revelation had stunned Drew. He barely knew which way was up, without the added burden of impending fatherhood. The world was no place for children. Evil lurked everywhere. Nowhere was safe.

Best not to think about the baby. Besides, the police hadn't yet left, although Matthew Thomas had requested a ten-minute break on his patient's behalf. Drew's fingers moved restlessly over the blanket on his bed, his gaze on DS Tucker and DC Tobin. Beside them was DC Jessica Smith, the Family Liaison Officer assigned to his case. Tucker glanced up, catching his eye. 'Are you ready to start again? Or do you need more time?'

Drew shrugged, desperate for the oblivion of sleep. He wanted them gone. 'Let's get on with it.'

'You've told us what you remember about the man who came into your prison. Dark hair, pale eyes, a scar through his top lip.' She paused.

Impatience surged through Drew. 'Do you know who he is? Why won't you tell me his name?'

'Because it may be difficult for you to hear.' She leaned forward. 'How much do you recall about your childhood?'

Uncle Hal, kicking a football towards him. Auntie Mel, baking chocolate brownies. His mother, her face fuzzy in his head. His father, known only through his signet ring. *Not much*, he thought.

'More's returning every day. But a lot's still a blur.' A layer of thick gauze lay between him and his memories. Terror lurked in his mind, but he couldn't name it.

Until DS Tucker did. 'Do you recall a man named Ian Morrison?'

The gauze lifted, and the horror became real. The monster from Drew's past seized him, dragged him back to the slime of years before. The cloying stink of Morrison's aftershave, masking his garlic breath. That scarred lip, those yellow teeth. His hands, rough and insistent as they shoved Drew to his knees. The sound of a zipper being pulled down.

This can't be happening... please don't make me do this... I don't want to...

A hand pushing his head towards the man's crotch. Then the command. 'Suck me, boy.'

Horror filled his ten-year-old self. Inside his skull he screamed words his mouth couldn't. *I'll choke... can't breathe... somebody help me...*

Help never came.

******

Drew first met Morrison through his uncle; the two men were golfing buddies. He said hello, uncomfortable at how the man's gaze raked over him when Hal Reynolds turned his back. Something dirty had smeared itself on him, and he'd never wash off the stain.

A week later, Morrison accosted Drew after he'd left school for the day. Too scared to protest, Drew found himself being led to the nearby park, at one end of which stood a dense grove of trees. A two-year-long nightmare began that afternoon. One that turned his soul ancient.

Afterwards Morrison asked him if he'd enjoyed their encounter. *Our special secret*, he'd called it. Too frightened to demur, Drew had said yes.

If you tell anyone, his abuser had said, *I will make your life hell. Wherever you are, I will find you, and you will suffer.*

Drew heeded that warning until he turned twelve. Then Morrison made his threat to strangle him. That same night, pale and shaky, Drew confided in Todd that he'd been molested. As always, his older brother knew what to do.

******

Now, fourteen years later, Drew became conscious of his screams as they crashed off the walls. Matthew Thomas stood at his bedside, conferring with Tucker. Drew squeezed his eyes shut to blank out Morrison's hated face. The man's warning—*wherever you are, I will find you, and you will suffer*—had often echoed in his brain over the years.

'Sorry,' he muttered, once able to speak.

'Don't sweat it,' Tobin said. 'We can do this another time.'

Drew shook his head while he struggled for words. His heart raced, and perspiration soaked his pyjamas.

'I'm sorry if that name triggered uncomfortable memories,' Tucker said. 'I think it's best if we leave now.'

He couldn't allow that to happen. Not when he was on the point of hearing his captor had been caught. With an effort, he dragged himself upright.

'Don't,' he said. 'I'm all right, really I am.'

'You sure you don't need a break, Drew?' Matthew asked. Tucker also looked doubtful. So did Tobin.

'Positive.' Drew threw all his emphasis into the word.

'I'll allow it. But go easy with the questions,' Matthew warned.

Drew turned to Tucker. 'Please. Tell me. Where is he? Have you arrested him?'

Tucker replied, but her words—*ruled Ian Morrison out from our enquiries*—made no sense. Drew shrank against his bedding, unable to comprehend what he was hearing.

'I don't understand,' he said. 'He was the one who abducted me. He came into my cell. Several times. I *saw* him.'

'That's impossible.'

'You're mistaken.' Drew's voice cracked. 'He did this. I *know* he did. Who else could it have been?'

Sympathy hovered in Tucker's expression. 'Not Morrison, that's for sure.'

'How can you be so certain?'

'Because a week after his release from prison, he was murdered.'

Shock pounded through Drew. He couldn't compute this. 'Why wasn't I told at the time?'

'Morrison's death happened in Cheltenham, where he'd gone to live with his mother. Gloucestershire police investigated the case, not Avon and Somerset.' Tucker released a long breath. 'Communication between forces isn't always as good as we'd like, I'm afraid.'

'How did he die?'

'His penis was sliced off.' In his peripheral vision, Drew saw Tobin wince. 'He was also stabbed in his femoral artery. Morrison bled to death at the scene.'

Despite his confusion, satisfaction sparked in Drew. The bastard had deserved his fate. 'Some vigilante killed him?'

Tucker shook her head. 'One of his former victims. Didn't bother to hide the evidence. Even offered a full confession. Said he'd happily do jail time for murdering Morrison.'

But he'd seemed so *real*. Then Drew remembered. When Morrison had appeared, Drew hadn't heard the door open first. Also, how could they have seen each other, if the room was pitch-black? If his eyes no longer worked?

He'd been so terrified that he'd failed to spot the obvious. Morrison's face didn't have a body. Drew had hallucinated him.

'Please,' he whispered. 'I need time alone.'

Tucker stood up, gesturing for Tobin and Smith to do likewise. 'We'll let you get some rest.'

After they'd gone, Drew slumped against his pillows. His abuser was dead. If Morrison hadn't abducted him, who the hell had? Was it, like he'd once suspected, some random psychopath?

Unable to answer himself, he dozed for a while. When he awoke, he spotted a man, most of his face hidden, peering into the ward, visible from the open door to Drew's room. The moment their eyes connected, the guy walked away. White-skinned, with dark hair, but other than that Drew would struggle to describe him. His mouth turned dry. Who was this guy? Why had he stared at him?

Panic swamped Drew, so fast his breath caught in his chest. With shaky fingers, he found the call button, and jabbed it hard.

A woman he'd not seen before appeared. She shrugged when he told her what happened. 'Probably a visitor, looking for the right ward.' Her tone was curt. 'Or an outpatient. You're not in danger, not here.' She studied the notes on his chart, her eyes flicking between them and Drew. He realised he'd lost her the moment she read the word 'hallucinations'.

Useless to protest further. 'Dr Thomas,' he managed. 'I want to see Dr Thomas.'

Another shrug. 'He's due to assess your progress later. You can talk to him then.' With that, she walked away.

Drew pulled the bedclothes over his head, shrinking under them, then thought better of it. He needed to watch the entrance to the ward at all times. That bitch of a nurse had been wrong. He wasn't safe, even in hospital.

CHAPTER 41

Ethan Parker's screams filled the basement room in the derelict warehouse. His world had dissolved into a blur of pain and terror. From his right eye, the one that hadn't yet been blinded, he watched the screwdriver disappear from view. Oh, God, no, not his knee again—

'Please,' he whispered. Blood from his busted nose trickled into his mouth.

'Don't mess me around, you little prick. You fucked up badly, you know that? I want you to admit what you did.'

Ethan would have sworn the moon was a melon if the pain would only stop. 'Yes,' he mumbled. 'It was me. And I'm sorry.'

'Not good enough.' Fire bolts of agony melted Ethan Parker's knee. Not for the first time, he passed out. Seconds later a bucket of icy water revived him.

'Great to have you back. You see, Ethan, actions have consequences. I believe you're beginning to understand that.'

CHAPTER 42

Holly parked her car outside Todd and Nessa's home, with DC Jessica Smith in the passenger seat. Jessica had arrived at the house earlier that morning to introduce herself as their Family Liaison Officer and to update Holly with the news about Ian Morrison. She told her she'd called Todd to inform him as well. Holly had hoped Drew's past could remain a secret from Nessa, given that he'd not wanted people to know, but secrecy no longer seemed an option.

Todd had texted while Holly was with Jessica, suggesting she come over so that they could discuss how to help Drew's recovery. She'd agreed, grateful for the chance to offload. To her surprise, Jessica suggested she should accompany them.

'I told Todd on the phone I needed to meet him as soon as possible,' she said. 'This would be an ideal opportunity, don't you think?'

Holly agreed. Two birds with one stone, and all that. Now, an hour later, here they were.

Nessa eyed her sister-in-law with a critical gaze after Holly stepped into the hallway. Her body language indicated a hug wouldn't be welcome. Holly couldn't recall the last time they'd embraced, unlike her memory, sharp and uncomfortable, of Nessa's scrutiny in the kitchen at Christmas. Anxiety squeezed the air from her lungs. *She suspects something happened between Todd and me. Wrong, of course, but how can I tell her?*

Holly introduced Jessica to Nessa, then took off her coat. She watched Nessa's gaze travel over the soft curve of her belly. She'd forgotten she'd made Todd promise not to tell his wife.

'You're pregnant.' Her sister-in-law's voice was flat. So much for Todd's assertion that Nessa would be overjoyed.

She nodded, her mouth dry. 'The timing's not great. I'm pleased, though.'

Nessa didn't reply, and Holly detected in her expression everything she wasn't saying. *Did Drew father your child? Or...*

'How far along are you?' A question loaded with subtext: *or was it my husband?*

Holly eyed her square on. 'Five months. Drew'll make a fantastic dad.' From her peripheral vision, she saw Jessica observing their interaction.

'I'm sure he will.' Still the frostiness, but melted somewhat. 'How are you holding up?'

'I'm fine.' She shook her head. 'Drew's the one you should be concerned with. He looks like hell.'

'Hardly surprising.' Nessa waved a hand towards the living room. 'Make yourself comfortable.'

Todd was sitting on the sofa. Holly considered whether to mention to him Drew's response to the news of his impending fatherhood, but decided against the idea. She was still too hurt. On seeing Holly, he got to his feet, giving her a quick embrace. 'Thanks for coming over.' He turned to Jessica and shook her hand. 'So you're our Family Liaison Officer. Good to meet you.'

Jessica smiled. 'Likewise, Todd. As I said on the phone, I'm here to help.'

'Damn right you are. The bastard who abducted Drew needs to be locked up, and fast.' Todd ran a hand through his hair. 'I'll make us some coffee.' He headed for the kitchen.

Holly sat next to Jessica on the sofa, opposite Nessa who chose one of the armchairs. The sound of a ring tone reached the room, followed by Todd's voice, too low to hear his words.

'Shane and Jack are having a nap, so with luck we won't be disturbed,' Nessa said. 'What's the news on Drew?'

Holly drew in a breath. 'He has a session with the physio guy first thing, then an assessment with his psychotherapist, Dr Thomas. The police want to talk further with Drew; he's not been able to tell them much so far. I'm heading over to Southmead this afternoon.'

'You've taken time off work?'

Holly nodded. 'My divorce cases can take a back seat. Drew needs me.'

'Todd and I will visit this evening. We won't bring the boys. They're desperate to see their Uncle Drew, but too young to understand. It's better they don't go while his head's still a mess.' She paused. 'That sounded insensitive. I meant for Drew's sake, not theirs.'

That was Nessa for you, thought Holly. *Not one to play safe with words.* Just as she was about to reply, Todd returned.

'Sorry about the coffees,' he said. 'DS Tucker called me. She asked if she can come round. Now.'

'Did she say why?' Holly asked.

'She said there'd been a new development, but refused to elaborate. I told her you were here.'

'But it's you she wants to talk to?'

'Yes, but she said your input would be useful. She'll be here by eleven o'clock, if the traffic allows.'

******

Tucker arrived half an hour later. Holly observed the tension around the woman's mouth. Whatever she'd come to discuss, Holly doubted it was good news.

Tucker addressed herself to Nessa once she'd sat down. 'I'd like to speak with Todd and Holly alone. If you don't mind?'

From her expression, Nessa did, but she got up with good grace. 'I'll leave you to it.'

'I'd love to meet Shane and Jack,' Jessica said. 'Why don't we go check on them, and get to know each other at the same time?'

Nessa smiled. Holly knew she never missed a chance to show off her beloved boys. 'Sure. Let's do that.'

'You said there had been a new development?' Todd said after the two women had gone.

'Yes. Your father was Barry Blackmore, right?'

Holly felt Todd stiffen beside her. She cast him a sideways glance. His face had paled, his mouth set in a tight line.

'If you know, why ask?' Todd replied.

Tucker ignored the hostility in his tone. 'Does the name of Rosalie Parker mean anything to you?'

'You know it does.' The antagonism in Todd's voice had shot up several notches.

Who the hell was Rosalie Parker? Unease prickled in Holly's brain. Had Drew been hiding other secrets from her?

DS Tucker leaned forward. 'Holly, let me fill you in on some details. Todd, a few of them will also be new to you. Certain facts weren't made public at the time.' She cleared her throat. 'Sixteen months ago the body of a woman was found in an industrial unit close to Farrington Gurney. Workmen hired to demolish the building discovered her when they searched the premises. The autopsy established she'd been dead for over twenty years.'

'And this woman was Rosalie Parker?' Holly asked.

'Yes. A part-time prostitute and mother of a young son.'

'But how does that relate to Drew?'

'I can't comment,' Tucker replied. 'Not at this stage.'

'Then why mention her?'

'I'm coming to that.'

Something clicked into place in Holly's brain. 'Had she also been chained to the floor? Was there sound-proofing? No light?'

'Again, I can't say.' Tucker's eyes confirmed Holly's hypothesis, however.

The facts didn't gel, though. 'My husband would have been a toddler when Rosalie Parker disappeared. Surely you're not saying the same person abducted both of them?'

Tucker turned towards Todd. 'How old were you back then?'

He exhaled an angry breath. 'You know damn well. I was thirteen.'

'Old enough to remember the police arriving at your house to question your father about Rosalie Parker,' Tucker said.

Holly stifled a gasp. She'd never once heard Todd speak about his long-dead father. When she'd asked Drew about his dad, he told her he barely recalled his mother. His father not at all. From the little he'd said, he clearly idolised the man, despite not remembering him. She recapped on what she did know. Barry Blackmore had died after Drew's third birthday, in an accident at the meat-packing factory he owned. Eloise Blackmore had succumbed to cervical cancer two years later, leaving the boys orphaned. Drew had always regarded his Aunt Mel and Uncle Hal as his parents. How Rosalie Parker fitted in, Holly hadn't a clue.

'Nothing was ever proved,' Todd said. 'But, yeah, I remember my father yelling abuse at the police. Overheard most of the conversation.'

'What exactly do you recall?'

'Dad admitted to being one of Rosalie's clients but not to knowing her whereabouts. Mum provided him with an alibi for the night she went missing.' Todd snorted. 'My mother would have sworn the moon was made of Swiss cheese if he told her to.'

'Was your father a violent man, Mr Blackmore?'

'He was a bastard.' Disgust hardened Todd's face. 'She'd never admit it, though. In the end, I stopped asking her about the black eyes, the broken bones. I couldn't bear to hear she'd walked into yet another door.'

Holly gasped. Todd's words were at odds with her husband's version of Barry Blackmore.

Tucker nodded. 'The investigating officers suspected your father was an abusive husband, from your mother's frequent hospital admissions. He was verbally aggressive with them too, as you've confirmed. He'd already refused a request to interview him under caution at the station.'

'I'm guessing that, with no solid evidence he'd abducted Rosalie, the police's hands were tied.' Todd's voice grew rough with emotion. 'I had no idea her body had been discovered. You found nothing at the crime scene to implicate my father? Of course you didn't. Otherwise you'd have questioned me again.'

'I can't comment on that.'

'I still don't understand,' Holly cut in. 'There's too big a time difference between her death and my husband's abduction. Besides, Drew was found alive.' She sucked in a breath. 'How did this woman die?'

'The autopsy revealed a fracture of her hyoid bone consistent with strangulation. We're unable to estimate how long she was held captive for prior to her death. But there was a pile of discarded food wrappings around her corpse.'

Horror crawled over Holly. 'So her abductor kept her alive? For what reason?' Then she understood. 'The bastard wanted to rape her whenever he chose. That's why he chained her up.'

Todd grimaced. 'It's the most likely explanation,' he said.

'But—' Holly gathered her thoughts. 'Drew's father was the main suspect in her disappearance, right? But he died years ago, as did this woman. So who abducted Drew? I'll ask you again. How are the two cases connected, apart from Barry Blackmore?'

Tucker leaned forward. 'Like I mentioned, Rosalie Parker had a son. After she went missing the boy, Ethan, got taken into foster care. He was ten years old at the time.'

'He'd have been an adult when her body was found,' Holly said. 'He was informed how she died, I take it? Including the stuff that wasn't made public?'

'Yes.'

'And you think he might have abducted my husband?' Holly leaned forward, her gaze on Tucker.

'Ethan told us he'd always suspected Barry Blackmore.'

Todd looked sceptical. 'What are you saying? That Ethan Parker imprisoned Drew to avenge his mother's death? Sins of the father, and all that?'

'It's a possibility.'

Holly couldn't contain her agitation. 'Where is he? Have you questioned him? What did he say?'

'There's a problem,' Tucker said. 'He's gone missing.'

A stunned silence filled the room, before Todd spoke. 'Since when?'

'He vanished not long after Drew was rescued.'

'What can you tell us about him?' Todd asked.

'I take it neither of you knew this man?' Tucker's gaze travelled between Holly and Todd.

'Ethan Parker? Doesn't sound familiar,' Holly said. 'Drew never mentioned anyone called that.'

Todd shook his head. 'I've never heard of him either. Do you have any photos we could see?'

'Not at the moment. He didn't have a passport or driving licence and wasn't on social media.'

'Isn't that a bit odd? Not to travel, or drive, or use Facebook?' Holly asked.

'The man was a loner, from what his landlord said. Lived by himself, no friends of whom we're aware, avoided contact with his neighbours. Didn't work, due to mental health issues.'

'My God. But he must still be in the area, surely? If he's been supplying Drew with food and water for the last four months?' This from Holly.

'Was he living in the disused abattoir?' Todd asked.

Tucker shook her head. 'There's no evidence of that. We're actively searching, but so far he's proved elusive.'

'Find the bastard.' Fury filled Todd's voice. 'I want the fucker caught.'

'We're working on a theory,' Tucker said. 'That Drew's abductor had an accomplice.'

Shock hit Holly. 'What makes you say that?'

'Someone released your husband. Cared enough to call an ambulance. That suggests two people were involved.'

'Why?' Todd asked.

'Whoever chained him up shows signs of psychopathic tendencies. And psychopaths can't feel remorse.' Tucker's voice indicated she'd met a few. 'They don't take pity on their victims.'

'Two of them working together.' Holly hadn't considered that.

Tucker nodded. 'It's rare, but sometimes these bastards operate in pairs. One of the two is usually more dominant.'

'But Drew only ever heard one guy outside his prison, right?' From Todd.

'That's what he claims.'

'Then who's the other fucker?'

'We don't know at this stage. But let's say the main man responsible teams up with Ethan Parker, but Ethan's the weak link. He feels guilty about how Drew's suffering, so he releases him. Guy number one discovers his sidekick's treachery, and murders him. Like I said, it's just a theory. One that might explain Drew's sudden release.'

'And the fact Ethan is missing,' Holly said.

Tucker stood up. 'Thank you both for your time. DC Jessica Smith will keep you informed. Now, if you'll excuse me, I have to go to Southmead. We hope to interview Drew.'

'We'll be there later,' Todd said. 'My brother needs to hear the truth about our father. From me, not the police.'

CHAPTER 43

Drew lay against his pillows, emotionally drained. DS Tucker and her sidekick DC Tobin had been questioning him for over two hours, frying his brain in the process. His memory was coming back stronger every day. That meant new things to tell the police, although it proved impossible to distinguish between reality and his hallucinations. Maybe he'd imagined the hairy wrist, the watch that he'd touched. And telling DS Tucker a man had abducted him hardly narrowed down the pool of suspects. Not when Ian Morrison was no longer in the picture.

At that moment, Holly arrived, with Todd in tow. His wife leaned over to kiss him, but he turned his head. He stared at the swell of her belly. He couldn't be a father. Didn't have what it took.

'We hoped you'd be finished.' Todd addressed his words to Tucker. 'Drew looks exhausted.'

Tucker nodded. 'We're done here. For now.' With that, she pulled Todd aside, speaking in low tones. Drew caught those unfamiliar names again, the ones DS Tucker had mentioned: Ethan and Rosalie Parker. He'd told her, truthfully, he hadn't a clue whom they were. Then: *You should be the one to tell him.* Todd saying: *that's why we're here.*

Once the two officers had left, Drew addressed his brother. 'What was all that about?'

'We have something to tell you,' Todd said, after he pulled out two chairs. Drew glanced at his wife. Her face looked pinched, miserable. This wouldn't be good.

Todd grimaced. 'I should have said *I* have something to tell you. Holly didn't know about this until a few hours ago. It's about Dad.'

Drew's worry intensified. He'd always been aware some mystery surrounded his father. Aunt Mel and Uncle Hal had never mentioned him. They'd responded to Drew's childhood questions with evasive answers. Todd was even less forthcoming, his face morphing into a tight mask whenever Drew asked about their dad. The most he'd ever volunteered was, 'He's dead, Drew. Uncle Hal's our father now.' Puzzled by his reticence, Drew had persuaded himself Todd found the subject too traumatic to discuss.

'What does Dad have to do with this?' he asked.

'He wasn't a good man,' Todd said. 'He used to hit Mum. Often, and hard. Enough to break bones, knock out teeth.'

Shocked, Drew dragged in a breath. Impossible. The father of his fantasies wasn't a wife-beater. 'Why would you say something so awful?'

'Because it's true. You're too young to remember what happened.'

Too angry to speak, Drew remained silent, his mouth pursed thin.

'One time she got back late from shopping,' Todd continued. 'I'd gone with her, helping to carry the bags. It was Christmas Eve, and the supermarket was packed. We took ages to get through the checkouts. All the way home I knew what the bastard would do, because he'd done it so many times before. Sure enough, when we walked through the door, he pounced. Slammed her against the wall, screaming at her what a useless bitch she was, how he didn't expect to be kept waiting for his meal. Then he punched her, breaking her nose. We spent Christmas Day in silence, her with black eyes and a cast on her face. You were only a few months old.'

'No,' Drew whispered. Todd was lying. But *why*?

Holly moved closer, taking his hand. Despite the gulf that separated them, he derived comfort from the gesture. His world had turned upside down, leaving him unable to cope.

'He slept with other women too,' Todd said. 'He'd arrive home late from work, reeking of perfume. Sometimes he stayed out all night.'

'I don't believe you.'

'I spotted him once, coming out of a pub, one Saturday lunchtime. A woman was with him. Blonde, much younger. He was smiling at her, but without any warmth to it. More of a leer. He seemed controlling, forceful, around her. The woman appeared cowed, almost frightened. He was probably all fists behind closed doors, same as with Mum.'

Drew remained silent. Partly because he hadn't a clue how to respond.

'One day the police knocked at our house,' Todd said. 'At first I hoped Mum had reported the abuse. She hadn't, of course. Instead the two officers spoke with Dad.'

'What about?'

'I'm getting to that. Mum hid with you in your bedroom, too scared to come out, but I listened from the upstairs landing. The only time I was ever glad the bastard had a loud voice, because I overheard their conversation. The police questioned him about the disappearance of a woman called Rosalie Parker.'

The same name DS Tucker had mentioned. 'Who was she?'

'A part-time hooker,' Todd said. 'Another sex worker realised she'd not seen Rosalie for a while, knocked on the door, didn't get a reply. Came back the next day, same result. She called the police, reported the woman missing.'

'What does this have to do with Dad?'

'The other prostitute told the cops her concerns about Rosalie's main punter. Said his name was Barry Blackmore, that he was violent, aggressive. Hence their visit to our house.'

'He wouldn't have cheated on Mum. Or hurt anyone.' Anger flared inside Drew. How dare his brother sully their father's memory?

'Drew.' Todd's voice had turned to steel. 'Ever wonder why none of us talked about him?'

'You didn't want to hurt my feelings. You knew how much I idealised him—'

'Because he was a grade-A arsehole, that's why. Yeah, you put him on a pedestal, and that was the fucking problem. How do you tell a child his father was the prime suspect in a woman's disappearance? Any time Hal or Mel tried to suggest he was anything other than a saint, you threw a tantrum. We all decided it was easier not to talk about him.'

'Are you sure Dad was involved?' Ice slid down Drew's spine as he waited for the answer.

'Nothing was ever proved. Dad told the police that on the weekend Rosalie went missing, he was in bed with an upset stomach both days. When they asked Mum, she confirmed his story. Too scared not to, of course. She'd overheard him shouting too, so she knew what to say. The cops had no evidence, apart from the neighbour's testimony about the bruises and Dad's relationship with Rosalie. They knew he was guilty, though.'

'How?'

'I watched through the banisters. The look on the senior officer's face said it all. Those guys get an instinct for who's innocent and who's not. Copper's nose, I think they call it.'

A sink hole opened in Drew's mind, into which his fantasies of Barry-the-perfect-parent vanished. How naïve, how stupid, he'd been.

'Dad died the following year,' Todd said. 'I hoped you'd never find out what a prick he was.'

Drew wiped tears from his eyes. 'I've been such a fool.'

'No. You didn't know any different, mate. Don't beat yourself up about this.'

Drew's fingers circled where his father's signet ring used to be. The skin felt filthy, tainted.

He recalled something DS Tucker had mentioned. 'The bastard's ring got shoved through your door, right?' he asked Todd.

His brother nodded. 'I'm guessing you don't want it back.'

'Bin it. Melt it down. Whatever. I don't give a shit.'

Holly stood up, breaking the tension. 'I'm going to get some coffee.'

'I'll come with you,' Todd said. He hesitated. 'Will you be okay alone for a while, Drew?'

Unlike before, he wanted his brother and his wife gone. 'Yes. I need space to think.'

After they'd left, Drew closed his eyes, his pain almost too awful to bear. Months in the Black Hole, his wasted legs, the rift with Holly. Now he'd lost his father for the second time, and in circumstances worse than any accident. Barry Blackmore had been the prime suspect in a woman's abduction, for fuck's sake. The dad he'd adored had been a delusion, alive only in his imagination. Drew's heart was missing a piece, yet felt twice as heavy.

He still didn't know how this related to his incarceration. Or even whether it did.

He turned his face into the pillow. Maybe if he blocked out the world, it wouldn't seem so cruel.

Ten minutes later Todd strode back into the ward, Holly trailing behind him. Drew forced himself to face them. His wife passed him a cup of coffee before sitting beside Todd. For a moment there was silence.

'Must be tough to discover how vile he was,' Todd said at last.

'Did Dad hit you too?' Drew dreaded the answer.

A pause. 'Yeah. When he got really mad. Mostly, though—' He closed his eyes, his face drained of colour. 'He did weird stuff.'

'Like what?' When his brother didn't reply, Drew placed his hand on Todd's arm. 'What aren't you telling me?'

Todd opened his eyes. 'This shit is hard to talk about, okay?' His voice sounded strangled, like the words were swimming through treacle.

'Tell me.'

Todd released a breath. 'He'd lock me in the cupboard under the stairs.'

'What? Like—'

'Yes. He'd grab me, shove me inside, then bolt the door. It was pitch-black in there. He'd not let me out until I apologised.' He shook his head. 'One time I lasted three days, using a plastic bucket for a toilet. But he broke me in the end.'

Drew almost puked. The father he'd revered had been a monster.

'He tossed in a bottle of water after the first day,' Todd said. 'A slice of dry bread after the second.'

'Like Rosalie Parker,' Holly whispered, her face ashen. 'And Drew.'

'Abuse runs in families,' Todd said. 'I'm not making excuses for the fucker, believe me. One time, though, his parents visited; the only time I ever met them. Our grandmother was a cold, hard bitch. Her husband was a shadow of a man, totally under her thumb. I said something she didn't like, and she went ballistic. Screamed how bad boys needed to be punished, then dragged me off to that fucking cupboard. Dad learned his abusive ways from her, don't you see? Along with his hatred of women. Shit like that scars kids, fucks them up.'

'You never told anyone?'

Todd shook his head. 'I was worried nobody would believe me.'

'Did Dad kill Rosalie Parker?'

From the corner of his eye, he saw Holly shoot Todd a warning glance.

His brother sucked in a breath. 'Probably. Like I said, nothing was ever proved, though.'

Todd told him how Rosalie's body had been found in an industrial building scheduled for demolition. 'Was she also chained up? In the dark?' Drew asked.

'DS Tucker didn't give us the details.'

'From her expression when I asked, I'd say the answer is yes,' Holly said.

Shock barrelled through Drew. This woman had also been held prisoner, shackled, alone in a darkened cell.

'How did she die?' he whispered, his voice hoarse.

Todd cleared his throat. 'She was strangled.'

Just as he'd once feared he would be. 'I need a moment,' Drew said. He couldn't look at his wife or his brother.

A silence fell around the bed. But not in Drew's head. Screams of fear filled his skull. In an instant, he was back in his prison, chains binding him to the floor, the foul-smelling bucket stinking out his cell. Loneliness and blackness overwhelmed him. No escape existed. He'd die in this fetid hole, alone and forgotten. Without a clue who had done this to him. Or why.

He became aware he could hear a man sobbing. Soothing hands grasped his shoulders, and he realised the noise came from him. 'Sorry,' he whispered.

Todd released his grip on Drew, then slid his arm around his brother. 'Nothing to apologise for, mate. You understand why we didn't tell you before?

'Yeah.' A question remained, though. 'Why now?'

'I'm getting to that,' Todd replied. 'Does the name Ethan Parker mean anything to you?'

DS Tucker had asked the same question. Drew shook his head. 'Should it?' Then he remembered Rosalie's surname. Something Tucker had said. 'Wait—he's a relative of the woman who went missing, right?'

Todd explained that Rosalie had been Ethan's mother. Drew heard how her son was also missing. How Ethan had suspected their father of abducting Rosalie. A man when her body was discovered, he'd been told the awful details of how she'd suffered, even if the public hadn't.

'It's likely he's also linked to your abduction,' Todd said.

His brother's phrasing struck Drew as odd. 'What do you mean, *also* linked?'

'The police suspect two people were responsible.'

'*What?*' Todd told him what DS Tucker had said about psychopathic duos, and how they operated.

'I can't help agreeing with her that the psychopath who abducted Drew murdered Ethan Parker,' Holly interrupted. 'Because Ethan released you. Out of guilt at what they'd done.'

'You're probably right,' Todd said.

Silence fell around the bed. Drew struggled to comprehend what he'd heard. Okay, so he'd suffered because of Barry Blackmore's crimes against Rosalie, but he couldn't understand Ethan's rationale. How did imprisoning him in that hellhole deliver justice for his mother? Barry was long dead, Drew linked to him by genes only. He hadn't even known the bastard. And who the hell had been pulling Ethan's strings?

'This man is missing, you said.' His voice cracked with terror. 'Am I safe? Can the police protect me?'

Todd shook his head. 'Not enough resources. While you're in hospital, they reckon you're okay. This is a busy ward, with lots of staff around.'

Drew didn't feel comforted. He remembered the man he'd caught staring at him. 'They're searching for this Parker guy, right?'

His brother nodded. 'Yes. But if someone wants to slip under the radar, it's easy enough to do.'

'If he's dead, then he won't be coming here,' Holly interjected.

'Or if he's lying low,' Todd said.

Drew wasn't convinced. 'If Tucker's theory's correct, what about the other whacko who abducted me?'

'Whoever he is, he can't hurt you, not while you're in hospital. You'll have people around you at all times. Either the nurses, or your physiotherapist, or Dr Thomas. Holly and I will come in every day. Nessa, too, as often as possible. The guys from the running club—Mike, Rory, Adam—they're all keen to visit.'

'Don't leave me. Please.' Drew was aware he sounded like a child, yet couldn't help himself. Once he'd craved company to end his isolation. Now he needed it to stay safe.

CHAPTER 44

The morning after he learned about Ethan and Rosalie Parker, Drew spent an hour with one of the hospital doctors and another with his physiotherapist. Beyond his door the ward bustled with medical staff, but he still felt alone in a world he didn't understand. Holly and Todd had promised they'd visit later and bring Nessa. Even so, loneliness gnawed at him, along with terror that Ethan Parker—or his partner in crime—might recapture him.

At least one of his unknown abductors now possessed a name, and a motive, but not a face. Despite Todd's reassurances, Drew didn't consider himself safe. Hell, he wasn't sure he'd ever feel that way again. Not until the police arrested Parker and the other guy involved.

His doctor had talked about discharging him within a couple of weeks. Drew had gained weight thanks to fortified protein drinks. Vitamin C had been prescribed for his scurvy. Antibiotic creams had healed the infected area around his anus. He'd received dental treatment too, with Todd offering to pay for tooth implants once his gums had healed.

'Can't have you frightening Shane and Jack,' his brother had said, with a grin, and Drew managed a weak smile. Todd always did know how to handle him.

The intensive physiotherapy had paid dividends. His legs were still feeble, and he could only walk using a frame, but after so long shackled to the floor, it seemed a miracle. And to use a toilet, to shower—Drew didn't think he'd take modern plumbing for granted ever again. The hallucinations had stopped, and his memories had mostly returned. Sight-wise, his depth perception was much better. His sleep patterns remained erratic, but no reason existed to prevent him returning home.

Apart from the fact the notion terrified him.

How could he defend himself with legs that barely worked? Would he spend his life watching for two men keen to punish him for his father's sins? Maybe he should install a state-of-the-art security system, then never leave the house... but no. His credit card debts, and lack of salary with which to pay them, wouldn't permit such an expense. Besides, a high-tech burglar alarm wouldn't deter his abductors, should they set their minds on snatching Drew. The bastards would find a way.

Perhaps he only had one guy with whom to concern himself. After all, Ethan Parker was missing. Holly might be right. If a two-man team had been involved, Drew would have been freed by the submissive partner. That didn't bode well for the man concerned, or for Drew. The more dominant guy would want his former captive back. Or, more likely, dead.

Drew turned over on his other side, his gaze drifting towards the ward doors. For a second, he saw a man staring at him through the glass panel. Most of his face was hidden; Drew glimpsed an eye, a cheek, the collar of a blue sweatshirt. Then the guy was gone, and Drew stared at the door, his heart pounding, sweat dampening his brow.

Panic engulfed him. His gut instincts warned him the man represented danger. Just as he'd feared, he wasn't safe, not even in hospital. Time to alert the police, and fast. He checked the clock on the wall: five to eleven. Dr Thomas was due any minute to take him to his psychotherapy appointment. Drew had always found the man friendly, approachable. He'd tell him what he'd seen, demand extra security to be put in place.

Within fifteen minutes Matthew Thomas had disabused him of that notion.

'Most likely it was an outpatient, or a visitor,' he said. 'Or one of the other consultants—we don't wear hospital scrubs, remember.'

Frustration filled Drew. 'He was staring at me. Why would he do that, if he was some random stranger?'

'I'm not denying what you think you saw. But you need to consider another possibility.'

'Which is?'

Matthew steepled his fingers over his nose. 'You're emotionally bruised. Mentally vulnerable. It's not surprising you see danger around every corner.' He paused. 'This man might have been a product of your imagination, nothing more.'

'He was real. I saw him.' Drew's tone was stubborn. Why wouldn't the guy believe him?

'We talked about this, remember? How isolation, coupled with sensory deprivation, results in hallucinations. Remember how we discussed the flashes of light, the visits from Holly? Not real, any of it.'

'Dr Thomas.' Drew fought his rising irritation. 'I haven't suffered anything like that for a while. Not since the first few days here. Why would the hallucinations come back?'

'Hard to say. Probably all to do with the brain resetting itself to its normal function. In other words, just a blip. Nothing to worry about.'

'He was staring at me.' How could he convince this man of the danger he faced? 'Ethan Parker. Or the other guy. One of them came to drag me off to that hellhole again.'

'Who's Ethan Parker?'

Drew enlightened him, but his words failed to persuade Matthew. 'Plenty of white men in their thirties around here,' his psychotherapist said. 'Not out of the question for one of them to glance into this ward. You only saw him for a second, right?'

'Yes, but—'

'You have to believe me, Drew. Nobody is stalking you.' He frowned. 'We may have to consider upping your medication. Or keeping you here a while longer. At least until we're sure the hallucinations are gone for good.'

Drew fared no better with Holly when she arrived later along with Todd and Nessa. 'He's probably right. Just a patient or visitor,' she told him. 'Please don't worry, darling. You're safe here.'

A sentiment echoed by Todd and Nessa. 'Nobody will hurt you in hospital, mate,' Todd said. 'Dr Thomas was most likely correct. One last hallucination before your brain returns to an even keel.'

'Concentrate on getting well,' Nessa told Drew. 'With any luck you'll soon be out of here. I have two little boys who can't wait to see you.'

Drew remained silent while Nessa prattled on about his nephews. He watched her face while she talked, grateful she'd come, but only half listening. He loved Nessa like a sister, but her dismissal of his fears frustrated him. Like he'd dreaded, he was alone with his terror.

It would be pointless to inform the police. They'd only ridicule him too. His gut told him the man was no visitor, outpatient or staff member. His abductor had paid him another visit.

******

After that, Drew kept an eye on the glass doors to his ward. Twice he spotted the man staring at him again. He only got a glimpse each time, unsure whether it was the same guy. Both times Drew suffered a full-blown panic attack, his chest constricting, heart thudding, his pyjamas drenched in sweat. He felt trapped, cornered by a psychopath, with no way out.

He didn't tell anyone what he'd seen. Nobody believed him, so what would be the point? His brain had done a U-turn; he now yearned to be home. No matter what it cost, he'd install a state-of-the-art security system on his return, and pray the police caught those two bastards soon.

Holly and Todd came every day. So did Nessa whenever her parents could babysit. Drew had told Todd he couldn't cope with anyone else, such as the guys from the running club, paying him a visit. He wouldn't be up to social chit-chat for a while.

His health continued to make good progress. His legs were still weak, and wasted, but his walking frame helped. As did the intensive treatment he'd received.

'You'll soon be strong enough to dispense with the frame altogether,' his physio had said, and Drew agreed. That morning he'd walked twice the distance he'd managed the day before. With any luck, before long he'd be able to run on his home treadmill, which should help strengthen his leg muscles. He possessed hand weights that would rebuild his upper body. His medical team had assured Drew he could continue both his physical and psychological therapies as an outpatient.

'I've had a shower seat installed in the bathroom, along with extra stair rails,' Holly had told him earlier. 'Everything's set for you to come home.'

He was almost ready to leave hospital. So why did panic still lurk in his chest?

Perhaps nowhere was safe anymore.

Part Three

Home

CHAPTER 45

In Holly's opinion, the hospital had discharged Drew too soon. His shirt hung slack on his thin frame; his trousers sagged at his waist. He'd regained weight, but still had several kilos left to go. What concerned Holly more was his mental health. His blank eyes, the way his gaze darted around. As though searching for something. Or someone.

He was scared, and vulnerable, of course. She understood, or she hoped she did. She'd lain sleepless most nights, picturing Drew in captivity, trying to comprehend his suffering. How awful, to lie shackled to the floor, in total darkness and silence, fed minimum rations. No human contact, no conversation, and for what? Some warped idea of justice? Drew's incarceration wouldn't bring Rosalie back. The police needed to find the two bastards responsible, and soon.

As for her marriage, Holly couldn't help but worry. She had not just Drew, but her baby to consider. In three months she'd be a mother, coping with both a new-born and her damaged husband. How on earth would she manage?

Don't go there, she warned herself. *Take it one day at a time.*

She placed her arm around her husband's waist. 'Let me give you a hand.' Drew shrugged her off, his expression irritable.

'I only want to help,' she said. His mouth tightened. This had to be frustrating for him, she told herself.

'Leave me alone. I can manage.' Drew's tone was petulant. He shuffled forward on his walking frame, his lips thin lines of resentment. Together they walked through the revolving hospital door into the chill outside. The sky was heavy with an incipient rainfall. Holly pulled her coat tighter around her swollen belly, a shiver running through her.

Nobody took any notice of them, thank goodness. DS Tucker had said she'd asked the local reporters to respect Drew's privacy, and Todd had already issued a statement on behalf of the family. A steady drizzle began as the two of them waited.

'Here's Todd and Nessa,' Holly said after a few minutes, a false note of cheer in her voice. Her husband didn't respond. The familiar blue Citroën stopped in front of them. Todd stepped out, followed by his wife.

'Drew!' Nessa's smile was wide as she threw her arms around him. 'I'm so pleased they've discharged you.' He made no reply, his expression morose.

'You're looking well,' Nessa continued. Holly winced at the lie.

'Let's get out of this cold and rain,' Todd said. 'Bet you can't wait to return home, mate. Although we'll stop off at our place first. Shane and Jack are dying to see their Uncle Drew.'

'Are your parents minding the boys?' Holly asked Nessa. Her sister-in-law nodded, her eyes fixed on Drew.

Todd opened the rear door for his brother, then slid into the passenger seat, Nessa behind the wheel. Holly glanced at her husband; perhaps taking him to visit the twins was a bad idea. His nephews adored him, but she doubted Drew could cope with two boisterous toddlers. Would the man she'd married ever return?

'How's your walking coming along?' Nessa asked, after she'd started the engine. His only response was a shrug. Holly saw Todd flash his wife a look. She fell quiet after that.

The minute the car pulled onto Todd and Nessa's driveway, Holly sensed the change in Drew. He remained in the back seat after everyone else got out. She stood on the pavement, unsure what to do.

To her relief, Nessa took control. 'Come on, brother-in-law.' She smiled at him. 'My boys can't wait to see their uncle.'

Drew's face was set and sullen. 'This was a mistake. Too much, too soon. Take me home, please.'

'But the twins are dying to spend time with you. Just five minutes, okay?' Nessa pleaded.

Holly saw Todd frown. 'We shouldn't push Drew,' he said. 'We'll go to your place if that's what you prefer, mate.'

Fear pooled in Holly's gut. She dreaded being alone with her husband. He'd become a stranger. 'It might be best,' she said.

'Take me home,' Drew insisted. The tension thickened, with Holly's nerves stretched tighter than piano wire. Nessa didn't reply, simply got back in the car, along with Todd and Holly. She restarted the engine and drove to Westbury-on-Trym.

'You guys need time to yourselves,' Todd said after his wife had parked. 'I'll call you, okay?' He directed his last comment at Drew, who merely nodded. So did Holly. If she spoke, she might cry.

The wind chill bit into her cheeks once they'd exited the car. She grasped her husband's arm while he inched the walking frame forward. To her relief, he didn't shrug her off.

Think positive, she told herself. At last she had her husband home. Time to love him back to health. Whatever it took.

******

Drew waited while Holly unlocked the front door, a blast of warm air greeting him from within. He positioned his frame inside the hallway, then stepped through. He gazed around the small space. The framed prints of Paris they'd bought on their honeymoon. A shoe rack, piled high with Holly's footwear. Twin spider plants that straggled over the windowsill. All so familiar, yet rendered foreign by his abduction.

'I'll make a pot of coffee,' Holly announced. Not bothering to reply, Drew shuffled towards the living room. The subsequent hiss of expelled air from the leather sofa as he sat down reminded him he was home. His eye fell on the handwoven rug, their battered bookcase, a silver photo frame. None of it meant anything anymore.

Holly soon returned with a tray bearing two mugs and a plate of sausage rolls. 'You need to regain the weight you've lost,' she said. 'I might be a crap cook, but I've stocked up on protein shakes and filled the freezer with ready meals—lasagne, curry, pizza. All your favourites.'

She set the tray on the coffee table and sat beside Drew. 'It's good to have you home, sweetheart.'

How was he supposed to respond? His wife had become a stranger. His abductor was all that mattered. A man who, right now, might be watching the house. From far away, he heard a woman's voice grow ever fainter. Drew spiralled back into the Black Hole, to darkness, silence, isolation. The stench of his own waste in his nostrils, those damn chains rubbing his wrists and ankles raw. Footsteps approaching his prison…

A hand landed on his arm. Drew screamed, desperate to escape. Then he realised the fingers clutching his sleeve belonged to Holly.

'Sorry,' he muttered.

His wife's face was white with shock. 'What's wrong?'

He forced himself to respond. 'Nothing. I'm fine.'

'You're not. Talk to me, please, Drew—'

'Drop it, will you?' He glanced away, ashamed. 'I missed what you said. You asked me something, right?'

She swallowed, her eyes bright with unshed tears. 'I was wondering—when's your next outpatient appointment at Southmead?'

'I'm meeting Dr Thomas in three days' time. So he can dig around in my brain some more.' Resentment filled his tone.

'You think that'll do any good?'

Drew shrugged. 'The hospital seemed set on that as the way forward, along with medication. I've got physiotherapy straight afterwards. Two birds with one stone, and all that.' He laughed, but the sound was as cold as the air outside.

She edged closer. 'Martin from two doors down said he'll give you a lift to Southmead whenever you need. It'll save on taxis until your legs are strong enough to drive.'

Drew was aware his expression had turned mutinous. 'Why can't *you* take me?'

'I need to get back to work. I can't afford any more time off. My boss has made that very clear.'

'What about me? You don't think *I* need you?'

'Yes, of course. You come first, you know that. But—' She broke off, her eyes on his face. 'What's wrong, love?'

He swallowed hard. 'I can't—' He bit his lip, his gaze on the carpet. *Hold it together, for God's sake. You can do this.*

Part of his brain disagreed. Within seconds the Black Hole overwhelmed him again—the silence, the loneliness— and Drew shattered into fragments. His hands clenched in fury, he pounded the sofa cushions, his shoulders shaking all the while. He heard his voice, strangled by panic, repeating the same words: *I can't... I can't...*

Drew felt Holly inch closer, then her fingers gripped his frenzied fist. She turned his hand to clasp hers, then pressed him tight against her body, as far as her pregnant belly allowed. To his surprise, the chant of *I can't* ceased, although shudders still wracked his thin frame. He rested against her, wrung dry. For a moment, neither spoke.

'I can't be alone,' he managed at last. 'For God's sake, stay with me, Holly. I'm begging you. Don't leave me.'

'I don't have a choice, love.' To Drew, her words crashed like rocks into the room. 'I've used up my holiday allowance. My caseload is huge, what with two colleagues out sick. Besides, we need the money.' In an echo of her husband, she continued, 'I can't—'

Drew pulled away. He stood up, his hands clutched on his walking frame. 'If you leave me, I'll kill myself.'

He watched as shock blanched Holly's face. Her face became a frozen mask. For a moment she didn't respond. Then: 'Don't say that. Please. Talk to Dr Thomas. He's there to help you—'

'I mean it. I don't give a flying fuck what you, Todd, or Dr Know-It-All Thomas say. Some guy was stalking me at the hospital. You think whoever abducted me will let me go so easily? Don't be so naïve.' He snorted, the sound harsh. 'The police can't help. You heard what DS Tucker said. Limited resources, no possibility of round-the-clock protection.'

Holly chewed her lip. 'You're afraid he'll try to snatch you a second time.'

'Of course he will. He'll have murdered his accomplice for letting me go. The reason Ethan Parker is missing.'

'You can't know that. Please listen to me, love—'

'No, *you* listen to *me*. The way I see it, I stand a chance of staying safe if I remain inside with you. Or Todd, or whoever.'

'You're asking the impossible.' Holly's voice was firm. 'I want to help you, but you're expecting me to become a prisoner in my own home.'

'I'll make sure we're protected. First, I'll install a top-of-the-range alarm system, then get locks on the windows—'

'We can't afford it. Have you forgotten how huge our mortgage is?'

'To hell with the money.' Drew's lips tightened with anger. 'Is that all you care about?'

'Of course not, but—'

'No buts. I can't let that bastard drag me back to that hellhole.'

'He won't, love. It's a crime scene, remember?'

'He'll have found somewhere else. Plenty of disused buildings around Bristol.'

'You can't live life as a recluse. What about your work? Our marriage?'

'I hated my job. And we won't have a marriage if that prick abducts me again.'

'Don't forget our baby, Drew. I'm pregnant, in case you've forgotten.'

He gestured towards her belly. 'As if I could. I'm reminded every time I look at you.' A low blow, but he was past caring.

Holly shot to her feet, fury in her face. 'You bastard. Don't you dare tell me you'll leave our child without a father, just because you're scared. I'm fucking scared too, Drew. You want to know why? I'm scared the man I married has gone forever. Scared I'll have to raise our son or daughter by myself. Scared the bank will repossess our home. Scared, scared, scared.' She stopped, clearly out of breath.

To hell with her fear. She hadn't suffered the Black Hole. Drew gripped his walking frame tighter. 'I'll say this for the last time. If you leave me alone in this house, you'll come home to find me dead.' With that, he shuffled from the room.

******

Holly lay in bed, unable to sleep. Since her fight with Drew, they'd not spoken. For food, she'd heated up a pepperoni pizza that she ate alone. Her sole consolation? Drew hadn't chosen to sleep in the spare room that night. Instead he lay beside her, his back turned. Random thoughts churned through her head—*request leave of absence, ask the doctor to sign me off sick, how will we manage for money?*—as the night wrapped around her. Drew had propped open the door and switched on the bedside lamp. The light made sleep impossible, but she didn't dare turn it off.

Neither could she risk dismissing his threat of suicide. Should she phone Matthew Thomas? But what about patient confidentiality?

Maybe she ought to ask her parents to fly over. Never mind what she'd told Karen about needing time alone with Drew. She couldn't cope with this by herself.

Her hands rested on her belly, feeling her baby kick. *Your daddy's not himself right now*, she told him or her. *When he's well again, he'll love you the way I do*. The fact Drew hadn't mentioned their child since learning of her pregnancy stung Holly. His mind was damaged, but even so...

Her husband sat up, swung his feet onto the carpet. 'I'm going for a piss.' Well, at least he was talking to her.

When he returned, he didn't get back into bed, but pulled open the curtains to stare out of the window.

'Is it still raining?' Holly ventured.

'No.' He turned away from the glass, then swivelled back. A hoarse cry wrenched itself from his throat. The glare from the nearby street lamp filtered into the room, allowing Holly to glimpse terror in his face. In an instant she was by his side, following the direction of his gaze.

'Is he still there?' Drew's voice was a whisper. His eyelids were squeezed shut.

'There's nobody outside, love.'

His eyes flew open to stare at the pavement. 'A guy was there. I saw him.'

Holly peered across the street, but failed to spot anybody. Impossible to tell whether anyone had been watching the house.

'It was just some stranger.' Holly prayed that was the explanation. It had to be, right?

'It was the same guy who stalked me at the hospital.' The blankness had returned to her husband's eyes.

'What did he look like?'

'I couldn't see his face. He wore a parka, with a big hood, pulled down low.'

'Then how do you know it was the same guy?'

'Who else could it have been?'

'Drew, you can't be certain of that.' Hadn't Matthew Thomas warned Holly her husband might exhibit signs of paranoia? 'You said yourself you only saw the man at the hospital for a split second each time. Same with this guy with the hood.' She steered him away from the window. 'Come back to bed, please.'

She didn't sleep that night. Neither, she was sure, did Drew.

******

In the morning Holly called in sick to work so she could stay home with Drew—what choice did she have?—then phoned her mother. Within minutes she abandoned the idea of asking her parents to fly over. Her horror mounting, she heard how Karen had discovered a lump in her breast. Holly did her best to provide reassurance, while floundering out of her depth. After the call ended, she stared out of the window, her expression blank. Too worried, too exhausted, to cry. An old proverb came into her head: *it never rains but it pours*. As she watched a spring deluge fall from the sky, she thought how true that was.

CHAPTER 46

The Watchman shifted in his seat, his brain pondering the previous evening. Had Drew spotted him? Probably not. The night had been dark, he'd worn concealing clothes, and had scurried off the moment Drew's bedroom curtains twitched open.

From behind his car's tinted windows he'd also seen Drew shuffle out of the hospital the day before. The man could barely walk and seemed exhausted. His former captive's face appeared thin, haunted. The Watchman was sure Drew would be on bed rest for a while, with limited trips out of the house. Good. That suited his plans perfectly.

He'd already decided how to play things; meanwhile he'd bide his time, and observe. At this stage of the game he needed to keep his distance for a while.

'How long will you wait?' Rick asked.

'We'll see. A few weeks, maybe. Then I'll make my next move.'

CHAPTER 47

A week later Drew lay in bed, his gaze fixed on a crack in the ceiling, listening to rain patter against the bedroom window. The alarm clock showed the time as ten past midnight. His sleep patterns remained out of whack; he'd doze off in the afternoons, yet be unable to fall asleep at night. Holly's breathing told him she wasn't sleeping, just avoiding conversation. They had become strangers, polite but distant.

At least he hadn't been alone. Todd had taken the morning off work two days after Drew's discharge from hospital. His brother kept him company while Holly consulted her doctor. She'd returned with a sick note for stress, signing her off for two weeks.

'He's concerned about my blood pressure,' she'd announced. 'Says there's a danger of pre-eclampsia.'

'Can't you take your maternity leave? Or is it too early?' Todd asked.

Holly shook her head. 'I'm not quite there yet. With any luck, after the two weeks are up, the doctor will issue another sick note.' She sank into an armchair, her hands rubbing her spine.

Todd handed her a cushion. 'Pregnancy backache's a bitch, isn't it? Nessa suffered hell before the twins were born.'

Guilt stabbed Drew. His wife was six months pregnant, tired and unwell, yet his brother cared for her better than he did. She'd told him about her mother, cried as she mentioned the biopsy and mammogram Karen would need. He'd longed to comfort her, but had remained frozen. His captor had switched off Drew's emotions.

Since that day, Holly hadn't left home, apart from to drive him to Southmead. Their local supermarket delivered whatever groceries they needed. If they ran out of something, they made do without. The enforced house arrest had taken its toll on his wife. Holly appeared subdued, pale, a shadow of her former self. She bore no resemblance to the woman he'd once nicknamed Prickle. He knew he should talk to her, but four months of separation had driven a wedge between them, and the gulf seemed unbridgeable. Bitter regret filled him when he remembered his threat of suicide. He hadn't meant it. He'd flung his ultimatum at her in anger and fear, but did she realise that?

Although sometimes, when Drew thought about the fact his abductors were still at large, death didn't seem such a bad idea. He spent hours each day staring out at the street, wondering if each man who passed—or, God forbid, lingered—was one of *them*. It became a ritual; if he didn't stand guard at the window the flashbacks struck more frequently, lasted for longer. He knew his behaviour worried Holly, but he couldn't stop himself.

'Your medication can take up to six weeks to kick in,' Matthew Thomas had told him. 'And you might not experience the full effects for several months.'

Not quick enough, not by half. Before long, he'd become a father, with the attendant stresses of parenthood. Small wonder terror clutched him. He couldn't care for himself, or Holly, never mind a child.

Drew reached out a hand, resting it on the curve of his wife's shoulder. Her body tensed, and she shifted away.

******

Two weeks later Holly lay across the bed from her husband, her thoughts dark. Nothing had happened to break the tension in the house. Her nightly phone calls with her mother—still no results from the biopsy—continued to worry her. Her daily texts with Amber and Elaine kept her sane as her world grew madder. The person beside her was a stranger—no, a robot—and she had no idea how to reach him. Conversations were limited to meal choices, television programmes and other banalities. They never discussed Ethan Parker, or his partner in crime. Police progress in finding either man had been non-existent, so what was there to say?

Drew appeared less on edge, which was one consolation. The medication must be kicking in at last. He still spent hours staring out of the window, his expression blank. Her suggestions for getting him out of the house—walks, shopping—went unheeded. He allowed Holly to drive him to physiotherapy, but the trip was fraught with paranoia. Drew's eyes would dart around, surveying the passers-by with suspicion, one hand clenched around the door handle. To her dismay, he'd abandoned his sessions with Dr Thomas.

'The man has never been forced to shit into a bucket for four months,' he'd told her, his tone curt. 'How can he possibly understand the crap in my head?' Holly's counter-arguments went ignored. So did Todd's.

Drew's brother had visited several times, along with Nessa, but only once with Shane and Jack. Holly had watched Drew with his nephews, how his body language was stiff and forced. The twins, clearly sensing his antipathy, had cried, and their parents had taken them home soon afterwards. Holly surmised, with a pang, that the boys reminded Drew he would become a father himself before long. A fact he seemed determined to ignore. She hadn't dared broach the subject. Drew's indifference had cut deep.

After that, Todd and Nessa came alone. Drew would chat with Nessa, Todd with Holly. Her relationship with him had returned to its former easy connection. Around Todd she felt human again. He'd discuss his work as a probation officer; she'd bitch about her divorce caseload, glad to be away from it. He'd enquire about her backache, she'd ask about his running. Holly would reheat something frozen for the four of them, and afterwards Todd helped her load the dishwasher.

That particular evening, as the two of them returned to the living room, she'd caught Drew's words: *It's good I can talk to you. I can't do that with Holly.*

Pain had hit her, followed by betrayal. Why couldn't her husband confide in her, rather than Nessa?

In a way, Holly understood. Nessa, with her easy-going nature, made people feel safe. Shouldn't she be glad Drew trusted someone, even if it wasn't her?

'Does Drew ever talk about his abduction?' she asked Todd the next time the two of them came over. She'd followed him into the kitchen after he'd gathered up their dirty coffee cups.

'No. I've tried, Hols, believe me. But he's made it crystal clear he won't discuss it.'

'He talks to Nessa.' She couldn't conceal her bitterness.

'She's a great listener. If it helps him—'

'Why can't he talk to me? I'm his wife, for God's sake.' To her horror, her voice shook with tears.

Todd pulled her close; Holly melted against his chest. His hand stroked her hair, his touch tender. It felt so right, so natural. Hadn't he always been there for her?

The door opened, shattering the moment. Drew appeared in the gap, his gaze fixed on his wife and his brother. Behind him stood Nessa, a frown on her face. Suspicion lurked in her dark eyes. Holly and Todd sprang apart, but too late.

'What's going on?' Nessa's voice sounded calm, but her mouth was pinched tight.

'Nothing.' Holly wiped a tear from her cheek. 'Just feeling a bit rough, that's all.'

Todd strode past his wife, back into the living room. Drew followed him. He'd not said a word the whole time.

When Nessa spoke she pitched her voice low, so the men couldn't overhear. 'Are you sleeping with my husband?'

'No.' No way would she wound Nessa by revealing she'd spent a night wrapped in Todd's arms, even though sex hadn't been involved. Her sister-in-law would still view it as betrayal. What wife wouldn't?

'I don't believe you. He's always had a thing for you.'

'A harmless crush. Nothing more.' Too late, she realised her words hadn't helped.

Nessa made an angry gesture towards Holly's belly. 'Maybe not so harmless.'

'What? No. You can't think—'

'Can't I?' Her sister-in-law stepped closer. 'All those times he stopped by your house when Drew was missing. Supposedly to make sure you were coping okay. But who's to say the sex didn't start before Drew's disappearance?'

Holly refused to break eye contact, despite her discomfort. 'You're wrong.'

'He'd arrive home, stinking of your perfume, and I never questioned him. Because I couldn't bear to hear him lie. Or worse, listen to the truth.'

'Nothing happened between us.' Holly steadied her voice. 'I love Drew. Not Todd.'

'Todd's besotted with you. You were alone. Vulnerable. Hurting.'

'It wasn't like that. I swear.'

'Yeah, right. You're telling me you didn't flutter your eyelashes and he came running?'

Holly shook her head. 'No.'

Anger twisted Nessa's lips. 'You're a liar.' She spat the words at Holly. 'I'll tell you one thing. Todd and I have been married for almost three years. We've been blessed with Shane and Jack, and we adore our boys. Our relationship's not all roses and rainbows, but it's solid, and it works. If you try to break us up—' Venom edged into her voice. 'I'll fight you, and it'll get ugly. Leave my husband alone, you hear?'

'I don't want Todd.' How could she make Nessa understand? 'I love Drew. I married *him*, remember.'

Nessa snorted. 'What a crap-fest of a wife you are. Ever asked yourself why Drew talks to me and not you?'

Yes, Holly almost protested, but Nessa turned on her heel and strode from the kitchen to rejoin the others. Stunned, Holly followed.

Drew and Todd seemed unaware of the tension between the two women. Holly sat beside her husband, unable to look at Nessa. Her sister-in-law remained standing.

'Our babysitter needs to leave early, so we'd better get going,' Nessa informed Drew. Todd shot his wife a quizzical glance, but said nothing. Neither did Drew.

Holly brooded over Nessa's anger all evening. Once they'd gone to bed, she couldn't stand the silence any longer. What must Drew have thought about the embrace?

'It wasn't how it looked,' she said to her husband's rigid back. 'Nothing's going on between Todd and me.'

He shrugged. 'Never thought there was.' As though he didn't care. 'If you don't mind, I need to sleep.'

The baby chose that moment to kick, and hard. It proved the catalyst for Holly's anger. 'The world doesn't revolve around you.' Her tone was harsh. 'Stop the self-pity, will you?'

For a second Drew didn't respond. Then he turned to face her, and Holly's stomach dropped at the ire in his expression.

'What the fuck did you say?' His voice dripped molten fury. Rage reddened his cheeks.

'You have no idea, do you?' he yelled, his breath blasting hot against her mouth. 'When was the last time some psychopath chained *you* up in pitch blackness? Do you know what it's like to shit into a bucket without the benefit of toilet paper? Not to use a toothbrush for months on end? To be so desperate for human contact that you beg whoever feeds you to say something—*anything*—to shatter your loneliness?'

When Holly, stunned into silence, didn't reply, he continued, 'The bastard never did, though. I stayed stuck in the blackness and solitude. Hungry, terrified and without hope. Don't you dare tell me I shouldn't feel like crap.'

'I'm sorry,' Holly whispered. He was right. She had no idea what he had suffered.

'I endured hell. For four long, awful months. I still do.'

All Holly's anger had gone. She edged closer. 'Can I hold you?'

He stared at her. She tried again. 'Don't shut me out. Please? I'm not the bad guy here.'

Still no response. She inched towards him, relieved when he stayed put. Holly wrapped her arms around Drew, her head on his shoulder. His body was stiff against hers. It was like hugging a surfboard.

'I love you,' she said. She never expected him to say it back, and he didn't. The rigidity of his posture relaxed a little, though.

'Towards the end I was slipping into madness,' he murmured.

Holly squeezed him tighter. 'I think you were found just in time.' Drew's mental health would never have survived years in isolation.

'My brain didn't function so well, what with the hallucinations, the silence, the blackness. I'd given up hope.'

She pulled away to look at him, stroking his wasted cheeks. 'Oh, my love. You've been to hell and back, haven't you? But, Drew, listen, please. You're not a prisoner any longer. What happened to you in that awful place—'

His face became shuttered. 'You're wrong. Every day Ethan Parker and the other guy remain free men, I'm still their captive.'

Something broke within Holly. 'I can't live this way.' Her voice shook with exhaustion. 'Even if you can't, or won't, leave the house by yourself, I have to.' She steeled herself. 'My boss has asked me to go in tomorrow. Says he needs to discuss the handover of my caseload during my maternity leave.'

Drew didn't respond, but his lips tightened. Holly pressed on regardless. 'Let's at least give it a try. I'll drive to work, come home the minute I'm done—'

'No!' He turned his back on her. 'If you were a proper wife, you wouldn't leave me.'

Anger crashed over Holly again. How unfair of him. 'Ditch the emotional manipulation, for God's sake. I deserve better.'

He didn't reply, his body set in rigid lines, rebuking her.

'Keep the doors and windows locked, and your phone close at hand. You'll be fine for a couple of hours.'

Sobs shuddered through her husband's frame. All the fight seemed to have drained from him. 'It's not just Ethan Parker that bothers me,' he said.

'What, then?'

He turned towards her again. The anguish in his eyes pierced her soul. 'I've told you—I can't bear to be alone. Solitude kills me. It's like I'm dead while still alive.'

Despite Holly's anger, she understood Drew's pain. She considered the options. Martin from two doors down had offered his help, but she baulked at the guy assuming a caretaker role with Drew. Their other neighbours were at work during the day. So was Todd. Impossible to ask favours from Nessa.

Holly decided to broach the unthinkable. She was out of line; it was way too early, but...

'We're two months behind on the mortgage, and I can't support us on my maternity pay.' She sucked in a deep breath. 'Well, here's a solution. You need to consider going back to work. Not right away, but soon.'

'*What?*' Drew's face flushed with temper. 'You can't be serious.'

'Just hear me out. You'd be with other people. No more loneliness. And while you're at work, your abductors can't get to you. You'd be bringing in money, funds we desperately need. It's the only way, don't you see?'

His expression remained hostile. 'I'm not ready. I can hardly walk.'

'Your mobility improves every day. And you work in computing, for God's sake. Desk-bound most of the time.' She paused. 'You could at least start job-hunting.'

'That's how the bastards got me before. Seized me from the car park at work.'

'Get a colleague to escort you to your car. Then drive straight home each evening.' Holly rolled away, desperate for sleep. Her bedside clock showed the time as one a.m., and she'd set her alarm for six. 'Like I said, I'm going into work tomorrow. I'll be back before lunch.' The stink of his suicide threat hovered in the air. 'Promise me you won't do anything stupid while I'm gone.'

No response. Then: 'Go if you must. I'll be okay.'

'I have to do this, Drew. You understand that, don't you?'

He didn't reply. Seconds later, she heard a snore, patently fake. Marriage, Holly thought, tears in her eyes, could be a lonely affair.

CHAPTER 48

'I'll be off, then.' Holly's voice dragged Drew from his introspection. He stared at her over the kitchen table, his morning cup of coffee stone-cold.

'The doors are all locked, and it's broad daylight. You'll be safe.' Holly's gaze was on the floor. He scrutinised his wife's face, and he didn't like what he saw.

He knew she'd not slept the night before—hell, he hadn't either—but she looked beyond rough. Her hair was dry and dull. Inky smudges underlined her eyes, amid sallow skin. A cold sore bloomed red and angry on her top lip. The mess in his head was exacting a harsh toll from his wife.

He couldn't blame her for wanting a respite. Perhaps a break might do them both good.

'Please tell me you'll be okay,' Holly said.

Part of him wanted to scream *no, no, no, don't leave me, help me*, demand that she stayed home with him. Oh, God, the thought of being alone...

'I'll be back before lunch.' She picked up her handbag, but hovered, waiting for a response.

Two hours out of the house. That was all his wife was asking. He stared at the cold sore, the blotches under her eyes, and his love for her shamed him with guilt. How he longed to hold her close, tell her that everything—their marriage, parenthood—would be fine.

Instead, he remained seated in their kitchen, immobile, mute.

'Drew?' Holly prompted.

'I'll manage.'

'You're sure?'

He wasn't, but what the hell. 'Just go.'

'Promise me—' Holly's fingers twisted around each other; he understood what she couldn't articulate.

'I'll be alive when you get back. You have my word.' With that, Drew manoeuvred his walking frame out of the kitchen, towards the stairs. He needed a shower.

By the time he returned, Holly's car was no longer on the driveway. Panic rose in Drew's chest, but he squashed it down.

'You can do this,' he told himself. Seating himself on the sofa, he turned on the television for company.

All too soon the walls closed in on him, their message clear: *you are alone. Adrift, abandoned, solitary.* Terror mushroomed in his head, blotting out the latest reality show. He might as well have been back in his prison. Sweat pearled on his brow, dampened his armpits. His heart pounded so hard he feared it might explode. A full-blown panic attack was seconds away.

Think, Drew, think, he told himself. What was that technique Matthew Thomas had taught him? Square breathing; that was it. In to the count of four. Hold for four. Release one, two, three, four. Hold. By the time he'd completed several rounds, the tightness in his chest had eased. The walls had receded to their normal position. His head felt clearer.

Weak sunshine streamed into the room as Drew walked to the window. He didn't spot anyone in the street who might be his abductor. Whoever was watching the house—despite Holly's scepticism, Drew was certain someone was—the guy came only at night. In the morning light, all appeared normal. A young mother pushed a pram along the pavement, a toddler gripping her hand. An elderly man struggled with several shopping bags. A teenager cycled past. Out there he wouldn't be alone.

Dare he risk it? His abductor had snatched him at night from a deserted car park. Surely he'd be safe enough at ten o'clock in the morning?

Half an hour, he told himself. Thirty minutes, then he'd return home. Holly was right. He couldn't stay cooped between four walls forever.

Drew edged his walking frame into the hallway. He put on his shoes and a thick fleece, then took his keys from their hook. Fear pounding through him, he pulled open the door and stepped outside.

The air was chilly, despite the sunshine, and Drew zipped his jacket higher. He turned left, his progress slow, his legs soon tired, but he pressed on. It didn't matter where he headed. All he cared about was the fresh air in his lungs, the blue sky above him. No walls to close in on him.

His newfound sense of freedom didn't last. As Drew neared the local shops, he encountered more people, throngs of them. Unease crept into his head. His abductor, or Ethan Parker, might be among them. The guy loading groceries into his car? That could be his jailer, ready to drive his former captive back to hell. Any kidnap attempt wouldn't take place in public, but Drew's fear refused to recognise logic. What the hell had he been thinking?

He'd been foolish to leave the house. Nowhere was safe, but at least back home he could hide behind locked doors.

A sob rose in Drew's throat, and a sound filled his ears. It took a few seconds before he realised the wail of despair came from him.

'Are you all right, love?' A woman's voice pulled him from his misery. She stank of alcohol, but her face was kind. She laid a hand on his arm. 'You don't look well.'

He couldn't respond, her sympathy hard to bear. He breathed in for four, held it for the same count. Out, two three four. Inch by inch, the panic receded.

From somewhere very far away, the woman spoke. 'Should I call someone? An ambulance?'

Drew shook his head. 'No. I'm fine. Really.' Before she could say anything else, he turned in the direction of home, dragging himself and the walking frame towards safety.

He'd learned a lesson. The outside world was too dangerous. From then on, he'd stick to where it was safe. Even if that made him a prisoner.

******

Holly didn't return until nearly one o'clock. Drew heard her key in the lock, but remained huddled in their bed, fully clothed, beneath the duvet.

'Drew? You up there?' Her voice grated against his nerves. Part of him wished she, and the whole world, would sod off and leave him alone.

When he didn't reply, he listened to her footsteps ascending the stairs. Perhaps if he feigned sleep, she'd leave him be.

His tactic worked. He sensed her in the doorway, although she didn't speak. After a few seconds she walked away. A whiff of her hurt lingered in the air.

Drew stayed under his duvet for the rest of the afternoon, sleeping. The doorbell was what eventually woke him. Drew peered at his alarm clock, which showed the time as seven thirty. Muffled voices—one Holly's, the others male— reached him.

'He's still far from well,' he heard Holly say. 'But come in anyway. I'll go check on him.'

Within seconds she appeared in the doorway. 'Your mates from the running club are here.'

That, Drew could deal with. In fact, he welcomed the diversion. Maybe he just had a problem spending time with Holly. What that meant for their marriage, he didn't know.

He threw back the duvet, grateful he was still fully clothed. 'I'll come down.'

When he entered the living room, Rory Bruce, Adam Scott and Mike Randall stood beside Holly. 'Good to see you,' Rory said. Drew liked the guy, although they'd not been friends for long. A recent addition to the running club, he'd grown a beard since Drew last set eyes on him, but still favoured his trademark baggy jumpers and jeans. He never said much, but Drew was glad he and the others had come.

'How're you doing?' Rory asked. He studied Drew's face, a frown on his. 'You don't look so great, man.'

'Hope you don't mind us barging in,' Mike said. He'd been the first to befriend Drew after he and Todd joined the club. 'We've not seen you for ages. Ever since—' He flushed and looked away.

'Yeah, Drew,' Adam chipped in, clearly keen to fill the awkward moment. 'When can we expect to chase your scrawny butt around the track?'

To his surprise, Drew laughed. God, he'd missed these guys. The banter, the camaraderie. Holly had already told him how the three of them had helped search for him.

'Not sure I'm up to that yet.' He turned back to Rory. 'How's that wife of yours? And the kids?'

Rory pulled a face. 'We've split up. I've moved out, filed for divorce.'

Shit. Drew remembered Rory had been a real family man, devoted to his daughters. The break-up had to have hit him hard.

'She's got the girls, and the house,' Rory continued. 'Doesn't seem fair, does it?'

Drew had no idea how to respond. Instead of words, he pulled Rory into a hug. 'Sorry to hear that, mate.'

Rory's body was stiff, resistant, before he pushed Drew away. 'Thanks,' he muttered.

'I'll leave the four of you to it,' Holly said.

The next two hours wrought a transformation in Drew, made him realise how self-absorbed he'd been. Shame filled him. The rest of the world had issues, too. Rory's wife had cheated on him. Mike had been made redundant. Adam's father had suffered a fatal heart attack. Real people, real problems. Life in all its glory; sometimes you got handed gold, other times crap.

'You three have done me the world of good,' he said, when ten o'clock came and he failed to stifle a yawn.

'Even if all we've done is bellyache about our lives?' Mike said, but with a grin.

'Glad to help, mate,' Adam said. 'We'll do this again soon, yeah?'

Rory clapped Drew on the back. 'We'll be round so often you'll get sick of us.'

By the time the three men left, Drew's mood had flipped a hundred and eighty degrees. He didn't feel so alone anymore. Rory, Mike and Adam were there for him. So were Todd and Nessa.

That only left Holly.

They'd edged closer the previous night, when she'd hugged him, said *I love you*. He'd almost said it back, but didn't. The words wouldn't come.

Drew remained seated on the sofa, reluctant to join his wife in bed. Her pregnancy still seemed an insurmountable hurdle. Had the Black Hole not happened, he'd have been overjoyed at the prospect of a child. His abductor, an ever-present shadow, still haunted Drew, though. How could he embrace fatherhood with the man as yet uncaught? The fucker had stalked him at the hospital. Now he lurked near the house most nights. The threat was real, and he hadn't a clue how to cope with it. Or how to mend his marriage.

He'd start small, he decided two hours later, as he slid into bed beside a sleeping Holly.

CHAPTER 49

True to his plan, the Watchman invested time in staking out Drew's home a couple of times a week. Usually after dark, on a street corner around which he could disappear should the need arise. Not always, though. The day before he'd witnessed Drew's pitiful attempt to leave his house and followed him to the shopping precinct, where he'd observed his public meltdown. The guy still looked tormented, and unwell. At the time, the Watchman had wondered whether he needed to postpone his plans.

'Will you?' Rick asked. 'Put things off for a few weeks, I mean?'

The Watchman smiled. 'Quite the opposite. I've changed my mind. It's time to step up a gear.'

'Is that wise? Shouldn't you wait?'

'No. Not when everything I—*we*—hoped for is within reach.'

'You're confident you can make this work?' From Rick's tone, the Watchman deduced his sidekick was getting anxious. Again.

'Trust me. Drew won't suspect what I'm up to. Keep things simple, that's the key.'

CHAPTER 50

Todd folded his arms and stared across the table at DS Tucker. He'd never been a patient man; right then he was struggling to control his fury. The room was cold, its walls grey and stark. His seat was hard and uncomfortable, his coffee tepid and weak. His anger had nothing to do with any of that, though.

'No, I don't need fucking legal representation. Why would I? Like you said, I'm not under arrest.'

'We asked you by phone if you'd voluntarily attend an interview under caution,' Tucker said. 'As part of that, you're entitled to free independent legal advice. It's in your own interests to have a solicitor present.'

'Screw that. You've read me my rights, spouted all that crap about how it may harm my defence if I don't mention something which I later rely on in court. I'm telling you now, there'll be no court case. Because I'm innocent. I'd never harm Drew.'

'Let's get on with the questions,' Tucker replied. 'If you remember, Bristol suffered a particularly bad snowfall on the evening of December the second last year. Where were you that night, Todd?'

Todd didn't respond. Fury blocked his throat, tightened his chest.

'Answer the question, please.'

'At Holly's house.'

'May I ask why?'

Todd scowled. 'Holly was distraught about Drew's disappearance. So was I. We supported each other.'

'I see,' Tucker said. 'What time did you leave?'

'I didn't.' Todd's voice turned defensive. 'You said yourself the weather was terrible. By late evening the roads weren't safe. So I stayed over. In the spare bedroom.'

Tucker harpooned him with her gaze. 'Was sex involved?'

'No. We're not having an affair.'

'Just providing mutual support, right?'

'Where are you going with this? Why aren't you concentrating on finding Ethan Parker and the other bastard who abducted my brother? Why hasn't either of them been caught?' Todd slammed his fist on the table. 'Drew's not safe while they're at large.'

Tucker continued as though he hadn't spoken. 'As you're aware, we spoke with Drew's neighbours after his disappearance. At the time they offered no useful clues.' She cleared her throat. 'One of them came forward recently. Said you became a frequent visitor to Drew's house.'

That'll have been old Mr Robbins next door, Todd thought; always spying from behind closed curtains. The nosy git must have noticed Todd's car in the driveway throughout the night of December the second. As well as all the other times he called round. Todd pictured the guy, watching, wondering whether he should inform the police. His urge to blab must have eventually gained the upper hand.

DC Tobin spoke for the first time. 'I see you wear a watch, Mr Blackmore.'

'What—?' Todd stared at his Timex. 'So do lots of people. What's your point?'

'And you have hairy arms.'

'Yeah, I've got body hair. What guy doesn't? Where are you going with this crap?'

'When we interviewed Drew, he told us that once he touched the man who delivered his food. Whoever it was, he wore a watch. Had hairy wrists.'

Todd shot to his feet. 'That's it? That's the reason behind this ridiculous line of questioning?'

'Sit down, Mr Blackmore.'

Todd ignored him. 'If your chief suspect is a hairy male with a watch, then good luck, because you'll have millions of men to interview. Fuck you.'

Tobin's expression turned steely. 'Lose the bad language, please. And I asked you to sit.'

After a few seconds, Todd complied. 'Drew hallucinated all kinds of things that weren't real. His mind was broken, don't you get it? Maybe he touched the guy, maybe he didn't. If that's all the evidence you've got, the investigation is screwed.'

'You told us you were home alone on the night Drew disappeared. That your wife had taken the children to her parents.'

Todd felt his face flush with temper. 'Yeah. Which I'm sure she's already confirmed.'

'So you had nothing to do with his abduction?' Tucker asked.

Todd was close to meltdown. 'He's my brother. Why the hell would I lock him in a fucking disused abattoir and leave him to rot, apart from the occasional sandwich and bottle of water?'

'Maybe,' Tucker said, her gaze gimlet-hard, 'you were having an affair with his wife. You needed him out of the way.'

Todd slammed the table with his fist again. 'I've told you nothing happened between us. If I'd wanted Drew off the scene, don't you think persuading Holly to divorce him would be simpler?'

'Could be we need to look closer to home for Drew's abductor,' Tucker replied. 'Perhaps you orchestrated the whole thing. With Ethan Parker, a man desperate to avenge his mother, as your puppet.'

Todd shot from his seat. 'What the *fuck*? Are you mad?'

'I'm guessing he was your accomplice, controlled by your more dominant personality. You don't strike me as the submissive type.'

'I love my brother.' Todd felt his face flush red with rage. 'I would never hurt him.'

'Then guilt got the better of Ethan,' Tucker said. 'So he released Drew. Made that anonymous phone call. And now Ethan's missing.'

'You're fucking insane,' Todd spat out.

'His betrayal infuriated you. A man you trusted, yet he was out of control. Did you kill Ethan Parker, Todd?'

'Jesus Christ, no! Of course not.' Before Tucker could reply, Todd continued his tirade. 'If you think I'm guilty where Drew's concerned, prove it. Cameras cover pretty much every inch of the roads in this country. If you can spot my car on the ones leading to that fucking abattoir, then I'll pay you a million fucking quid. Because you won't.'

'Cars can be stolen,' Tobin chipped in, his face impassive. 'Number plates cloned. And no CCTVs cover the approach roads to the abattoir. It's pretty isolated.'

'Tell me how I'm supposed to squeeze in daily trips to Chew Magna. Talk to my boss, my wife, my mates. They'll confirm that, between work, family and friends, my time's fully accounted for.'

Tucker shrugged. 'Maybe you got Ethan to do the day-to-day stuff.'

'This is all bullshit. Conjecture. You have no evidence for any of it.' Todd grabbed his jacket off the back of his chair. 'You told me I had the right to leave at any time. Well, fuck the pair of you. I'm out of here.'

*****

Holly stared at her phone. Todd had texted, asking if he could come round. 'Drew's at physio, right? I need to talk to you. Alone.'

He didn't say why, and she hadn't probed, because she wanted to see him too. She needed his perspective on Drew.

That evening her husband was at a two-hour appointment with his physiotherapist, for which he relied on her to drive. His legs were strong enough to operate a car—he'd recently ditched the frame and had started walking on his treadmill—but he still refused to leave the house by himself. Holly hadn't told Drew she'd called Rory Bruce, begging him to drop by with his running mates. On reflection, she was glad she had. The evening had turned out well. Drew had taken her hand that night after he climbed into bed. She'd been awake, but had pretended otherwise. He'd not said a word, and they'd fallen asleep that way. The simple gesture, the touch of his skin on hers, gave her hope. Not much, though. The wall between them remained, even if not as impenetrable. Drew talked more, but not about anything that mattered. At times her loneliness still threatened to overwhelm her.

She'd arranged lunch with Amber and Elaine for next week, which helped but wasn't enough. Was it so very wrong to yearn for Todd's arms around her?

Her gaze dropped to her pregnant belly. *Yes*, was the answer.

She picked up her mobile and tapped out a text. 'Need to leave by seven to pick him up. Is that OK?'

Within seconds, she had a response. 'See you in five.'

Todd's expression was murderous when Holly opened the door. He swept straight past her into the kitchen, ignoring the hug she offered. With his body angled over the sink, he poured himself a glass of water and gulped it down. Then he turned towards Holly. His face was red with rage, his fists balled at his sides. A thick vein throbbed at his temple. 'Screw the police,' he said. 'They haven't a fucking clue.'

Holly pulled a chair from the table and sat on it. She gestured for Todd to do the same. 'About what?'

With that, he told her. Holly sat immobile, unable to speak. She couldn't believe what she was hearing. 'Tucker interviewed you under caution? She suspects you of involvement in Drew's abduction?'

'Yeah. It could have been worse, I suppose. At least she didn't arrest me. I'm guessing they didn't have enough evidence.'

Horror gripped Holly. 'Oh, my God. I've been questioned too. I just didn't realise.'

She told Todd about DC Jessica Smith's visit the day before. Their pleasant chat that, without Holly's knowledge, had concealed a hidden agenda. *Thank goodness the weather's improved after all that snow we suffered,* Jessica had said when Drew was out of the room. *Do you remember that terrible storm at the beginning of December? The second, wasn't it? Were you safe at home that night?* Holly had confirmed she was. That Todd had called round, then stayed in the guest room, thanks to the icy roads. Her cheeks had flushed when she recalled the kiss that followed shortly before Christmas, and she'd become aware of Jessica's scrutiny. Then the conversation moved on, and Holly thought no more of it.

'DS Tucker suspects I kidnapped Drew. She must be wondering if you were complicit in that,' Todd said.

Anger hit Holly. The idea was repugnant.

'There's more. Nessa knows,' Todd said.

'Knows what, exactly?'

'That I spent the night here once while Drew was gone. I told her nothing happened, but she didn't believe me. Well, of course she didn't.'

Shock hit Holly. 'You told her? Why, for God's sake?' She hoped Todd didn't still harbour hopes about her.

'Seems she'd guessed something had changed between us. She wormed it out of me. You know how persistent she can be.'

'You idiot. You should have kept your mouth shut.'

'Don't judge me, Hols.' His voice held a wealth of weariness. She felt a stab of pity for him. Unrequited love must be a bitch.

'I've not told Nessa about the police interview,' Todd continued. 'How can I tell her—or Drew—that I'm a suspect in his abduction?'

Holly stared at Todd's watch, at the thatch of hair trapped under its leather strap. Her earlier suspicions sneaked back into her brain, full-force. She quashed them, angry at herself.

She glanced up, caught Todd staring at her. 'You think I did it.' His tone was icy, devoid of emotion.

Holly shook her head. 'I don't, I swear.' Her voice betrayed her, though.

'You're lying. I saw it in your face. My God, Holly.' Todd got to his feet, reached for his jacket. His face was closed, the shutters pulled down.

'Please, Todd—'

'Shut the hell up. Not another word.' His expression turned to contempt. He strode past Holly into the hallway. She heard the front door open, then bang behind him.

CHAPTER 51

The Watchman sipped his coffee, a smile on his face. Everything was coming together just as he'd hoped. It might be a cliché, but slow and steady really did win the race.

'Yeah, right. But is the finishing line in sight?' Rick asked.

The Watchman grinned. 'You bet. And like I said before, this time my plans include Todd.'

Rick frowned. 'He'll prove more difficult, don't you think?'

'You're not wrong there.' Besides Drew, the Watchman had also kept Todd under observation.

He'd tailed the guy earlier, had witnessed his angry exit from Bridewell. The Watchman couldn't be sure, but he thought the police had probably been fishing for clues. After all, they couldn't have any solid evidence against Drew's brother. All to the good. For his scheme to succeed, the Watchman needed Todd on the right side of the law.

What he'd seen concerned him, though. The guy could be a hothead at times.

'He's a loose cannon. Who's to say he won't end up wrecking your plans?' Rick said.

The Watchman shook his head. 'Not gonna happen. I'll make very sure of that.'

CHAPTER 52

On the evening of the following day, Tucker and Tobin arrived at the house. 'We'd like to speak with Drew, please,' Tucker said, once Holly opened the door.

She waved them inside. 'What now? More wild accusations?' Her tone was pure acid. Todd was innocent, she'd already decided. No way would he have hurt his brother.

'We have some news,' Tucker replied. 'Is Drew at home?'

Holly gritted her teeth. 'He's upstairs. I'll go get him.'

Holly returned a minute later with her husband. The two police officers were standing in the living room. She didn't ask Tucker or Tobin to sit, still angry with them. Drew parked himself on the sofa, with Holly next to him.

'Have you arrested my abductors?' Drew asked.

'No,' Tucker replied. 'But we've found Ethan Parker.'

Drew released an audible sigh. 'Thank fuck for that. You've got him locked up, right?'

'No. If you'll let me explain—'

Her husband slammed a fist into the sofa. 'Why not? How come the bastard isn't in custody?'

Holly winced at his fury. He had a point, though. Why were the police dragging their heels?

'Because he's dead,' Tucker replied.

Beside her, Drew gasped. Shock rendered Holly silent. She'd suspected as much, but even so...

'A couple out walking discovered Ethan's body buried in a shallow grave. If it hadn't been for their dog digging, he might not have been found for months.'

'How did he die?' Drew asked. 'Was he murdered?'

'I can't reveal the details,' Tucker replied, but her eyes said *yes*.

Holly drew in a sharp breath. 'So the other guy—?'

Tucker nodded. 'We still believe someone besides Parker was the driving force behind Drew's incarceration.'

Holly tensed. They were veering into dangerous territory. Drew would be crushed to know the police suspected Todd.

'Then who abducted me?' Drew's brow creased, his skin unhealthily pale. 'Rosalie Parker only had one child, right?'

'Correct.'

'She's the connection here, surely? Otherwise why subject me to the same hell she endured?'

'What about her other relatives?' Holly asked. 'Did she have any brothers or sisters?'

Tucker shook her head. 'She was an only child. Her parents both died when Rosalie was in her twenties.' She stood up, as did Tobin. 'Thank you for your time. Either myself, DC Smith or DC Tobin will keep you posted.'

After they'd gone, Drew remained immobile on the sofa. Holly took his hand. To her horror, his fingers trembled, along with his whole body.

'I'm scared,' he said. 'So fucking frightened, Holly, every minute of the day. Whoever abducted me murdered Ethan Parker. He'll kill me too.'

Holly had no idea how to respond. Perhaps touch might work better than words. She stood up, reached out her hand. 'I know it's early but I'm exhausted. Come to bed. Please.'

He followed without demur. Once in their bedroom, Holly took off her necklace and put it in her jewellery case. Her gaze fell on Drew's wedding ring, nestled inside one of her bracelets. Beside her, she felt him stiffen. He'd seen it too.

She waited, but he made no move to extract the ring. Sadness stabbed through Holly. *Give him time*, she told herself.

They undressed, then slid between the cold sheets. Drew lay on his back, his gaze on the ceiling. Holly curled against him, her swollen belly pressed against his side, one arm across his body. They remained that way for several minutes, his breath warm against her hair. Then the baby kicked. Hard.

Drew reacted as though a red-hot poker had prodded him. 'What the hell was that?'

Holly traced the curve of his cheek. 'That, sweetheart, is our child. Saying hello to its daddy.'

'My God.' His hand slid over her stomach. The baby kicked again.

To Holly's horror, Drew rolled away, his back to her. 'This world is a shitty place,' he said. 'Who'd want to bring a kid into it?'

The coldness in his voice frightened her. She had to try, though. 'You'll feel differently after the birth.'

He didn't respond. Holly barely slept that night. Neither, she was certain, did Drew.

******

Two days later, Drew sat with Holly and Todd in an interview room at Bridewell police station, awaiting DS Tucker.

'I wonder why she wants to talk to both of us together,' Drew said to Todd.

'No idea.' His brother's tone was clipped. For some reason, Todd seemed furious whenever Tucker was mentioned.

'I guess it's easier to talk to all of us at once,' Holly said. Drew had been surprised, but pleased, when she'd asked if she could accompany him. Tucker had agreed straightaway.

'I just want to run through some stuff, and it'll be easier at Bridewell,' she'd said when she called. 'If you'd like Holly there, I have no objection.'

Drew shot a glance at his wife. He noted her rigid posture, the tension in her face. She'd not exchanged a single word with Todd. Both of them were acting weird, and it puzzled him.

The door opened, and Tucker walked into the room, accompanied by Gary Tobin and Jessica

Smith. 'Good morning, everyone,' she said. Drew and Holly muttered their responses. Not so Todd. His arms remained folded, his expression hostile.

Tucker took the vacant seat next to Holly and placed a folder on the table. Tobin stood behind her. Jessica sat at the back of the room.

'I'll come straight to the point,' Tucker said. 'We checked into other women who went missing around the time Rosalie Parker disappeared. Some have since turned up, others haven't. We concentrated on those with sons.'

Drew breathed out heavily. Bristol might contain other Rosalies, their skeletons chained up in a clone of the Black Hole. Victims of his father, the man he'd once adored. Bile rose in his throat.

'How many other missing women had sons?' Holly asked.

'Three. Of those, we discounted the first straight away. Her child died of meningitis during his teens. The son of the second one emigrated to Canada eight years ago. The third is this woman.' She pulled the folder towards her and extracted a photograph, laying it on the table. 'Michelle Davenport. Part-time prostitute reported missing a year after Rosalie Parker. Leaving her young son motherless.'

Holly's hand flew to her belly in a protective gesture. 'The poor child. What he must have suffered.'

Drew glared at her. 'That 'poor child', as an adult, might have abducted me.' He turned back to Tucker. 'No father on the scene? I presume not, given this woman's profession.'

Tucker shook her head. 'This story has a happy ending, though. Of sorts, anyway.'

'Which is?'

'Michelle Davenport resurfaced a while back. She'd been living in Croydon.'

'Does her son know she's alive?' Todd asked.

'Yes. He was reunited with her not long afterwards.'

'So he couldn't have kidnapped me? He didn't have a motive,' Drew said.

'We need to cover all bases,' Tucker said. 'Michelle Davenport was found alive shortly before you were released. At the time of your abduction she was still on the Missing Persons list.'

'Was my father implicated in her disappearance?'

'No concrete evidence was found to link them. That's not to say a relationship didn't exist.' She turned to Todd. 'Does the name of Michelle Davenport ring any bells? In connection with your father?'

Todd shook his head. 'No.'

'What was her son called?' Drew asked.

'Kyle. Kyle Davenport.'

'I don't know anyone with that name.' He glanced at his brother. 'Todd?'

'Me neither. So where is he now?'

'We've not been able to trace him,' Tucker replied. 'He's no longer at the same place where my colleagues visited him about his mother. Moved out a while ago and left no forwarding address.'

'So he's gone missing?' Drew said. 'Like Ethan Parker?'

'You don't think that's one hell of a coincidence?' Todd shouted. Drew had already told him about Ethan's murder. 'Is Kyle Davenport also going to turn up dead?'

Tucker pulled out another photo. 'Let's hope not. This is from his driving licence, but it's years old. Taken in his early twenties. We've not been able to find anything more recent. He's not on social media, and CCTV stills from when he visited his mother in hospital are too fuzzy.' She passed the photo to Drew. He stared at the thin face, the sullen expression, the hank of hair that flopped over his forehead. Nothing about the guy looked familiar.

'Sorry,' he said, passing the licence to Todd. 'I don't know this man.'

'I don't recognise him either,' Todd said.

Disquiet settled over Drew. Kyle Davenport, most likely, had abducted him, and murdered his partner in crime, Ethan Parker, along the way. Saliva flooded his mouth, and he rushed from the room, heading for the nearest toilet.

When he returned, he caught the final fragments of something Tucker was saying to Todd.

'We often need to ask difficult questions,' she said. 'We're now examining the other lines of enquiry I've outlined.' She shut up the moment Drew walked in.

'What was that all about?' he asked his brother once they'd left Bridewell.

'Nothing for you to worry about.' Drew recognised the closed look on Todd's face. He knew he'd not get anything else from him. His brother was hiding something, though.

CHAPTER 53

Holly watched Drew's fingers shake as he prised the top off a boiled egg the following morning. After the visit from Rory, Mike and Adam, she'd been hopeful he'd turned an emotional corner. Now, on this damp May morning, she doubted that. The man opposite her had become a stranger again. Since Tucker's revelations about Kyle Davenport, he'd been insistent she should stay with him at all times.

'Want to know what I think?' he'd said the night before. 'DS Tucker's right. Two men, not one—Kyle and Ethan—abducted me. Ethan released me, and Kyle murdered him in retaliation. I won't be safe until he's arrested.'

Holly wasn't sure what to believe. One thing was certain: she no longer suspected Todd. She'd seen the fury in his eyes as he'd stared at Kyle's photo. The concern in his face as Drew had rushed from the interview room. Not the reaction of a guilty man.

The stress of it all was wearing her out. Later she'd stared, unable to sleep, at the red digits on her bedside clock, hour after hour. Exhaustion had become her constant companion. She was almost seven months pregnant, for Christ's sake, and her back ached like a bitch. She realised Drew had suffered emotional trauma, but she needed his support, damn it.

At least one worry had been eliminated. The biopsy results had shown her mother's lump was benign. Thank God for that.

Holly drained her coffee. 'I've got an antenatal appointment at nine. Followed by a training session for my maternity leave cover. Can you manage by yourself, just for today?'

'I don't want to be alone.' His expression was sullen.

'Then call your friend Mike. Didn't you say he got made redundant? Maybe he can spend time with you.'

Drew shook his head. 'We spoke a couple of days ago. He's visiting his grandparents in Yorkshire.'

An idea occurred to Holly. She hadn't wanted to go this route, but...

'How about I call Nessa and ask if she can come over?' she said.

Drew's hand stopped midway to delivering a spoonful of egg to his mouth. He stared at her, then lowered the spoon onto his plate.

'She'll be busy with the twins,' he said.

'She can bring Shane and Jack with her.'

He still didn't speak, but the strain in his expression relaxed somewhat.

'It's not a long-term solution. But it'll do for today.'

Drew cleared his throat. 'Kyle Davenport will find me, no matter where I am. I won't be safe here. You should have let me install that alarm system.'

'We don't have the money. Besides, Kyle might be another victim. Like Ethan Parker.'

Drew didn't look convinced. She couldn't blame him. It seemed unlikely.

'I'll call Nessa now.' Better not to give him a choice, Holly decided. She reached for her phone.

Nessa answered on the first ring. 'Hello, Holly.' Her voice was a clipped monotone.

Holly outlined her request, her chest tight with tension. Nessa didn't respond for a second or two. Holly held her breath.

'I'd be glad of some adult company,' her sister-in-law said at last. A pause. Then: 'I'm doing this for Drew. Not you.'

'I get that.' She was grateful, but Nessa's coldness alarmed her. She'd already confronted Todd with her suspicions. What if she told Drew?

******

Drew hugged Nessa hard, after Holly had left, the scent of his sister-in-law's patchouli perfume strong in the hallway. 'Sorry to impose on you like this.' He glanced behind her, surprised by the absence of a buggy. 'Where are Shane and Jack?'

'Mum and Dad are in Bristol for a few days. They're looking after the twins. I adore my boys, but they're exhausting.' Nessa laughed. 'When Holly called, I jumped at the chance for a break.'

She led the way into the kitchen. 'Make yourself useful and put the kettle on. I could murder a coffee.'

He complied, busying himself with mugs and spoons. 'You seemed a bit on edge around Holly.'

Nessa sat opposite him. Her eyes didn't meet his. 'I didn't sleep well last night, that's all.'

Drew couldn't shake the impression that Nessa was lying. That puzzled him. She'd always been a straight-talker.

He loaded a tray with their coffee and took it into the living room, Nessa following him.

'We need to talk,' she said once they'd sat down.

Unease prickled at Drew. 'About what?'

'It's about Holly. You won't like what I have to say.'

So he hadn't imagined her coldness towards his wife. Drew took a gulp of coffee. 'Better get it over with, then.'

'Your wife is almost seven months pregnant. She looks, to be blunt, like shit. You need to get your act together, Drew.'

He sat, stunned, while her words echoed through his head.

'She's exhausted. Working full time for most of her pregnancy in a stressful job. Now she's supporting you, while you sit around hosting your own personal self-pity party. You think that's fair?'

Nessa didn't wait for an answer. 'You've been to hell and back. Nobody's denying that. But Holly, Todd, me—we suffered too.'

Drew stayed silent. Nessa was in full flow, and any interruption wouldn't be well received.

'You need to pull your head out of your arse. Get back to counselling, go running, whatever it takes to move past your abduction. Above all, you should make your marriage a priority. Holly's dying inside, and you're too blind to notice.'

She was wrong. He'd noticed, but that wasn't the problem. 'I don't know what to say to her anymore.'

Nessa snorted. 'You'll be a father in just over two months. Talk about baby names, for God's sake. Discuss what colours to paint the nursery. Stop thinking about yourself all the time.'

'I don't.' The denial came automatically, but Nessa was right. Drew recalled with a pang how he'd vowed, in the Black Hole, to embrace fatherhood. Rekindle his relationship with his wife. A moment far back in time, almost out of reach, but not if he tried. If he took on board Nessa's advice.

His sister-in-law had fallen silent, her gaze fixed on his face. A haunted look sat in her eyes. Her keenness to mend the marriage of a woman she seemed to dislike all of a sudden puzzled Drew. But then, he reflected, Nessa had a generous heart. He'd do well to listen to her.

'You're right,' he admitted.

A small grin twitched the corners of Nessa's mouth. Drew sensed the lecture was over. *Phew.*

'So what are you going to do about it?' she asked.

Drew blew out a breath. Good question. 'What you said, I guess. Go back to counselling. Talk more to Holly.'

'That's a great start.'

'I do love her.' He'd not meant to say that, but it was true. His little Prickle. He recalled his wonder at feeling their baby kick.

'Don't tell me, tell Holly. The sooner the better.' She patted his hand. 'Can I give you a piece of advice?'

Drew laughed. 'You're going to anyway, right?'

'A wise man once realised, as he walked free from prison, that if he didn't leave his bitterness and hatred behind he'd still be in jail. Learn from Nelson Mandela's example, Drew.'

******

Holly arrived home at five thirty. She looked exhausted, Drew noted. Shame hit him, before he remembered his promise to Nessa. He'd make this right, be the husband Holly deserved.

'How's your day been?' he asked.

She slipped off her shoes, slid them into the rack by the door. 'Way too long.' Her nose twitched. 'Is that curry I smell?'

'Nessa's cooked us a lamb dupiaza. We've had a good time, haven't we, Ness?'

Nessa emerged from the kitchen, her face impassive. 'Hi, Holly.'

Drew noted her shift from warm to cold. Strange, given the way she'd argued his wife's corner earlier. Holly, too, seemed tense.

'I'll leave you to it,' Nessa said, as she left amid a waft of patchouli.

Once she'd gone, Drew pulled his wife into his arms. He caught the shock on her face before he kissed her, long and deep. Inside her belly, he felt the baby move.

'I love you,' he said. 'And I want things to change. Between us, I mean. And for me too.'

Holly pushed him away, staring into his face. A myriad emotions flitted across hers: surprise, hope, suspicion. 'What's brought this on? Did something happen today?'

Drew shrugged. 'Just been doing some thinking, that's all.'

'Nessa said something, didn't she?' Was that fear he detected in her voice?

He took her hand. 'Yeah. A few things.'

'Anything in particular?'

'She told me to get my head out of my arse. Consider it done.'

Holly didn't respond. Instead, she pulled out a chair at the kitchen table and sat down. A wince crossed her face.

'Damn backache,' she said.

Drew stood behind his wife, his hands rubbing circles over her spine. Nessa would be impressed, he decided. 'Does that feel good?'

'Mmmm. Don't stop.' For a few moments, silence fell over the kitchen.

'You always were comfortable around Nessa.' Holly twisted round so she could look at him. 'I wish you'd confide in me, not her.'

Drew remembered Nessa's frostiness towards Holly. Maybe he should ask if the two women had fallen out. Holly didn't give him the chance. Tears swam in her eyes; he moved in front of her, all thoughts of Nessa gone. His arms wound around his wife.

Holly's tears soaked his shirt. 'I've missed you, Drew. So much.'

'Shhh.' His hand stroked her hair. 'I'm back now. Things are going to change between us, sweetheart.'

'You promise?'

'Yes. Whoever abducted me stole enough of my life. He's not taking any more.'

'I was scared I'd lost you for ever.' Her voice was a mere whisper. 'The man I married disappeared months ago, and I don't mean when you were taken. You were pulling away from me— from *us*—before that.'

'I was afraid. Of parenthood.' He shook his head. 'I said nothing about it to you, but Ian Morrison screwed me up. A lot. So did Hal and Mel's deaths.'

'I get that. I miss them like crazy too.'

'My emotional hurt was the reason I let my spending spiral out of control.' He bit his lip, embarrassed. 'I've debts you don't know about.'

'Actually, I do. You want my opinion?' Holly's fingers brushed his cheek, her touch tender. 'You didn't allow yourself to grieve. Not properly.'

'You're right. I racked up debt to numb the pain.' How stupid of him. 'I'd already lost my parents. Then my aunt and uncle died. To bring a child into the world and risk more loss? I didn't think I could cope.'

'Our child needs its father, Drew.'

He stroked her hair. 'I want this baby so much. And a couple more besides. Most of all, I want *you*.'

Holly rested her head on his shoulder. 'You've always had me.'

CHAPTER 54

A fortnight later, Drew hummed while he cubed chicken breasts for the evening's stir-fry, his mood buoyant. Since his chat with Nessa, his resolve to turn his life around had stayed high, unswayed by the failure of the police to find Kyle Davenport. From what Jessica Smith had said, no concrete leads had emerged. No matter, because Drew refused to play the victim. His abductor still haunted his head, but he wouldn't let the bastard beat him. Far better to move on with his life. Drew had considered whether to resume counselling, and he'd discussed with Todd rejoining the running club. Whether they should both train for the London marathon in two years' time. His legs grew stronger daily, and he'd gained several kilos. He'd applied for three computing jobs, any one of which would bring in money while he set up his own software business. And—a huge weight off his shoulders—Todd had settled Drew's debts.

His brother shrugged when Drew thanked him. 'Repay me once you find work. That's all I ask.'

As for Drew's mates, Mike, Adam and Rory were frequent visitors, either together or singly. Their support, cloaked in good-humoured ribbing, helped. Earlier that day Rory called round during his lunch break, armed with sausage sandwiches.

'Me and the other guys—we're here for you,' he'd said before he left.

Every morning Drew forced himself out of the house, often to walk across the Downs. He never went out alone after dark, but during the day he felt safe enough. Whenever he stared out over the Avon Gorge, the sense of freedom he experienced overwhelmed him. He felt blessed: a loving wife, a child on the way. His marriage seemed back on track. Like a desert after water, it had blossomed, along with Holly. Drew had painted the spare bedroom to prepare for their child's arrival, and they'd discussed baby names.

'Maybe Eloise if it's a girl?' Drew suggested. 'In memory of my mum?'

'I like that idea. How about Oliver for a boy?'

Overall life was good, thanks to Nessa. He still suffered flashbacks, he'd need medication for the foreseeable future, but for the first time in months he had hope.

A key in the front door. Holly was home, following her trip to buy baby clothes. Drew sliced mushrooms into the wok and checked progress in the rice cooker. Perfect.

His wife walked into the kitchen. 'Smells good.' She dumped her bag on the table. 'Sorry I'm late. Traffic was terrible.'

'Doesn't matter.' Drew hugged her, kissed the top of her head. 'The food's almost ready.'

They ate in a companionable silence, before Drew's mobile shattered the peace. Nessa's name came up as the caller, but when Drew answered, she laughed.

'It's Todd I'm after, not you. Tapped your name into my phone by mistake. My brain's fried.'

'Shane and Jack running you ragged?'

'When *don't* they? You doing okay?'

'Yeah, thanks to you. Want to talk to Holly?'

Nessa coughed. 'Er, no, not right now. I have to go, sorry.' She ended the call.

They finished their food in silence, Drew's brain focussed on Nessa's weird behaviour. He recalled her previous coolness towards Holly. The fact the four of them hadn't enjoyed Sunday lunch together for ages.

Something else occurred to him. His brother also acted reserved around Holly now. He'd first noticed it at Bridewell police station. Gone were the smiles, the quick touches on her arm, the easy affection. At times the two of them seemed like strangers. Nessa's words came back to him. *Holly, Todd, me—we suffered too.*

Did something bad happen while he was incarcerated? Something his family had kept from him, deeming him too fragile to cope?

Drew reached across the table to hold Holly's hand. 'Can I ask you a question?'

She smiled. 'Sounds ominous. Fire away.'

'Is everything all right between you and Nessa? Things seem a bit strained lately.'

The colour drained from his wife's face. She dropped her gaze, her fingers playing with her fork.

'Everything's fine,' she said.

'Are you sure?'

She pulled her hand from his. 'I said so, didn't I?'

Her irritation surprised him. 'What about Todd?'

A flush stained her cheeks. 'What do you mean?'

'Everything okay between you two?'

'Of course.' Holly pushed back her chair, leaning across to grab Drew's plate. 'I'll load the dishwasher.' Shock filled Drew. His wife had just lied to him.

Like Nessa, she'd never been the deceptive sort. Perhaps his wife and sister-in-law had squabbled about something trivial, Todd had intervened, and Holly was embarrassed to admit it. Weird, though. He'd not noticed any conflict before his abduction. Nessa and Holly were too different to be close friends, but they normally rubbed along together well enough.

What about Todd, though? His brother had always shared a special bond with Holly, but no longer. Why were the two of them estranged?

Guilt stabbed Drew. He'd been so focussed on his own pain he'd failed to recognise the people he loved were suffering.

He observed his wife closely throughout the rest of the evening. They chatted, watched television, but Holly still seemed tense. Later she switched off the light the second they got into bed, pleading tiredness. He was certain she was still awake, though.

Drew lay beside her, wondering if he should dig deeper or let it go.

He made a decision; he'd talk to Todd tomorrow. The two of them had arranged a post-work drink to discuss his return to running. If something was wrong, Todd would tell him.

******

Holly stared at the bedroom ceiling, storm clouds of worry gathering inside her. Everything had been going so well. Drew had delivered on his promise; he'd been loving, attentive, excited about their baby, even buying—and reading—a copy of *The Expectant Father*.

'He's turned back into the man I married,' Holly told Amber and Elaine when they met the day before. Their friendship had blossomed into something Holly believed would deepen after she'd had the baby. Amber had recently discovered she was pregnant, and Elaine and her husband were trying for their first child. Holly harboured high hopes that motherhood would bond the three women even closer.

As for her parents, they'd booked flights to the UK, arriving a week before Holly's due date. 'Not every day I become a grandmother,' Karen told her daughter. 'Can't wait to see you, darling. Drew too.'

Family, friends, marriage—everything seemed set for a happy future. Drew's probing had changed that.

Holly shifted restlessly, her instincts warning her of trouble ahead.

******

'We'll go for a jog on the Downs this Sunday. Just a couple of kilometres at an easy pace. How does that sound?'

'Fine.' Drew drained his pint. Around them the Red Lion hummed with laughter and conversation. Perhaps this wasn't the right time or place to voice his concerns. But Holly's behaviour had bugged him all day. She'd seemed more relaxed over breakfast; he'd almost persuaded himself he'd imagined the whole thing. But when he factored in Nessa's coldness, the fact that Holly and Todd no longer touched...

What the hell. No harm in asking, especially if Todd could provide the answer.

'Can I shoot a question your way?'

Todd shrugged. 'Sure. What's on your mind?'

'Holly and Nessa. They're acting weird around each other. And you and Holly don't seem close anymore. Did something happen while I was missing?'

His brother looked away. He drained his beer, taking longer than necessary to set his glass on the table. When he did meet Drew's eyes, his expression was shuttered.

'It was a difficult time,' he said. 'We had no idea where you were. If we'd ever get you back. Stuff like that—it changes people.'

'I don't understand. Wouldn't it have brought the three of you closer?'

'You need to give us time, mate.' Todd gestured towards the bar. 'Another pint?'

The subject seemed closed, and Drew was reluctant to force the issue. He couldn't shake the conviction that his brother, like Holly, was lying.

CHAPTER 55

The following day, when Drew knew Todd would be at work, he drove to his brother's house. Nessa would tell him what was going on, if he pressed hard enough. Perhaps then the four of them could get back to normal.

To his surprise, Nessa was as close-lipped as Holly and Todd. Like them, she found it difficult to look him in the eye.

'Todd's right,' she said while they drank coffee in the living room. 'He was frantic when you disappeared. So was Holly. We all suffered.'

Drew still didn't get it. He tried the same rationale he'd used with Todd. 'Surely that would bring the people who love me together. Not drive them apart.'

'People deal with stuff in different ways. That can create barriers.' Nessa's lips tightened. 'Maybe it's a good thing.'

'What do you mean?'

She still refused to meet his gaze. 'I was never comfortable with how Holly and Todd acted around each other. Their behaviour sometimes bordered on inappropriate. Just my opinion.'

Her comment surprised Drew. He recalled the easy banter his wife and his brother had always enjoyed. Their occasional flirting had seemed harmless. Secure in his love for Holly, and vice versa, he'd never been the jealous type. He'd assumed that Todd had long since moved past his crush on Holly.

Nessa collected their coffee mugs. 'I'll get us both a refill.' She headed towards the kitchen.

Drew mulled over her words while she was gone. They had unsettled him. And dredged up a memory.

Holly and Todd, hugging behind a closed kitchen door. At the time he'd been so self-absorbed he'd barely noticed. Now he remembered something else.

After Todd and he had left the kitchen, Nessa stayed behind. She'd returned a few minutes later, her expression tight, unhappy. Holly had followed, pale and tense. Since then everything had changed.

He sifted through the facts. Nessa had also seen Holly and Todd embrace. She'd always tolerated their flirting, even if it made her uncomfortable. So why the sudden dislike of Holly? How come Todd never joked around with her anymore?

One reason sprang to mind. Drew rejected it at first. Impossible. No way. But it was the only explanation that fitted. His wife and his brother had slept together. And Nessa had found out.

Drew's world flew off its axis and hurtled into free-fall. His sister-in-law's words came back to him: *people deal with stuff in different ways.* Holly's evasiveness, Todd's reaction to his question—everything pointed towards betrayal.

Anger pulsed through him. When Nessa returned, he looked her square in the eyes.

'Did Todd have an affair with my wife while I was locked in that shithole?'

Nessa released a long breath, pain in her face. She placed their mugs on the table, then sat beside him.

'I don't know for certain,' she said.

'But you believe so?'

'Yes.'

'Do you think—?' He closed his eyes, unwilling to say the words. 'That the baby might be Todd's?'

'Holly says it isn't. But I'm not so sure. They might have got together before your abduction.'

Molten jealousy erupted within Drew. So much for him not harbouring the green-eyed monster. He didn't trust himself to speak.

'Todd's always had a thing for her,' Nessa said. 'It hurt, but I persuaded myself he'd never act on it. Stupid of me, right?'

Drew's fury boiled over. 'Fuck both of them! I was chained up, naked, losing my mind, while my brother screwed my wife? He might have fathered the baby she claims is mine? I can't get my head around this.'

Nessa covered his hand with hers. 'If it helps, I think it was pretty short-lived.'

'It's no fucking consolation at all.' He shook his head. 'What made you suspect them?'

'I first noticed something wasn't right one time after taking Shane and Jack to stay with my parents. Todd seemed weird afterwards. Nothing I could put my finger on. Then it happened the next time I stayed in Bridgwater. I confronted Todd, but he denied it.'

'You didn't believe him?'

'No. You know what a terrible liar he is.'

Drew recalled Todd's evasiveness the night before. 'Yeah.'

'In the end, I wore him down. Insisted he tell me the truth. He said they comforted each other, nothing more.'

'But you suspect he's lying.'

'Yes.' Nessa's tone was flat. 'I do.'

'How do you live with him? Believing he's cheated?'

'I can't pretend it's easy. But I have to consider Shane and Jack. I can't wreck their lives over a fling.'

She was right, of course. 'Besides,' Nessa said, 'I love my husband.'

A sneer twisted Drew's lips. 'Looks like he grabbed his chance with Holly the minute he could. Some husband he is.' Nessa flinched, and remorse seized him. 'I'm sorry. That was insensitive. Don't mind me. I'm just lashing out because I'm so angry.'

'Todd cares about me. Not the same way I love him, but I accept that. What choice do I have? And he's a fantastic father.'

'I'm going to demand he tells me exactly what went on. The whole truth.'

'Please don't. Whatever happened, I'm confident it's over. I've moved on, or at least I'm trying to. Can't you do the same?'

'No.' Nessa looked stricken. Drew felt sorry for her, but one way or another, he'd prise it out of Todd. Then he'd confront Holly.

Right then he hated his wife. And his brother. 'Fuck them. Fuck both of them to hell and back.'

******

After leaving Nessa, Drew drove to the Probation Service building where Todd worked, parked next to his brother's car, and waited. Rain drizzled against the windscreen, matching Drew's mood.

He didn't know which betrayal wounded him the most. He'd have staked his life on Holly's fidelity. As for Todd—Drew couldn't comprehend such treachery. His brother had always been a rock for him. The one to whom he'd revealed Ian Morrison's abuse. Who'd comforted him after Hal and Mel died, despite his own pain. What the hell had Todd been thinking?

Not once did Drew give a thought to Kyle Davenport. The Black Hole had gone from his mind. All he could picture was Holly. With his brother.

Todd appeared a few minutes after five. Drew lowered his window. 'Get in the fucking car.'

Todd's eyebrows rose, but he complied. 'What's up, mate?' he said, once inside.

Drew's lips tightened with anger. 'Have you been sleeping with my wife?'

Up until then, he'd hoped Nessa had been wrong. He watched panic flash into Todd's eyes, and knew she hadn't.

His brother didn't reply at first. 'We never had an affair,' he said at last.

'A one-night stand, then. Either way, the two of you ended up in bed.'

'Yes, but—'

Fury boiled within Drew. 'I'm your brother, for fuck's sake. How could you do that to me? To Nessa?'

Todd shook his head. 'You've got this all wrong. Holly believed you'd abandoned her. I comforted her.'

'With your dick?' He restrained the urge to punch Todd. His brother was bigger, and stronger; it wouldn't end well.

'No! We never had sex. But—' His eyes slid away, and Drew knew he was concealing something.

'You're lying,' he spat. 'Nessa thought so too.'

'I admit I kissed Holly. That was wrong of me.'

Drew's mouth curled in a sneer. 'Yeah. And we all know where a kiss can lead.'

'Except she pushed me away. Made it clear she wasn't interested.'

'I don't believe you. When did it start? You were fucking her before I got abducted, right?'

'No. Whatever Holly and I had, it ended years ago. She married *you*, remember?''

'The baby.' Drew could hardly bear to ask. 'Is it mine?'

Todd threw up his hands in frustration. 'How can you doubt it? Holly adores you.'

'She's got a funny way of showing it.'

Todd started to speak, but Drew forestalled him. 'Don't. I want nothing more to do with you.'

'You need to listen, mate. We didn't have sex.'

'Get out of my car. Before I punch your fucking lights out.' He'd do it, too, and screw the consequences.

'Oh, for God's sake. We'll discuss this once you've calmed down.' With that, Todd yanked open the door, slamming it behind him. He strode towards his car, anger in every step. Within seconds he'd driven off, leaving Drew still furious.

So it was true. His wife and his brother had slept together, while he'd been enduring hell. Time to force Holly to admit the truth. A conversation that would end their marriage.

CHAPTER 56

Drew returned home only to find the house empty. When he checked his phone he found a text from Holly. 'Gone to get stuff for dinner. Baby Blackmore restless today—getting kicked a lot! Love you loads xxxx.'

Screw her. The bitch could go to hell and take his brother's brat with her. He sat down to wait.

Half an hour later he heard her key in the door. Drew marched into the hallway, ready to confront Holly. She still had her coat on, her keys in one hand, as she placed her shoes in the rack. His anger must have showed, because she stared at him, her face pale.

'What's wrong? Has something happened?'

'You slept with Todd.' Drew shoved his wife against the wall, his face an inch from hers. Fear sparked in her eyes.

'Let go of me, Drew, you're hurting my arm—'

Drew's fingers clutched his wife's elbow tighter. He didn't care if it hurt.

'Admit it.' His voice was a growl of anger. 'You fucked my brother. Now you're pregnant with his child.'

If Holly's face had been pale before, it was now ashen. 'No,' she whispered.

'You're nothing but a cheating bitch. All that crap about a new start. When all the time you wanted Todd.'

Shock snaked into her expression. 'That's not true. I've only ever wanted you. I love you.'

Drew pushed her away. Once he'd felt the same. Right then she disgusted him.

'I didn't have sex with Todd. You have to believe me.' Desperation sounded in Holly's voice.

'So I'm being paranoid, am I? You're saying this is all in my head?'

'If you'll just listen—'

Drew couldn't think straight. Not with such anger inside him. 'Fuck you. And screw this marriage.'

With that, he let go of Holly, who shrank back against the wall. He grabbed his keys, jacket and phone, then yanked open the door.

'Drew, please. We can work this out.' Sobs choked Holly's voice. 'I love you. What happened with Todd meant nothing.'

He stepped into her personal space. 'So you admit it. You betrayed me. With my own brother.'

'No! Not the way you think. You have to let me explain—'

'You destroyed our future. For what? A casual fling?'

'You're twisting my words—' But Drew didn't wait to hear more. Instead he strode off down the path. Holly stood, crying, in the doorway. 'You slept with Todd,' Drew yelled at her over his shoulder. 'I'll never forgive you.'

******

Drew knew the second he left the house he intended to get blind drunk. Next door, Mr Robbins was wheeling his rubbish bin onto the pavement, his attention flitting between Drew and Holly. *That'll give the old gossip something to chew on*, Drew thought sourly, as he stalked off into the night. Not once did he stop to consider whether Kyle Davenport might lurk close by.

Fury filled him. All he wanted was to find an anonymous boozer, one he'd never been in before, where it wouldn't matter if he got barred. Nowhere local, then. The weather typified a cold spring night, a steady drizzle falling around him, and Drew was glad he'd stopped to put on a jacket. He trudged along until he found himself outside the Spotted Cow in Redland. As good a place as any. Drew pushed open the door.

The place was almost deserted. A trio of elderly men were at the far end, clutching pints of Guinness and talking in low voices. A middle-aged couple sat in silence to their left, not looking at each other. Nobody paid him any attention as he approached the bar. Behind it a man was stacking glasses. Drew could drink himself into oblivion, and no one would notice, or care. An excess of alcohol might not mix well with his medication, but so what?

His mobile sounded from inside his jacket. He pulled it out, rejecting the call when he saw Holly's name on the screen, but his phone rang again seconds later. This time Todd's name flashed up. With a muttered curse, he switched his mobile to silent, and shoved it into his pocket.

Three whiskeys later, Drew was feeling the effects of the booze. The first two had slid down his throat in a couple of gulps. He took the third more slowly, mindful of the watchful stare of the barman. By then the alcohol had blurred the boundaries of his misery. His heart still hurt, though. His wife had bedded his brother, and he couldn't forgive her betrayal.

Who had made the first move? Had Todd exploited Holly when she was at her most vulnerable?

But no. Had she been any sort of a wife, she wouldn't have slept with another man. If he'd gone missing for years, Holly moving on would be understandable. Not after a matter of weeks, or months. And not with his own brother, for Christ's sake.

'Bitch,' he muttered.

Drew's phone vibrated in his pocket. When he took it out, he saw he'd missed three more calls from Holly, and the same number of voicemail messages. Well, screw her. He drained his drink and approached the bar, his legs unsteady. To his relief, his request for a fourth whiskey came out unslurred. The barman, after a long look at him, tonged ice into a glass and held it against the Jack Daniels optic.

A few seconds after Drew slumped back in his seat, his phone vibrated. When he checked it, Todd's name appeared on the screen. Drew rejected the call with an angry swipe. Would there ever come a time when he didn't want to punch Todd's lights out?

Soon after came another call from Holly. With a muttered curse, Drew switched off his phone, and gulped back his whiskey. He ordered his fifth Jack Daniels.

The world grew increasingly fuzzy. Maybe he should simply stay drunk. Far less painful than reality.

'You sure that's a good idea?' the bar man asked when Drew requested his sixth whiskey.

'Best I've had in years,' Drew slurred, pulling a tenner from his wallet. The guy shrugged, then took the money. Business clearly wasn't brisk enough for him to get picky about whom he served.

When the bell for closing time rang, Drew slid off his seat and stumbled towards the door, desperate to sleep off the booze. The drizzle had turned into driving rain that soaked him to the skin before he'd staggered more than a few hundred yards. The walk sobered him up a little, enough for him to steer himself home.

Drew stood outside his house, oblivious to his drenched clothes, the chill in his body. The living room and hallway lights were on, indicating that Holly hadn't gone to bed. She must be waiting up for him. How touching. Where had that concern been when she'd slept with his brother?

He took out his phone and located the voicemail feature. He listened to Holly's messages, her words muffled by tears.

'Drew, I love you. Come home so we can talk.' Silence for a few seconds, then a strangled

318

sob. 'Don't break up our marriage. Please.' The others were in the same vein.

Screw the cheating bitch. Drunk and in the mood for self-flagellation, he called up Todd's message.

'Don't be a prick, Drew. Holly loves you, not me.' Sadness in his brother's voice. 'Go home to your wife. She needs you.'

Holly must have called him after Drew's angry exit. Sod both of them. No way could he face his wife; instead he'd find a hotel. When his head was clearer he'd take stock, decide what to do.

CHAPTER 57

Kyle Davenport, a.k.a the Watchman, observed Drew from the comfort of his car, glad to be sheltered from the rain. What he'd seen and heard that evening disturbed him. First Drew's angry exit, coupled with the harsh words he'd flung at Holly. His former captive clearly suspected his wife of sleeping with Todd. Not good. A rift between the brothers didn't fit with Kyle's plans.

Then came Drew's drunken stagger home. A great opportunity for Kyle, but one he'd missed, thanks to the driving rain and his own uncertainty how to proceed. No point in worrying about that now.

What the hell was Drew playing at? He was soaked to the skin, but continued to stare at the lighted window downstairs. Kyle waited, still unsure what to do. Then his quarry headed in the direction of the shopping precinct. Kyle started the car and followed him at a steady pace.

Soon it became clear Drew's destination was the local taxi rank. Kyle pulled into a parking space and killed the engine. By then the rain had eased to a drizzle. He tugged the hood of his parka over his head and stepped from the car. Drew was only a few metres away. Around the corner from the taxi rank, and out of sight from the drivers.

Never mind a cab. Kyle's car was ready and waiting. He'd wasted enough time already. The moment had arrived. Soon he'd have Drew right where he wanted him.

He stepped forward, his heart hammering. Too late. Drew stumbled around the bend in the road, opened the door of the nearest taxi and slid inside. Seconds later it drove off. Kyle's curses issued into the night air.

CHAPTER 58

Drew awoke the following morning with a cotton-wool mouth and a pneumatic drill pounding in his head. Along with anger. His brother had slept with his wife. Oh, they'd denied it, but he didn't believe them. He refused to be that gullible. While he'd been losing his mind, they'd been thumbing their noses at him and Nessa.

A tear trickled down his cheek, and he brushed it away, his fingers angry. He was a grown man, for God's sake. No way would he cry on account of a wife who couldn't keep her legs together. Or his shit of a brother.

If only he had someone who'd understand his pain. Normally, he'd turn to Todd. As things stood, Drew was alone with his hurt.

Maybe not. An idea occurred to him.

'Gonna talk to Rory,' he muttered. Hadn't the guy also been cursed with a cheating wife? He'd text Rory once his hangover eased, ask if he could visit. They'd chat, share their sorrows, offer mutual support. Guys together and all that. Yeah. He had a plan.

Drew curled into a ball, willing the world to leave him to wallow in his misery. He closed his eyes and allowed sleep to overcome him.

He awoke to the phone beside his bed shooting knives into his skull. A reminder that check-out was in half an hour, or the hotel would charge him for another night. He threw back the duvet with a curse. Fifteen minutes later he'd showered, dressed, and taken the lift to the lobby, where he bought a packet of paracetamols and dry-swallowed a couple. After he'd settled his bill, he headed to the restaurant.

Drew toyed with his mobile while he ate his full English breakfast. Another two texts from Holly, neither of which he read. The idea he'd hatched earlier, of discussing his marital problems with Rory, returned. The man had gone running every week with Todd while Drew was missing. Perhaps his brother had let something slip about Holly, meaning Drew could gauge how long they'd been sleeping together. Whether the baby might be Todd's, not his. Yeah, he should do this.

He sent Rory a quick text. The guy was off work that week, so should be around. In less than a minute, Drew had a reply. Along with Rory's address.

Once he'd finished his breakfast, Drew walked outside to the line of taxis. Shortly afterwards he stood in front of a large Victorian house in Horfield, staring at the four doorbells. Rory had told him weeks ago he'd moved into a rented flat after discovering his wife's infidelity, and Drew empathised with the guy. Chances were Rory needed a friendly ear too.

He pressed the bell marked 'Three'.

Within a minute, he heard footsteps descending the stairs, then Rory opened the door. 'Hey, man. Come on in,' he said, with a grin. Drew followed him to the third floor of the four-storey building. A whiff of old cooking lingered in the stairwells, along with the smell of damp.

Once inside Rory's bedsit, Drew glanced around, and his empathy for Rory multiplied. The place was clean and tidy, but cramped. Under the window was Rory's bed; squashed to one side was a tiny table with a chair at each end. Opposite the bed was a fridge, a small sink, and a counter on which sat a two-ring gas burner, a kettle and a toaster oven. No cupboard space existed; tins of food stood stacked several high under the counter. Piles of books and papers covered the table. Drew pulled out one of the chairs and sat down.

'It's great to see you. Coffee?' Rory enquired.

'Make it black. And strong.'

Rory busied himself with mugs and the kettle, while Drew seated himself at the table. The other man didn't attempt to make small talk, to Drew's relief. His head still throbbed, but the pain was bearable.

Minutes later, Rory plonked a mug in front of Drew, then sat opposite him. 'You okay, man? You don't look so good.'

Drew's misery poured forth. How his wife and his brother had been conducting an affair. His doubts the baby was his. Whether he should leave Holly.

'I'd bet money on it being over between them,' he finished. 'Even so, how the hell am I supposed to move on?'

Rory blew out a long breath. 'You say they both deny anything happened?'

'Yes. But they would, wouldn't they?'

'Do you have any proof?'

'Nothing concrete. Holly thinks I'm being paranoid, but that's bullshit.'

'What makes you say that?'

'Nessa also thinks they had an affair.'

'I don't agree.'

The other man's words surprised Drew. 'Why not?'

Rory took a sip of coffee. 'After you disappeared, Todd was a mess. Me, Mike and Adam, we'd go for a pint with him after our run. He started drinking heavily. Said stuff once the beer got him talking.'

'Like what?'

'How he'd always wanted Holly, but had settled for Nessa. But that your wife loved you, not him.'

Drew was silent. This cast a different light on things.

'Nothing he said gave me the impression they'd been having sex,' Rory continued. 'Quite the opposite.'

Drew yearned to believe him. Doubt still clawed at him, though. 'So why are they so weird around each other? Why all the tension?'

Rory shrugged. 'No idea, man. But you going missing was hard on Todd. Sometimes he was mad as hell, other times he seemed like he was about to cry. Must have been rough on Holly too, don't forget. I reckon they took comfort in each other, but not the way you suspect.'

Was Rory right? Both Holly and Todd had denied an affair, and Nessa had no proof. 'I don't know what to think,' he admitted.

'Talk to her. Listen to your gut instinct.'

Drew remained silent, pondering Rory's words.

'If Holly's cheated, I'd be the first to condemn her, given the crap Louise has put me through. Living in this dump, only seeing my kids at weekends—it's been hell. Don't end up like me, man, not if you can avoid it. You've got a baby on the way, a lovely home, a wife who's nuts about you. Are you going to throw all that away on a mere suspicion?'

Put like that, Rory had a point. *People deal with stuff in different ways.* Perhaps whatever had soured Todd and Holly's relationship, and spiked Nessa's anger, wasn't anything to do with sex.

'I want to believe her.' Drew's voice sounded hoarse.

'Well, that's a start. Take my advice. You and Nessa might be jumping to conclusions.'

Drew's phone vibrated in his pocket. Another text from Holly. 'I love you. Nothing happened with Todd. Please come home.' Followed by three emoji hearts.

Matthew Thomas had warned him PTSD symptoms could manifest in paranoia. The hug in the kitchen, Nessa's suspicions—they didn't, as his Uncle Hal would have said, amount to a hill of beans.

His heart squeezed in his chest. Rory was right, damn him. Hadn't he vowed two weeks ago to mend his marriage? Shame crept into his brain. He'd behaved like a child throwing a tantrum. Well, no longer.

He reached out a hand, clapped Rory on the shoulder. 'You're a good mate. I'll talk to her the second I get home.'

'You do that.' Rory's voice sounded strained. He cleared his throat. 'You deserve to be happy, after the hell you've suffered.'

An awkward silence fell. Then Rory stood up. 'Back in a minute. I need to piss, and the bathroom's on the next floor.' He walked across the tiny space and through the door.

Drew sucked in a breath, aware he should text Holly. Better still, talk face to face with her. He'd take a cab home, apologise for his behaviour, then try to mend their marriage.

He stood up, ready to leave once Rory returned, grabbing his jacket from the back of his chair. As he did so, he knocked a pile of stuff off the table: a battered paperback, a wallet, a bunch of keys. They clattered to the floor, the book and the wallet both landing face down and open. Drew picked up the book and placed it back on the table. His fingers retrieved the wallet, which was a simple folding one with no catch. Something snagged his eye. A credit card, slotted behind a clear plastic section.

The name on the card read Kyle Davenport.

Drew's breath caught in his chest with shock. He rifled through the other cards. They all bore the same name.

What the *hell*? How come Rory possessed the wallet of a man who'd gone missing?

His gaze fell on the bed, on which lay a mobile phone and a second wallet. Drew opened it, checked the name on the cards inside. Rory Bruce on every one.

His brain flew into overdrive. A *third* man—Rory—must have been involved in his abduction. Had manipulated Kyle Davenport into keeping Drew captive. Now Kyle couldn't be found. And Ethan Parker had been murdered. Rory Bruce was eliminating his co-conspirators, it seemed.

But that scenario was impossible, surely? Until recently, the guy had been happily married with two kids. A house in Redland, a job as a civil engineer. And Barry Blackmore couldn't have murdered Rory's mother; Rory had mentioned his parents, both still alive, several times. Drew struggled to understand Rory's connection to Ethan, Kyle and the abducted women. There didn't appear to be one.

This didn't bode well for Kyle Davenport. Would his body, like Ethan Parker's, also be discovered in a shallow grave in the near future?

More to the point, why had the bastard who'd held Drew captive tried to save his marriage?

For that, he had no answer. None of this made sense.

Drew's mind spiralled back to the Black Hole. His breath grew ragged, a panic attack waiting to strike. That *couldn't*, wouldn't, happen. He needed to get out the hell out of here. Let the police deal with Rory Bruce.

Footsteps sounded on the stairs. Drew slid the bunch of keys into his jacket pocket. His eyes fell on the wooden sash window, which had been painted shut. He remembered they were on the third floor, which was good. Very good. He schooled his features back to normality.

The door opened. Rory walked towards Drew, a smile on his face. 'You should get on home. Make things right with your missus.'

Drew side-stepped him, positioning himself closer to the exit. Then he punched his fist against the other man's nose. The crack of shattering bone sounded out. Rory staggered backwards, blood spurting from his nostrils. His eyes were wide with shock. Drew seized his chance, running through the open door, pulling Rory's keys from his pocket. He slammed the door shut, noting the two locks: one Yale, the other Chubb. He inserted the Chubb key in the bottom lock, twisting it closed. Followed by the Yale one. Tortured moans issued from inside Rory Bruce's bedsit.

Drew ran down the stairs and out onto the street. He hailed a passing cab. 'Bridewell Police Station,' he told the driver.

CHAPTER 59

Rory Bruce stuffed a handful of sleeping pills into his mouth, then washed them down with a slug of whiskey. His busted nose hurt like hell, but Rory was past caring. Death offered a way out, and he'd take it and say a heart-felt *thank you*. Drew had seen too much. If he hadn't pieced the puzzle together yet, he, along with the police, soon would.

So this was how his story ended. His eyes flitted over Kyle Davenport's wallet—the mistake he'd made that had given the game away. Not that it mattered anymore. Nobody would care about his death, whether he lived or died. Irrelevance summed up his miserable existence.

He lay back on his narrow bed and closed his eyes, waiting for oblivion. Seconds later a reason to stay alive flashed into his brain.

CHAPTER 60

Drew burst through the doors of Bridewell police station. He'd called DS Tucker from the taxi, barely able to string a sentence together, so great was his agitation. What if Rory had a spare set of keys? Or escaped through the window somehow? Perhaps, even now, he wasn't safe.

Tucker and Tobin managed to calm him down. They plied Drew with endless questions while he spilled his story. Tucker assured him she'd dispatch a squad car to Rory Bruce's bedsit. That the police would question Rory as to the whereabouts of Kyle Davenport.

He'd taken advantage of a coffee break in the proceedings to text Holly. 'Will be home soon. So sorry. Can we talk?'

A minute later her reply pinged through. 'I'd never cheat on you. I love you, always will.' Followed by: 'Even though you're an idiot at times.' Three smiley faces.

Well, he couldn't argue with that. Thank God his wife possessed more sense than him.

'We'll be in touch once we've spoken to Mr Bruce,' Tucker told Drew before he left Bridewell.

Another taxi, this time to home. He sucked in a deep breath as he walked up the front path. He'd not mentioned Rory Bruce in his text; that could come later. His marriage took priority. Time to salvage it.

He slotted his key in the lock and pushed open the door. The scent of his wife's perfume met him, and he breathed her in deeply, his eyes closed. Holly was his everything. He couldn't lose her.

'Drew?'

She stood in the doorway to the living room. Her eyes were red with weeping.

Drew melted, remorse pounding through him. He ran towards his wife, pulling her into his arms. Her hair tickled his nose, as did the scent of her shampoo. The child in her belly pressed against him.

'I didn't have sex with Todd.' Her words, ragged with hurt, filled Drew with guilt. Of course she hadn't; he'd been a fool to think otherwise.

'I know that now.' He took Holly by the hand and led her to the sofa. He noticed her pale skin, the exhaustion smudged under her eyes, and shame hammered inside his head. His gaze flitted to her stomach; the enormity of his impending fatherhood struck Drew. Not with fear, but with joy. He was about to embark on parenthood with this woman, who'd stuck by him during his darkest times. First, though, he needed her forgiveness.

Drew smiled at his wife, attempting to pour the love he felt into his expression, then pulled her into his arms again, her head against his shoulder. 'I'm sorry, Prickle. I've been a fool.'

She wiped a tear from her cheek. 'It's so good to hear you call me that. Like the old Drew is back.'

'Matthew Thomas was right. About the paranoia, I mean. I put two and two together and made five.'

'Yes. You did. A DNA test will prove this baby is yours.'

'No need. I believe you.'

'It was wrong of me to seek comfort from Todd. I'm sorry, sweetheart.'

'It doesn't matter. Not anymore.'

'Can you forgive me?'

'Yes. If you'll do the same for me.'

Her response was instant. 'Deal.'

Later, much later, he told Holly about Rory Bruce. 'I think,' he said, 'that the nightmare might just be over. Now we can move forward. Together.'

******

Anticipation seized Drew, wouldn't let go. Rory Bruce, the fucker who'd wrecked his life, had been arrested, from what Jessica Smith had said when she'd phoned. Well, thank God for that. It was now the day after, and DS Tucker had arrived at Drew's house along with Jessica and DC Tobin, saying she had things they needed to discuss. The four of them—Holly was upstairs, putting on her make-up—sat in the living room, swapping the usual chitchat. Then Tucker got down to business. 'How well do you know Rory Bruce?'

The question surprised Drew. It seemed a strange place to start. 'He became a mate of mine after he joined the running club. I've never met his wife or family, though.'

He saw Tobin and Tucker exchange glances. 'He isn't married,' Tobin said.

Confusion hit Drew. 'Yes, he is. Her name's Louise. He's got a couple of kids too, Amy and Sophie. They all used to live in a big house in Redland. He filed for divorce recently. The reason he's living in that bedsit.'

Tucker shook her head. 'Whatever he's told you, it's likely to be lies. Rory Bruce's real name is Kyle Davenport.'

'That can't be right.' Drew's voice rose high, denial running through his body. 'You've made a mistake.'

'No mistake. He's admitted it, told us Rory Bruce was an alias. We found a birth certificate in the name of Kyle Davenport. He's Kyle, all right.'

Drew couldn't respond. He'd assumed Rory had killed Kyle. Now Tucker was saying they were the same guy?

'We discovered other stuff,' Tucker continued. 'Your wallet, phone and keys, from when you went missing. A log of the visits he made to you while you were his prisoner.' She grimaced. 'He does labouring jobs for cash, pays his rent the same way. Uses different names, changes his appearance. Hence why we couldn't find him.'

Drew heard Holly's footsteps on the stairs. Seconds later she appeared in the doorway. 'What's the latest on Rory Bruce?'

Before Tucker or Tobin could respond, Drew cut them off. 'He's Kyle Davenport. They're the same person.'

Holly's face turned grey with shock. 'What? How can that be?' She slumped into the remaining armchair. Tucker recapped the gist of the conversation for her.

'He always seemed such a nice guy,' Holly said, once Tucker had finished. 'Hard to believe he's a kidnapper. That he murdered Ethan Parker.'

'I guess he's denying everything?' Drew's tone turned sour.

'No,' Tucker said. 'Far from it.'

'What's he saying?'

'Not much.' Tucker leaned forward. 'This is where you come in, Drew. He's told us he'll give us a full statement and confess to kidnapping and imprisoning you. Along with his reasons. He also says he has information pertinent to the Rosalie Parker case that he'll share. But he'll only do all that after—' She drew in a breath. 'After he's talked with you.'

'No way.' Holly spoke before Drew got the chance. 'That bastard put my husband through hell. Now he wants a cosy chat with him? About what, for God's sake?'

Drew remained silent. His brain refused to entertain the idea.

'We don't know,' Tucker conceded. 'But I admit we're keen to hear whatever he might say about Rosalie Parker.'

'We realise this is asking a lot, Drew,' Jessica said. 'But please think before you say no. Depending on what Kyle tells you, we might gain vital facts for our investigation into Rosalie's murder.'

'Where is Kyle Davenport now?' Drew asked.

'Under suicide watch at Southmead Hospital's psychiatric unit,' Tucker replied.

Drew couldn't believe what he'd heard. 'Why? What happened?'

'He tried to take his own life. We found him unconscious, along with an empty bottle of sleeping tablets. Luckily the pills didn't have time to kill Kyle before the paramedics reached him.' She paused. 'We suspect it was a cry for help rather than a genuine suicide attempt. Which is more or less what he told us. Part of him wanted to die, but he also hoped we'd save him.'

'And he insists he has to talk to me?'

'Yes. He's agreed a police officer can be present, along with a mental health nurse. Other than that, he's not been forthcoming.'

'Don't do this, Drew.' Holly frowned. 'There's no need.' She turned to Tucker. 'He's admitted he abducted my husband, right? Why subject Drew to more torment?'

'Like I said, we're also investigating Rosalie Parker's murder,' Tucker said. 'And the statement he's promised us would be helpful. Without Kyle's confession, we'll have to go to trial, which poses the risk of any competent lawyer citing a mental health defence. Kyle attempted suicide, remember. He's being detained in a psychiatric ward.'

'He can rot there. He almost destroyed my marriage.' Holly's tone was bitter.

'The thing is, he doesn't seem mentally disturbed,' Tucker said. 'When we spoke to him, he appeared calm. Claimed the suicide attempt was a stupid mistake. We're hoping the hospital will discharge him soon, so we can hold him at our Keynsham custody suite instead.'

'I'll visit him. If that's what you want.' Drew hadn't intended to say that, but knew it was the right decision. He needed to eyeball Kyle, stare into the face of the man who'd tortured him and understand *why*. His gut told him the effort would prove worthwhile, in ways he couldn't yet comprehend.

CHAPTER 61

From his bed in Southmead's psychiatric unit, Kyle Davenport, formerly known as Rory Bruce to Drew, considered his situation. Thoughts looped round in his head, which remained stuck on the past few days. Why the hell hadn't he destroyed his old identity? But he knew the answer to that. It defined him, ran through him like veins in marble.

Kyle Richard Davenport. Known as Rick for the first seven years of his life, but only by his mother. She'd called him Kyle after a television actor and Richard after her dad, even though he'd kicked her out following an argument. After Michelle registered her son's birth, lonely and missing the father she loved, she decided she preferred Richard to Kyle. Over time she shortened it to Rick. At school, and later in foster care, he was Kyle, but remained Rick at home. He'd liked the distinction; it made him his mother's special boy. She'd said so, hadn't she? *He's all I have.*

Hate and love for her still battled in his head, mostly the latter. She'd had a shit life. Now she faced the grim descent into dementia. Put like that, he couldn't hate her. He only wished they'd been granted more time together.

Kyle's mind spiralled back to when it all started. Once he'd been a terrified child who yearned to be a hero and kill Mr Nasty. It wasn't until his teens that the Watchman born. All thanks to his obsession with comic books. Fourteen-year-old Kyle read the Watchmen series, and, intrigued, delved deeper. He discovered that watchmen predated the police, being organised groups mandated to stamp out crime. With that, a modern-day version of the Watchman sprang into life. Kyle reinvented himself as a combination of a comic book superhero and a bygone law enforcer. The only one who could obtain justice for his mother.

Except his attempt to do so had heaped horror on Drew Blackmore. Once he'd realised the truth, the part of him that would always be Rick freed Drew, but too late to undo the damage inflicted by Kyle.

'Told you before,' Rick said inside Kyle's head. 'You should have gone to the police. Drew didn't deserve that shit.'

He was right. Kyle would serve a long stretch inside for his crimes, which seemed only fair. Actions had consequences, after all.

Perhaps prison wouldn't be so terrible. In jail he'd never be alone. For the frightened kid he'd once been, that meant the world.

First, though, Kyle had stuff he wanted to say to the man he'd wronged so badly. Things Drew needed to know.

CHAPTER 62

Drew paused on the threshold of his home, staring at the view beyond his door. Sunshine had replaced the drizzle of the last few days, albeit accompanied by a cool breeze. He searched within himself for a sign of his former agoraphobia and found nothing. Now that Kyle Davenport was in police custody, safety had returned to his world. Drew could step outside without fear.

'Are you sure you don't want me to come?' Holly's voice startled him; she'd sneaked up behind him while he'd been lost in thought.

'I'll be fine. You should rest, sweetheart.' Disappointment flashed in her eyes, and he hugged her close. 'I need to face Kyle Davenport alone. Besides, I don't want you—or our unborn child—anywhere near him.'

She nodded, but didn't look convinced. He continued to hold her, grateful beyond words. He'd made the best damn decision of his life when he'd married this woman. Over the coming months, they'd rebuild their relationship, ready for their future. Him, Holly and the baby. Together as a family.

He tilted up his wife's head to kiss her. Then he walked, his pace steady and confident, towards his car.

******

Drew sat on a chair in a corridor at Bridewell police station, waiting to be escorted to an interview room. From what he'd been told, Kyle Davenport had been discharged from Southmead and been taken straight to Bridewell. He had reiterated his intention to give Tucker and Tobin a full statement after he'd spoken with Drew. Sweat dampened Drew's palms, even though three police officers would be present. His former ebullience was long gone.

Closure, he reminded himself. Once this was sorted, he and Holly could move forward.

At last a man came to fetch him, and Drew walked behind him, his legs shaky. Inside the interview room, DS Tucker and DC Tobin were sitting along one edge of a table. Across from them sat Kyle Davenport. A woman and a man, neither of whom Drew recognised, occupied the two chairs either side of Kyle. Jessica Smith had positioned herself close to the door.

'Take a seat, Drew,' Tucker said. She gestured towards the woman. 'This is Caroline Bradshaw, a registered mental health nurse. She's here for Kyle Davenport's benefit. And this is Sam Miller, Kyle's legal representation.'

Drew found the courage to look into his abductor's face. The guy looked like he'd not slept, his eyes red and ringed with exhaustion, his skin dry and sallow. Thick surgical gauze masked his broken nose. His beard—probably grown to mislead the police, Drew decided—needed a trim. Small wonder he hadn't recognised the clean-shaven, much younger and thinner version he'd seen on the guy's driving licence.

Eventually Kyle took a deep breath. He raised his eyes to meet Drew's.

'You have to understand,' he said. His voice, not surprisingly, emerged thick and nasal. 'Barry Blackmore abducted my mother. I convinced myself he killed her.'

The words came flooding out. Drew heard about Barry's abuse of Michelle, how a terrified seven-year-old had been too traumatised to reveal what he'd witnessed. Later, after discovering Barry had died, how Kyle recalled something he'd read during his religious phase. That the sins of fathers would be visited on their sons.

Kyle told how he'd joined the running club under the guise of Rory Bruce to familiarise himself with Drew's life, his routines, where he worked.

Next came Kyle's reaction on learning his mother was still alive. How he'd crushed sleeping tablets into Drew's water for the last time. Cut him loose, left food and warm clothes. Later, once he remembered Drew's wasted legs, he called the emergency services.

That puzzled Drew. 'You acted alone? No accomplice?'

Kyle shrugged. 'Of course I did. Story of my damn life.'

'What about Ethan Parker? Rosalie's son?'

'What about him?'

'Don't try to deny he was your sidekick. You tracked him down, manipulated him into going along with your plan.'

Confusion filled the other man's face. 'What? No. You've got this all wrong.'

'Then, when you discovered he'd released me, you murdered him. Right?'

'I haven't killed anyone. I never even met the guy.'

Drew's mouth twisted in derision. 'Yeah, right. You expect us to believe it was a random mugging gone bad? When his body was found in a shallow grave?'

Sweat glistened on Kyle's forehead. 'It wasn't me, I swear.'

The guy was a consummate liar. And one hell of an actor. A deeply disturbed individual whose moral compass had broken years ago. Well, screw him, Drew decided. He'd leave Ethan Parker's murder, and Kyle Davenport's culpability, to the police.

Time to ask the question that burned inside his brain.

'You prick,' he said, his voice a snarl. 'Do you have any idea how badly you've fucked up my life?'

'I'm sorry. If I could change things, I would. But I can't.' He glanced away. 'I eventually released you, though.'

'You mean Ethan Parker did, you bastard.'

'No. It was me who set you free.'

Drew didn't believe Kyle. Ethan Parker *must* have been involved. 'Why abduct me? Why not Todd?' Not that he'd ever wish such hell on his brother.

'Todd had kids. You didn't. I'd never deprive a child of its father.'

'Except you almost did.'

Kyle scrubbed a hand over his jaw. 'I didn't know Holly was pregnant.'

'You expect me to forgive you?' Drew's voice turned hard. That, for him, was a step too far.

'No. Just to understand. I loved my mum, even if she was clueless about parenting. But her abduction damaged me. Broke me. Years in foster care didn't help.' His voice cracked on the last sentence.

Caroline Bradshaw leaned in, whispered in Kyle's ear. Kyle made a dismissive gesture. He turned back to Drew.

'There's something you should know.' He seemed reluctant to continue, though.

'Whatever it is, spit it out,' Tucker said.

Kyle's eyes locked onto Drew's. Drew's gut clenched, a visceral realisation that the next few seconds would be life-changing.

'I visited my mother in hospital. After the police told me she was alive.'

Drew waited. The tension in the room squeezed tighter.

'She suffers from early dementia, brought on by alcohol abuse. But she remembers stuff from years back. Better than she does her own name.' He pulled in a deep breath. 'I asked her a question. The one that's bugged me all my life.'

Anxiety churned through Drew. 'Which was…?'

'She refused to tell me when I was a kid. If I asked, she'd get angry, yell at me to shut up. Or else she'd belt me one.'

'Tell you what?'

'Who my father was.'

In that moment, Drew *knew*. Revulsion filled his soul.

'The dementia allowed her to talk at last,' Kyle continued. 'She told me Barry Blackmore got her pregnant.'

Drew shoved the table away, causing it to slam into Kyle. He stood up, his fists clenched. 'You're a liar.'

Why would Kyle lie, though? A DNA test would prove the truth or otherwise of his words. Besides, the man had summoned Drew for a reason. Something beyond remorse.

'Sit down, please, Drew,' Tucker said.

He ignored her. Thanks to this bastard, he'd almost lost his mind and his marriage. He yearned for the chance to shove a dose of Kyle's own medicine down his fucking throat. Chain him up in complete darkness for months and see how he coped with *that*. Now he was claiming they were related?

'They met when she was twenty, and had a brief fling. She was estranged from her family, living on benefits in a council flat,' Kyle said. 'The two of them lost touch for a while. She turned to prostitution to support herself after I was born. He ended up one of her regulars.'

Liar, Drew wanted to say, but didn't. His mouth was too dry. He poured himself a glass of water, then sat down.

'She never told him I was his son. Or even that I existed. Too terrified of how he'd react.' Bitterness laced Kyle's voice.

Drew gulped back his water, every nerve in his body on edge.

'We're brothers,' Kyle said. 'Half-brothers, anyway. When I found out Barry Blackmore didn't kill my mother, I released you straightaway.'

Drew found his voice. 'Shame you didn't turn yourself in. Or swallow a bottle of pills back then, instead of later.'

'You've no idea. What it's like to crave a family, instead of being an only child. To grow up in foster care, certain your mother is dead.' A shudder shook Kyle's frame. 'That's why, after I freed you, I stuck around. To make sure you'd be okay.'

Something clicked into place for Drew. 'You were at the hospital. It wasn't a hallucination.'

'Yes. I watched your house most nights too. Followed you when you got drunk the other evening. I needed to make sure you were safe.'

'You weaselled your way into my home. Pretended to be my friend.'

Kyle nodded. 'When Holly asked me to visit with Mike and Adam, I was ecstatic.'

Drew couldn't believe the man's gall. 'Yeah. So you could gloat.'

'No. To get to know you better. I wanted that with Todd, too. Even if I could never disclose the truth.' He swallowed. 'I had it all planned out. A new address, along with false ID as Rory Bruce. Then I fed you that story about my phony marriage breakdown. I thought—' He broke off, his gaze on the floor.

'What, exactly? That we'd all live happily ever after? Yeah, right.'

Kyle shook his head. 'I wanted to be part of my brothers' lives. In some small way, at least.'

'Shared genes don't make us a family.' Drew spat out the words. 'I hope you rot in jail, you prick. Where you belong.' He eyeballed Tucker. 'Take his statement, because I'm done here.' Before she could respond, he strode out of the room.

Drew found the nearest toilet and locked the door, resting against it, his eyes closed. Then he crouched over the bowl and vomited.

CHAPTER 63

Back home, Drew threw himself on the sofa, his head a mess. Hate and revulsion were his most dominant emotions. *We're brothers.* Drew felt soiled by the DNA he shared with Kyle Davenport. A lifetime of showers wouldn't wash him clean. As a boy he'd endured Ian Morrison. Then, as a man, a horrific abduction. Now this latest shock.

He sank his head in his hands, desperate for someone to confide in. Holly was in town, shopping for baby clothes with her friend Amber. Todd, then. They'd not communicated since their fight, and his brother needed to hear what had transpired at Bridewell. Drew grabbed his mobile and fired off a text. 'Can we talk? Got important stuff to tell you.'

To his relief, Todd replied straightaway. 'Sure. Will leave work early. I'll be there ASAP.'

True to his word, he arrived half an hour later. 'You look like shit,' he said, once Drew opened the door.

Drew laughed, despite his mental turmoil. 'Tell it how it is, why don't you?' He stood aside to let his brother pass. Todd followed Drew into the kitchen.

'Coffee?' Drew enquired. 'Or something stronger?'

'Beer, please. A pint won't stop me driving. Besides—' He grimaced. 'I suspect this might be a difficult conversation.'

348

Drew cracked open a Budweiser and passed another to Todd. He took a swig from his own, gathering his courage, then gestured for his brother to sit down. An uneasy silence stretched between them.

'You said you had something to say?' Todd prompted.

'Two things, actually. First, I know you didn't sleep with Holly.'

'Halle-fucking-lujah. Well, that's good to hear. You believe me now?'

Drew nodded. 'I've been an idiot. And I'm sorry.'

'Yeah, you were a dickhead all right. I told you, mate—Holly loves you.' Todd took a gulp of beer. 'You should have let me explain.'

'I got a bit paranoid. Jumped to conclusions,' Drew admitted. 'Holly says she forgives me, though.'

'A wise woman, your wife. You should listen to her more often.' The hint of a smile lifted Todd's mouth.

'That's not the only reason we need to talk.' Drew told his brother how Kyle Davenport, a.k.a. Rory Bruce, was his abductor. He watched shock fly into Todd's face.

'Fuck.' Todd shook his head after Drew had finished. 'He seemed so on the level. The wife, the kids. He lied about all that?'

'Yup. All part of his cover story.'

'The bastard.' Todd's expression was grim. 'Did he admit to murdering Ethan Parker?'

'Nope. He denied all knowledge of him.'

349

'Well, he would do, wouldn't he? The fucker's a grade-A liar. Deserves to burn in hell.'

Drew nodded. 'Can't argue with that. We'll have to settle for him rotting in jail for several years.'

'So why did he change tack? Invent a phony marriage breakdown?'

This bit wouldn't be easy. 'I guess the time had come to shed the pretence.'

'What do you mean?'

Drew sucked in a deep breath. 'Michelle Davenport told him she had an affair with our father. He claims he's our half-brother.'

'No way.' Todd slammed his fist on the table. 'I don't believe it.'

'Why would he lie?'

'Didn't you say his mother has dementia? How do we know this isn't the ramblings of a diseased mind?'

'A DNA test will prove it either way. To build their case, the police will check his against ours. We'll find out for sure then.'

Todd was silent for a while. 'He always reminded me of someone,' he said at last. 'Never did figure out who. Now I think of it, he's got Dad's nose.' He exhaled sharply. 'God, I feel dirty. Knowing we're related to the fucker who made your life hell. That he's our half-brother.'

Drew reached out a hand, squeezed Todd's arm. 'You're the only brother I'll ever want. Or need.'

******

'Come over for lunch on Sunday,' Todd said, right before he left. 'And bring Holly.' That boded well, Drew thought. Time for the four of them to get back to normal around each other.

He remembered he had a phone call to make. That done, he went upstairs, got into his running gear and switched on his treadmill. He ran until his legs buckled under him. Exhausted, his clothes drenched with sweat, he felt purged of Kyle Davenport. For the time being, anyway.

Just before six thirty, Drew heard his wife's key in the door. 'Drew?' she called from the hallway.

He walked to the doorway of the living room. 'In here.' He watched his wife unwind her scarf. Stared at the curve of her throat, the swell of her belly. He loved every inch of her.

'How did it go at Bridewell today?' Worry lurked in Holly's eyes.

Drew cleared his throat. 'Good. I've been—' He chose his words carefully. 'Released. For the second time.'

Confusion replaced concern. 'I don't understand.'

Drew took his wife's hand and led her to the sofa. She looked less tired, not so pale, he noted. 'Can I get you a coffee, sweetheart?'

She shook her head. 'Just tell me what happened.'

So he did. About Kyle's professed remorse. The fact he'd locked eyes with Drew, apologised for his crimes. Finally—and most difficult—how Drew shared DNA with his abductor.

Holly's eyes flew wide with shock. 'You're half-brothers? Really?'

'So he claims.'

'You must feel...' She shook her head. 'I have no idea what, to be honest. Talk to me, Drew, please. We've done so little of that lately.' She glanced away, but not before he glimpsed the sadness in her face.

'Amen to that.' Drew cleared his throat. 'I've come to a decision.'

'Which is?'

'I called Matthew Thomas earlier. I'm going to resume our counselling sessions.'

'Thank God you've seen sense,' Holly said. 'All the shit in your head—you can't cope with it alone.'

'I realise that. You're the best wife ever.' He smiled at her. Impossible to say certain things enough. 'I love you so much. You know that, right?'

Holly didn't respond, and for a second fear clawed at Drew. Then she pushed him away. 'Come with me.' She took his hand in hers.

Drew followed Holly upstairs and into their bedroom. He watched as she opened her jewellery box. Seconds later he saw his wedding ring nestled on her palm.

'May I?' Holly sounded nervous. She gestured towards his left hand.

Drew nodded. Without it, his finger was naked. Incomplete.

Holly slipped the ring over Drew's knuckle, her touch cool. He stared at the platinum band, too choked to speak. Instead, he pulled her into his arms, his embrace saying what he couldn't.

What had Todd said about listening to Holly? Drew's abduction, the abuse by Ian Morrison, the revelation that Barry Blackmore had been a monster—he'd bottled up his pain his whole life. Time for that to stop. Especially now he needed to process Kyle Davenport's revelations.

Besides, he would soon become a father. His child, and Holly, deserved the best version of himself he could offer.

It had been a cold, dark and silent winter, he reflected. One from which he'd emerged changed forever. But the nightmare, although not over, was fading. Now he glimpsed light, where before only blackness had existed. His captor was headed for jail, but Drew was determined to step free from prison. What had Nessa told him about Nelson Mandela? Time to leave his bitterness and hatred behind. A new life beckoned.

His palm rested on Holly's belly, their child stirring beneath his fingers. He pictured himself with a tiny hand grasping his. He couldn't wait.

Winter was over, thought Drew. *Roll on summer.*

CHAPTER 64

Back in Keynsham's police custody suite, Kyle mulled over his meeting with Drew. His half-brother's mention of Ethan Parker had surprised Kyle. His mind travelled back to when he'd lurked outside the guy's home. He'd been so tempted to talk with Ethan, persuade him to join his plan; then, at the last minute, he decided not to. Had walked away, gone home instead. The idea seemed fraught with risk. Besides, hadn't Kyle always operated alone?

He'd learned about Ethan's murder from a television report. Despite Drew's scorn about his innocence, Kyle assumed some random guy must have killed Ethan. However it happened, the man's death had nothing to do with him. Despite that, he mourned Ethan. Hadn't Barry Blackmore blighted both their lives? In a way, they'd been brothers, albeit unlinked by DNA. Just ones who never met.

Kyle never expected Drew to welcome news of their shared genes with jubilation. He'd done what he needed to do, though. Drew deserved to learn the truth from him, not a police officer.

He wondered how Todd would react to the knowledge he had a half-brother.

CHAPTER 65

Todd whistled as he glided the paint roller back and forth in the twins' bedroom. He enjoyed decorating; the motion of his arm acted like meditation, soothing him. Nessa was downstairs, preparing vegetables for Sunday lunch; the aroma of roast lamb wafted up the stairs, making his mouth water. Sounds drifted up from his boys playing in the kitchen: the occasional wail from Jack, muffled laughter from Shane. Drew and Holly should arrive within the hour. A perfect family scene would ensue. Everything was good in Todd's world.

He'd talked to Nessa two days ago.

'I love you,' he'd told her. 'I always have. But—' He stopped, surprised when she placed her fingers against his lips.

'Don't.' Her eyes slid away. 'If you're planning to divorce me, just spit it out.'

He stared at Nessa, unable to speak. Affection for his wife swirled through him, thick and wonderful. Not the same as the passion he'd once felt for Holly, but love nonetheless. She'd given birth to his boys, created the stable family he'd always craved. Sweet, lovely Nessa, with her bohemian skirts, her silver bracelets, her hemp sandals. Strong, solid, loyal. Every inch of her was precious. How had it taken him so long to realise her worth?

Todd pulled his wife close, feeling her body shake against his. She was crying, and shame filled his soul.

'I was going to say,' he whispered into her hair, 'that I've not been the husband you deserve. But I plan to be.'

She pushed him away. Her cheeks were mottled, her nose red. He'd never loved her more.

'I don't understand,' she said.

Todd took her hands, folding her damp palms into his. 'I'm committed to our marriage, our sons. I've given you reason to doubt me, I know. Not anymore. From now on, I'll be the man you want. You'll never have cause to worry.'

Nessa chewed her lip, her expression uncertain. 'What's brought all this on?'

Good question. 'So much happened over the winter. Made me realise my priorities.'

She wiped away a tear. 'What about Holly?'

'I don't want her.' The truth. 'She's having Drew's baby. They're happy together.'

'You loved her.'

'A stupid crush, nothing more.'

'The two of you shared a bed. How can I believe it was just for comfort?'

She had every right to be angry. He'd been weak and foolish, but no longer. He squeezed her hands tight. 'Look at me.'

Nessa raised her eyes to his. God, they were gorgeous. 'I will spend the rest of my life proving how much I love you.' Then he kissed her, long and hard. Somehow, after that, their marriage began to mend.

Todd swished the roller back and forth, still whistling. He'd not felt the need to tell Nessa everything.

It had been wrong of him to want sex with Holly. Drew's disappearance cut Todd to the bone, made him angry. Like Holly, he'd needed comfort, had been all too human. Not anymore, though. It wasn't just the fact Holly had spurned him. *I love Drew. Not you. It will never be you.* The words had stung, but hadn't proved the final rejection. For Todd, that had been when, for a second, he'd seen doubt in her eyes. When she'd believed he'd abducted his own brother.

In that moment, he'd hated her. Any love he'd once harboured fizzled and died.

Blood was thicker than water, so they said. Todd's loyalties had always been, would always be, with Drew. He could never hurt his younger brother.

From the moment Eloise Blackmore brought her baby home from the hospital, Todd had adored Drew. Sworn to protect him. He'd witnessed his father beat his mother, suffered the force of Barry's fists himself. Endured days of imprisonment in the cupboard under the stairs. The man was a bastard, but he stopped short of harming a baby. Todd knew such restraint wouldn't last once Drew left his toddler years behind. He recalled the police questioning his father over Rosalie Parker the year before. Drew wasn't safe around such a monster.

One Saturday night Barry, fuelled by booze, turned particularly violent. The house was detached; to the best of Todd's knowledge, their neighbours were unaware of the abuse that took place at the Blackmore residence. Todd listened to his mother's screams, her pleas for her husband to stop hurting her. The commotion woke Drew, who began to howl.

'That kid needs to shut up, or I'll ram my fist down his throat,' Todd heard Barry shout at his wife. Concerned, he slipped into Drew's bedroom, pulling the terrified child close. He rocked him back and forth, humming his brother's favourite nursery rhyme. It worked. Drew slept, and the sounds from his parents' room ceased.

The next morning his mother emerged with a black eye, her bottom lip split, moving like a ninety-year-old. She wouldn't look at her eldest son.

'Your dad's gone to work,' she said, when Todd asked over breakfast. Nothing unusual in that. Barry often spent Sunday mornings at the meat packing plant, catching up on paperwork while the place was closed.

He stared at his mother's bruised face. In contrast, his brother's was perfect, unblemished. The way it should stay. In that moment, he knew what he had to do.

He waited until they'd finished breakfast, then told his mother he'd promised to visit a friend from school. She nodded, still not meeting his eye. Todd slipped into his father's home office, took the spare keys to the meat packing plant from their hook. Then he set off.

His father's workplace stood at the rear of an industrial estate in St Philip's. Few people were out and about that Sunday morning. Nobody noticed the fourteen-year-old kid, hunched into a hoodie, who crept around the back of the building. Keys in hand, Todd unlocked the side door, and pulled it open. Slowly, carefully. Then he padded up the metal stairs. Although big for his age, he made no sound. From inside Barry's office came a belch, low and rumbling. Todd smelled the stink of his father's sweat, rank and acrid, in the air.

He surveyed his surroundings. Boxes and rolls of packing material, not visible from where his father sat, stood stacked several layers high on the landing. Todd reached out, pushed the top box off its perch. On its way to the floor, it hit into one of the packing rolls, creating a domino effect. The noise boomed around the silent interior.

'What the *fuck*?' Todd heard his father stride across his office. He never noticed his son, hidden behind boxes on the other side of the door. Only the mess he'd created. He did, however, feel Todd's hands shove into his back, propelling him towards the open stairwell. Barry scrambled to regain his footing, but failed. He pitched into the void, tumbling through space, his head banging off the metal steps until it slammed into the wall at the bottom of the stairs. His body lay inert, his neck at a weird angle. A pool of blood oozed from his shattered skull. Todd had never seen anything so glorious.

He didn't waste time. He sprinted down the stairs, leapt over the blood and out the side door. He locked it behind him, then ran to his mate's house. He didn't return home until late afternoon. When he did, he hung the keys he'd taken back on their hook, then went to play with Drew.

The early shift discovered Barry's body on Monday. The police questioned Eloise, but a till receipt proved she'd shopped at Tesco that Sunday morning. So did the store's CCTV cameras, showing Eloise, her bruises hidden behind dark glasses, pushing Drew in his buggy. Todd convinced the police he'd been with his mate, whose grasp of time was notoriously hazy. The coroner ruled Barry's death a tragic accident.

That was the first time Todd killed for Drew. The second was Ian Morrison.

He'd watched his brother turn into a haunted shadow under Morrison's influence. Twelve years in jail and the loss of a testicle had seemed insufficient retribution. Not given Drew's mental scars.

When Morrison was released, Todd had been ready. Revenge, he discovered, really did taste better when served cold. Even if by proxy.

In his work as a probation officer, he encountered many men who failed to adapt to life outside prison. Reluctant to operate too close to home, he checked out possibilities from his colleagues' caseloads. One, a guy who'd knifed another man to death in a bar fight, caught his attention. Aged eighteen at the time of his conviction, he'd served fifteen years in jail, and had recently been paroled. Top dog inside the nick, he was struggling to cope outside. The two of them talked. In return for cash paid to his disabled mother, the man agreed to help Todd.

A week after Morrison's release, the guy attacked him in a dark alleyway. Sliced off his dick, slashed open his femoral artery then left him to bleed out. As a final touch, he pissed and spat on the corpse. Police identified his DNA, found the knife in his possession. He told the arresting officers he'd been one of Morrison's many unnamed victims. They had no reason to suspect otherwise.

Ethan Parker was the third time Todd killed for Drew.

He'd lied to the police when he'd said he'd not known about Rosalie's death. As he listened to DS Tucker recount the grim details of Drew's captivity, he'd speculated whether Rosalie ever had a child. One who might have sought revenge. Later he discovered the answer online within minutes, and acted swiftly. In Todd's mind, Ethan became the prime suspect. Convinced of his guilt, he tracked him down. Tortured him for information. Turned out the guy was innocent, but Todd killed him anyway. Merciful, really, given his injuries.

Now he only had Kyle Davenport to deal with. He guessed Kyle's sentence for kidnap and false imprisonment would be ten to fifteen years of jail time. Not that it mattered. He was happy to wait.

Kyle would pay with his life for what he'd done to Drew. Todd would make sure of that once the guy was released. Actions had consequences, after all.

'Lunch is almost ready,' Nessa called up the stairs. 'Drew and Holly should be here soon.'

Todd placed his roller in the paint tray. 'Coming, love. I'll give you a hand with the boys.'

Ah, family. Nothing was more important. He'd kill for his.

POSTSCRIPT

I hope you enjoyed *Silent Winter*! If so, please consider leaving a review on whichever sales platform you bought the book from, and/or Goodreads.

Please note that this book conforms to British conventions of spelling, punctuation and grammar. You'll see favourite not favorite, tyre not tire, maths instead of math, etc., none of which are incorrect, just different.

If you've enjoyed this book, why not visit my website at www.maggiejamesfiction.com, where you can also find my blog - I post regularly on all topics of interest to readers, including author interviews and book reviews. While you're there, why not sign up for my Special Readers' Group, and receive a free copy of *Blackwater Lake*? The newsletter is sent monthly and when a new title is released, so you won't get bombarded with emails. It includes fiction recommendations, news about my latest books and personal life, and discounts on my novels.

You can also connect with me on Facebook (Maggie James Fiction) or via Twitter (@mjamesfiction).

ACKNOWLEDGEMENTS

Huge thanks to Mary Moss, Will Patching, Simon Leonard, Mark Tilbury, Terry Hetherington, Colin Garrow and Gary Powell for their invaluable help and feedback.

Also thanks to the real-life Karen Harris for her unfailing support and friendship.

ABOUT THE AUTHOR

Maggie James is a British author who lives near Newcastle-upon-Tyne. She writes psychological suspense novels.

Before turning her hand to writing, Maggie worked mainly as an accountant, with a diversion into practising as a nutritional therapist. Diet and health remain high on her list of interests, along with travel. Accountancy does not, but then it never did. The urge to pack a bag and go off travelling is always lurking in the background! When not writing, going to the gym, practising yoga or travelling, Maggie can be found seeking new four-legged friends to pet; animals are a lifelong love!

Find out more at Maggie's website and blog: www.maggiejamesfiction.com.

Printed in Great Britain
by Amazon